THE LAST DESCENDANT

BOOK ONE OF THE BLOODPRINT SERIES

KRISTINA KAIRN

For Dee and Nay.
It's never too late to chase a dream.

PROLOGUE

Abby walked down the hall, but none of the adults noticed. Things always slowed and quieted in the evenings. During the day, the hospital buzzed with fluorescent lights, beeped with machinery too complicated for her to understand, and bustled with the fabric of disposable scrubs and hazmat suits. But at night, either out of exhaustion or respect, their sequestered children's ward became peaceful.

She liked the feel of the cold white linoleum floor under her bare feet, and sometimes pretended it was the first snow of winter. Anything to forget what was really happening.

The fourth room on the right waited.

Her head leaned into the doorway, and right on cue, his head carefully rolled to face her. Somehow he found the strength to smile. She smiled back, and then she looked back down the hall. The angel bowed her head in approval, silver white hair undulating behind her gray, muted face. The angel placed two fingers to her mouth.

Abby tiptoed into the room and climbed onto the foot of

the bed. She was shorter than most but was used to the extra effort required to scale normal heights.

"Hi, Jack," she said.

Jack wheezed in deeply, which was odd because the oxygen tubes ran air into his nose. Maybe he wished to inhale her scent, inhale her comfort. Or maybe he wanted to fill his lungs on his own without any help.

His skin looked grayish green like Play-Doh that had been left out. An ugly color for a child to wear for his courage. At least he wasn't crying blood.

"I'm sorry about your hair," Jack said.

Abby raked her fingers through her hair. It was smooth but greasy from not being washed for a week. She hadn't lost any of it, not like the other children. She still didn't understand his comment and tilted her head.

"About pulling your hair all the time," Jack explained.

It was strange to finally speak to the boy who used to spend his mornings tormenting her at the bus stop. Tugging on her hair until she kicked him so hard in the shin he lost all his laughter.

"It's okay." It was now. It really was.

"Why aren't you sick like the rest of us?"

Her lip involuntarily pulled down, but she would not cry or suffer in front of him. Too many were crying. Too many had suffered.

"I don't know." She stared at her hands.

Jack glanced at the machinery monitoring his life. They always checked the machines before they left, like checking in with a parent for permission. Abby hated those machines.

His fingers reached out for her hair. "They were always so neat and shiny. Your braids. That's why I pulled them."

She would not cry. She would not show this boy, this

neighbor, this new friend, her fear. She smiled and leaned her head down. He stroked her hair.

"Is there really an angel here?" he asked.

She nodded.

"It stops all the pain?"

She nodded again. She didn't have the strength to speak.

His eyes welled up, and he struggled to breathe, and he shed pink tears. She wiped them away with her fingers.

"How come you see the angel and we don't?" he asked.

She took a deep breath. "Because I'm going last, after I help everyone. I always get picked last for being too small." With the fear pulsing in her veins, the white lie floated out of her mouth so easily.

"I don't think you're small."

The hair on her arms stood tall. The angel floated across the walls and hovered in the corner in front of the boy. But he didn't see it.

Abby scooted up the bed and lay next to Jack. His body was just a shell of skin and bones, nothing like the big bully who taunted the playground.

They lay in the quiet, until the boy began to hum a familiar tune. He stroked her hair and she picked up the song.

Buy me some peanuts and some Crackerjack...

Their voices fell in harmony with the beeping of the machines.

I don't care if I never get back.

The angel sat at the edge of the bed, her face always hidden in the shadow of light.

Let me root, root, root for the home team, if they don't win it's a shame...

Abby's heart raced even though she knew the outcome, but she always wanted to fight. She wanted to shove the visitor of death out of the room. Shove it out of the hospital. Shove it back to heaven. She wanted her classmates to live.

Jack's breath became shallow, almost invisible to detect. His hand stopped stroking her hair.

For it's one, two, three strikes, you're out at the old ball game.

She sang the last line alone. The room grew bright as day, then faded back to darkness. The machines didn't beep. They droned the harsh note. Someone in disposable scrubs would come soon. Her body shook uncontrollably but she pushed herself out of the bed.

Jack's eyes stared at the ceiling, empty but content. She carefully pushed his lids shut and kissed him on the mouth. His mouth already cold from a game no one could win in this hospital.

She shuffled out of the room as the medical people swooped in. It was the third room she had visited that day. Twelve visits in the last three days. The drone of death rang through her ears.

Abby turned the corner and saw the angel again.

Not another. Not now. I'm tired. Please, let me be. She prayed the angel heard her pleas. Her first night with the angel had taught her the angel didn't heed prayers.

Her fat tears hit the floor and splashed her toes.

The angel moved down the hall, ebbing between two doors on the left. It turned to Abby then chose a door.

Abby screamed. "No. No. No."

Her shrieks shattered the hospital's silence and decorum.

"No. You promised." She wailed. "You promised to take me."

The angel entered her brother's room.

1

NORMAL

James Stuart wanted to listen to the thrum of his heart, but all he heard was the quiet hiss of air as Colonel Pride came down the hall. The sound occurred every other step from the titanium prosthetic leg balancing the Colonel's six-foot-four frame. James's dead heart wouldn't beat until later anyway, a consequence of his cursed condition. The door opened, and the Colonel entered the bedroom. James didn't turn to greet him. He didn't want to imply anticipation or excitement. James kept his eyes on the River Cam, waiting for nightfall, waiting for his ghosts, their innocent faces bearing accusation. But he was as much a victim of *her* as they had been.

"I found her," the Colonel said and handed James a dossier.

"Are you certain?"

"The family changed their name after leaving Sturgis. Didn't really bother to hide it so much. They just wanted to give her a chance at a normal life."

A normal life. James closed his eyes and inhaled. He loved the scent of the Colonel – the fealty, the courage, the apprehension. He was happy they were at the beginning of their relationship. The Colonel would be a difficult companion to let go, but they all were in their own way.

"Can we get her to take the job?" James asked.

"I think after what's happened, she's up for a change. She's corresponded with Tousain before."

"Tragic to survive twice." He eyed the Colonel. There was no change in his expression. "And DI Cooper?"

"He's come in for treatments. There is very little of his blood that isn't..." the Colonel hesitated for the right word.

"Contaminated," James said.

"What will happen to him?"

James didn't have an answer, so he ignored the question. Miracles came in all forms, and George was just that – a miracle. Perhaps hate could save them both. Love certainly hadn't gotten him very far. Insurance was always prudent, so he needed the American.

He continued to read the Colonel's report, his index and middle fingers running down the page. "What kind of girl survives that kind of tragedy and grows up to be a pathologist?"

The Colonel didn't hesitate. "A woman looking for answers."

James rubbed his face. Was this exhaustion or hope? It'd been so long, he really wasn't sure. It almost felt human. The fog began to claw its way up the river. The familiar faces of the dead would come soon. He tossed the dossier onto the bed.

"Remove your shirt," James said. His tone held no hint of menace.

He watched the Colonel because it was still uncomfortable and awkward for the retired Royal Army officer. Soon the Colonel would acquiesce with no hesitation. James savored their innocence for as long as possible, and when every touch, kiss, or embrace became needful or too easy, he would let them go.

The Colonel placed his silk tie neatly on the back of the oxblood leather chair in the corner of the room. It marked where he felt most relaxed in the room. James knew it would take weeks for him to lay on the bed, perhaps months. He wasn't sure they had months.

The Colonel snapped his shirt to iron out the wrinkle in his fidelity. In the end, their arrangement would make his marriage stronger. He folded the crisp shirt, placed it on the seat of the chair, and quickly glanced at James affirming his commitment.

"Tell me about Kandahar," James said.

The Colonel's steel gray eyes locked on James with a powerful earnestness that only whet his appetite for the man's blood and memories.

"It's a miserable, beautiful kind of hell."

It took a few years of war to teach the Colonel what a century of misery had taught James. If James didn't know better, he would swear his heart was beating.

"What does hell smell like?" James asked, luring pain to the surface of the Colonel's skin.

"Shit layered on shit."

"How is that beautiful?"

A tight nerve twitched on the Colonel's upper lip, flushing a ripple of desire through James's veins.

"Operating in that kind of place takes a different level of faith."

"In God?"

"No, in men."

"Kneel."

James's shadow ate the distance between them. Even on

his knees, the Colonel was chest high. Out of courtesy, James wiped his lips dry with the back of his hand. He walked behind the Colonel and planted his feet on either side of the officer's knees.

James heard the Colonel unzip his trousers. He didn't want to make the mistake of ejaculating into them again. It made his departure from the house on his first visit dangerously close to his last. Neither of them wanted that.

The Colonel's hair smelled of pomade and primal panic. James wrapped his arm around the Colonel's chest quick as a whip and pulled his head to the right. He drove his fangs into the Colonel's taut neck, deep into the jugular vein. The salt of sweat and the copper of blood no longer registered. James drank until the memories came, and euphoria set in.

In a matter of seconds, he tasted cumin and fenugreek on rotted meat. He tasted the heat of frustration against the cool of the dark caves. He tasted the dryness of sand mixed with the oil of spent ammunition. He saw a foreign land for a few moments. Tasted the thrill and beauty of war, and he consumed the Colonel's shame like it was a glass of Claret.

The Colonel groaned as he swayed back and forth. When his body grew stiff, he stilled, and James sucked harder for the very last second of the man's memories. The Colonel shuddered, the scent of poppy fields quickly replaced by the scent of semen.

James staggered to the edge of the bed, eyes heavy with satiation, wiping blood from his chin. He listened to the Colonel's heart pound like thunder until his own stopped beating again.

2

NEW HIRE BLUES

There was nothing noteworthy about my third week at the Hastings Clinic. I had gotten lost twice on my way to the restroom, but that was due to the monochromatic interior design scheme. Maybe they wanted us to be so bored with the color palette—varying shades of white, shiny silver metal accessories, black lettering on white, and textured white on white art pieces—that we'd keep working to stay awake. Maybe they were running an asylum on the weekends. I was even beginning to resent my last name, Whiting.

As I began my third week, the only striking characteristic about the Scandinavian chic, antiseptic clinic was the man who had hired me. He'd recruited me out of Stanford as if his life depended on it, and yet, Dr. Mathieu Tousain still couldn't be bothered to show for a proper introduction.

Riding up the elevator, one of his second-year residents, Padma Venkat, who I had mistaken as an HR rep on my first day (that did not go over well), was talking with another second year and I patiently waited for them to wrap up their conversation. Even the harsh LED light bounced off Padma's shiny black hair, making me wonder why mine didn't have that kind of luster. Mine was always pulled back in a tight ponytail anyway. Her lilac silk blouse accentuated a figure fit for a fashion model.

"Is there something I can help you with, Dr. Whiting?"

Dammit, I must've been staring.

I turned and apologized. "I was wondering if Dr. Tousain was around today?"

Her brown eyes were surrounded by an enviable amount of lashes. She pursed her coral glossed lips. "You haven't reached him yet?" There was a faint note of irritation in her tone. I think she was still upset about the HR comment or that we were the same age and yet I was her senior.

"He hasn't returned any of my calls." Geez, I sounded desperate.

"He's been tied up with that press release."

"Yeah, that's what you said last week."

Padma crossed her arms. "Well, I'm sure he'll turn up at some point."

"Does the research library have his citations for his last published paper?"

"The universal immunity paper?" Okay, I wasn't giving her enough credit.

"I attended his lecture in New York last October. I've been wanting to see the research ever since." I had wanted the medical records he had cited for much longer.

"I'm sure the research library has whatever you need. But you might need his permission if he had it classified."

The elevator pinged. We arrived at the fifth floor, home of the pathology department. We exited.

"Where is the research library?" I had only explored our floor and the employee gym one building over.

"The second floor."

I waved goodbye and waited for her to turn the corner before hitting the elevator button. Without a boss to meet, I had some time to kill. How big could the research library be?

The research library of the clinic was the entire second floor, all ten thousand square feet. And Padma had lied. Well, she misspoke. I think she believed I would find Tousain's research papers in the flipping library. Some of it was there, and some of it had not been logged in, or "formally submitted." Trust me, when someone says that to you in a British accent, you can't help but feel stupid.

I was looking for a specific citation regarding a viral outbreak in 1999 in Sturgis, South Dakota. I was born in Sturgis. I remember the outbreak. When camera crews from every major network show up *anywhere* in South Dakota, it's hard to forget. Hell, it was the last state for Obama to visit in his epic eight-year term. Not a lot happens in South Dakota.

Tousain had cited the outbreak incorrectly. I wasn't saying he made it up. Doctors, especially clinician's, made up stuff all the time. Their job was to prove it. And I wanted to see the Sturgis medical files, which required his security clearance. The morning hadn't been completely wasted and I headed back up to my lab. I had a spectacular view of the spires of King's College Chapel, but I continued to feel like the dull cousin visiting from America.

Dr. Tousain hadn't been in the clinic since I arrived. I stalked, I mean, I checked his office once, maybe three times a day. There was a layer of dust in his office rivaling my old shelf of conference freebies back at Stanford. And on my seventeenth day as a new employee, as I exited the elevator, I was a little alarmed to see a swarm of police officers lingering around the hall surrounding his office.

Not good.

One tall police officer glanced at me as the elevator pinged and I stepped out, the doors closing behind me.

Of course, I looked down at my printouts and proceeded to my lab like nothing out of the ordinary was happening.

"Excuse me, are you Dr. Whiting?" the officer asked.

Why did he know my name?

"Yep." The tall police officer was in his early thirties, brown hair with no traces of gray, blue eyes that were a little bloodshot, probably from lack of sleep because he didn't look unhealthy. He had the build of an Olympic swimmer—broad shoulders, long arms, big hands, thin waist, squared-off hips. Hair that held the scent of chlorine.

"Do you have a few seconds?" he asked.

"Uh, sure, can we walk and talk?" I pointed down the hall to my lab.

"American?"

"Yes. Does that make me a suspect?" Had I really just said that?

"Suspect?" His stare was amused and alarmed all at once.

"Sorry, I don't encounter the police that often, especially at work. I assumed there was a crime committed."

I shoved open the door to my lab, relieved I hadn't barfed up breakfast thanks to my nerves.

"Well, we hope not. When was the last time you saw Dr. Tousain?"

"I haven't seen him. I'm new here."

"Right. Dr. Venkat made me aware of that. Have you spoken to him?" Judging by his frown, Padma had made a less than pleasant impression. Good, I was on better footing than the police as far as Padma was concerned.

"Not since I was made an offer of employment. A month ago, maybe."

He jotted notes. I didn't think cops really carried little black notebooks. Interesting.

"And was this done over the phone or video conference?"

I shook my head. "No, it was all done over email."

"He didn't interview you?"

"Yes, of course." I rubbed my cold hands. I needed to stop fidgeting. "But that was two months ago. Over Skype."

He continued to note every word.

"And you've been trying to get a hold of him since you arrived on the eleventh of July?"

I chewed my bottom lip. He could've gotten this information from Padma. Or Tousain's secretary. Or HR. "Yes."

"And you've visited his office every day since?"

My mind was an erased white board. "Huh."

"Are you alright?"

"How do you know that?" I tried to cover up my agitation with an airy laugh.

"We've reviewed security camera footage." He pointed to the discreet orbs hiding in plain sight in the hall. The ones I seemed to have not noticed. My profession revolves around observation.

"Right." I nodded while compiling a suitable reply. "His office is next to the vending area." I pulled open my bottom drawer that was overflowing with culinary vending delights. "Cadbury Finger? Royal Tea Biscuit?"

"No thanks." He peered down. "Do you always alphabetize your snack drawer?"

I kicked the drawer closed. "I wanted to meet my new boss. And I was a little anxious."

He smiled. I searched his face for any threat and his hand for a wedding ring. I wasn't sure why. I'm not supposed to like cops.

"Are you enjoying Cambridge?" he asked and closed his small notebook.

"Pardon?"

"Cambridge? How are you liking it? I'm guessing it's very different than where you're from."

"It's very green. Nothing like Silicon Valley, although there's the same sense of innovation." I sounded like a lame recruiter.

"So you're from San Jose or Palo Alto?"

He knew his California geography. "Stanford."

"Go Cardinals." Damn, he was smart. He reached his hand into his blazer, while I stood stupefied. "I'm a big American college football fan."

"Really?" I took his business card. I think I had attended one of those games with my dad a long time ago. "Detective Inspector George Cooper. So not a DCI yet?" I quipped. He scrunched his brows. I have a horrible habit of accidentally offending others when I'm nervous. "I watch a lot of British mysteries. Big BBC fan."

The nice smile returned. "If you think of anything that might help us in our investigation, please call."

"But I don't know what you're investigating."

He rubbed his temple with the side of his hand. "Right. Sorry, how did that slip my mind? Dr. Tousain has gone missing."

"Missing? For how long?"

"That's what we're trying to determine."

"Trying to determine. No one reported him missing?"

His eyes cased my office. "He didn't show for a lecture three weeks ago, and the clinic didn't contact us until yesterday."

"How did no one notice for three weeks?" My voice

broke. Had I flown five thousand miles and given up my home for nothing?

"He doesn't have any family, and he seems to work a lot. I guess that's the cautionary tale."

"To not work too hard?"

He laughed. "No, to make friends." His eyes scanned my office once more. "Have you not finished unpacking?"

"Yeah, last week. Why?"

He shook his head. "No reason. Anyway, thank you for your time. I'll let you get back to work."

I turned on my laptop and intentionally didn't watch him leave. There was no reason to be anxious or to be perspiring. My instinct had been right. Something had gone wrong. There had to be another way to access Tousain's research. I was sure there was another department head I could contact. I began to search the clinic directory when someone tapped on the glass of my lab door.

It was the detective again. I waved him in and took a deep breath.

"Sorry, just curious. What is it that you do?"

"I'm a pathologist."

"Like dead bodies?"

My insides tensed and I think I slammed my eyes shut. "No. No corpses." I stopped my head from shaking. "Disease. I study the pathology of disease and immunology."

His mouth turned down as if he had ingested something unpleasant. More likely he hadn't understood what I had just said.

"You're in search for cures?"

"Yes." Okay, he was really smart.

"So if I ever had a question about cancer or a viral outbreak that leads to a zombie apocalypse, I could give you a call?"

"Uh, sure. But there is no evidence that would ever lead to corpses reanimating post mortem. Life is always necessary. Even viruses need living hosts."

"I meant it as a joke, Dr. Whiting. Thank you again."

This time I watched him walk down the hall and join the other officers lingering around Tousain's empty office.

"Disease isn't a joke to me, detective," I whispered into my coffee cup.

3

A PRIEST AND A DOCTOR

M athieu Tousain was the most senior employee at the clinic, having been hired their founding year in 1995. He'd also acquired all the medical records from Sturgis General Hospital when it shut down twelve years ago. And after spending all afternoon trying to locate the department head to get access to his research, I came upon a strange finding.

The only way to request access was to contact a man by the name of James Stuart, who just happened to be the Chairman of the Board. Since Tousain was employee number one, no one outranked him but the Chairman. Great.

I had drafted five different emails, all varied in tone and professionalism. I really didn't want to step in it on my seventeenth day of employment with one of the most prestigious research clinics in the world. Literally, I didn't want to sign my own professional death warrant by being too pushy and get flown home to a small storage unit in Cupertino.

I was hoping the buzz of police activity would've lured Padma over for a visit so I could subtly ply her with questions, but I probably didn't strike her as the water cooler type. She would be right. It wasn't like I had yakked it up with colleagues at Stanford either. But I was trying to turn a new leaf, and I had made a habit of visiting said water cooler to no avail. It was time to go fish.

The floor was morgue silent. The decision to explore the break room was the least uncomfortable. Humans are creatures of habit, and I knew the vending area like no one else. Option A1 was a Cadbury chocolate covered honeycomb bar called Crunchie. They were mildly addictive. Option B3 was vinegar-flavored chips, but the locals called chips "crisps," which I still couldn't wrap my tongue around.

There were no protein bars or granola or nuts or fruit, unless you considered strawberry flavored KitKats fruit. All of the sandwiches were coated with butter, which was an awful kind of surprise at dinnertime. I had already sent an email suggesting the vending options be changed, and was politely thanked for my feedback, and directed to the large "newly-renovated" employee cafeteria two buildings over.

I knocked on the door of the lab for the second-year residents. There was no answer. Actually, there had been no lights on in anyone's lab all the way down the hall. Was there like some company meeting I was missing? I checked my phone.

No messages. No company-wide email.

I had already picked the most promising email and sent it off anyway—to the Chairman's admin. I wasn't a complete idiot. There was no reason to let the silence kill me, so I made for the break room. I turned the corner, passed the elevators, and stared at the frosted glass walls of Tousain's darkened office.

Missing for weeks? Had I really just given up what at least on paper looked like a very promising Silicon Valley life to end up at this dead end? I wasn't good with new beginnings. I liked stasis. I was a creature of some very disciplined habits. Avoiding change had been a long-cultured one.

Something moved in the corner of Tousain's office, like a shadow in my periphery. I reached for the door and stopped when I noticed it had been sealed with police tape. Something moved again.

I pressed my forehead to the glass and peered in. My huffing fogged the glass, but I swore there was someone in there. When I heard the clang of my knuckles knocking on the glass, my heart thrummed in my ears. What the hell was I doing? What if someone was in there? What was I going to do about it? This was dangerous. I didn't do dangerous. I studied disease, but I did it under layers of protection. Because I was a coward.

I swiftly took a step back and watched the room. And watched. There was a little irony in that moment. That was what I did for a living. I got paid to observe things under glass.

"It's like a tomb in there."

I jumped. I may have even screamed a little.

Behind me, stood a man nursing a hot cup of coffee and a caught-you-off-guard smirk. He had short, fashionable blonde hair and green eyes. The smile would've been more dangerous if it weren't for his dimples. "Sorry, I didn't have you fingered for a screamer."

"Sorry, who are you?" I asked.

"Nate Rothschild. I'm around the corner. Hematology."

With some reluctance, I shook his hand. "Abby Whiting—"

"Pathology. The American acquisition." He batted his eyelids. "Do you always go snooping around crime scenes?"

"What? No. Are you always this direct?"

He sucked air through his teeth. "Why beat around the bush? Plus, Padma is shit at giving new hires tours. We should've met on your first day. She probably didn't think we should meet. You free this Saturday? I'm hosting a tarts and vicars party."

If he had punched me in the face, I would've been more prepared. I only blinked and then jumped when my phone rang.

"New hire anxiety? Or is this new Burberry cologne having its usual effect?" he asked.

I stepped back and looked at my screen. "That can't be right." I said to my phone.

The phone rang again. The piercing sound vibrated up my arm and jangled my head, making me question my ability to function under pressure.

The screen said James Stuart.

Odds of the Chairman of the Board calling a few minutes after I had emailed his assistant, requesting access to research papers that had not been "officially submitted", were minimal. Statistics were my friends. It had to be his assistant.

"The vicar himself, you should probably answer that," Nate said. He was leaning toward me and had obviously seen my phone. "I'll come scare you later. Nice to meet you, nervous Abby from Stanford."

"Hello?" My voice was mousier than usual.

"Hello, Dr. Whiting. This is James Stuart. I was wondering if you're available to meet?"

I stared at my stunned reflection in the glass of Tousain's deserted office.

"Dr. Whiting?"

"Yes. Yes, I'm free." Holy. Shit.

"Good. Can you come to the hospital chapel?"

What? I mouthed. I don't do chapels or churches. Then I remembered I was standing in front of a security camera. "Sure." I tried slipping my phone into my back pocket, but I was in the new-hire trousers and not my jeans.

The hospital chapel wasn't in the hospital, which thankfully, I had learned from the clinic directory. After ten years of clinical research, I had managed to avoid hospitals altogether. I got a little anxious in hospitals. The whole point of doing what I do was to prevent people from ending up in them.

The chapel was on a small grassy knoll at the center of the clinic. The clinic was composed of five buildings: one was the main building to welcome the public and media, another was an employee gym and cafeteria, two research buildings, and one large hospital.

The chapel was off to the left of the hospital. It didn't just stand apart in the small campus of modern building. It stood alone in its uniqueness. My eyes darted up and down the small Gothic building. The damp Cambridge air had taken its toll on every elaborate arch, pointy peak, and sooty crevice. Centuries of existence had been scratched into the sandstone. The old building was more suitable for Charles Darwin, not someone from Silicon Valley.

I pulled the door open slightly and peered inside. There was an old couple sitting with a priest. They were too far away for me to make out their faces. They were speaking in hushed voices and were the only people in the church. I quickly and quietly closed the door. I checked my phone. It had taken me twelve minutes to walk to the chapel. The Chairman was probably a busy man.

So what was the right move? Call him back and apologize for taking so long to find the chapel? Go look for his office?

The door to the chapel opened and the elderly couple exited followed by a handsome man, but what caught my eye was the white clerical collar. I didn't think priests were ever that young or attractive. They weren't typically found in research clinics either, but I would've considered attending his church.

"There you are, Dr. Whiting," said the priest. "I'm James Stuart."

I dropped my phone, my jaw, and my sensibilities.

"No," I whispered. The one step I had forgotten in my earnestness to get those files was to Google photos of James Stuart. I didn't even question why there hadn't been one in the employee directory. That was poor judgment on my part.

"Really, I'm James Stuart." He picked up my phone and held it out to me. "This happens all the time."

"You can't be. You're too young." I wasn't sure where these words were coming from because I had received them at so many points in my career. And I had resented them.

"I'm much older than you'd believe." He seesawed my phone at me like shiny lure. "Please, I don't bite." He smiled and his teeth glistened and I attempted to swallow.

"But you're a priest." Where were these questions stemming from?

He fingered his collar and shook his head. "Sorry. Does this help?" He pulled the stiff clerical collar from his shirt, but it didn't matter. He had already made one hell of a first impression. I would always see him as a man of God.

"I was hoping you could help me solve a problem," he said.

"Did you get my email?" This was more of a can-I-stall-for-time question than a question question.

"I'm having my assistant look into the citations you referenced." He palmed the back of his head and released a sigh. There was a graceful innocence in the gesture, like he was a little overwhelmed. "Mathieu was always a stickler about his work. Very private. Not very good with sharing." He had the most perfect shade of strawberry blonde hair I'd ever seen. If there were human cherubs, well, he'd certainly qualify, but the hair on my arms remained at attention. Which was probably more related to the sequence of the day's events. There were just too many anomalies.

"How can I help you, Mr. Stuart?"

"Well, with Mathieu missing, we really need someone to oversee his patient."

"Patient?"

"Just one. A special case."

"I don't work directly with patients. Can't really remember the last time I was in a hospital." Well, I could. I just didn't want to think about it.

"He has a very rare blood disease. He's been under Mathieu's care for some time and the heart of his research for the last nine months."

My curiosity was more than peaked. And was I really capable of saying no to this man?

"Here is his medical file." Mr. Stuart held out a medical file that was well over two inches thick. This was not a healthy patient. My chest tightened.

I took the file. It was heavy. There were a decades worth of lab reports—blood transfusions dating back to 1995. All too much to consume in front of Mr. Stuart. I glanced back at my building.

"I think it would be easier if you met him."

I nodded but turned to walk back to the comfort of my lab while I read through the reports.

"Dr. Whiting?"

I looked up and Mr. Stuart gestured to the door of the hospital.

"You want me to meet him right now?"

4

SELF-EXAMINATION

Patient number 8267 was on site. Given his illness, and the amount of blood transfusions he required, it only made sense. Since this was a personal favor to the very man who I was employed by, it also made sense to go visit the patient. I followed Mr. Stuart to the hospital and stopped short of the entrance.

"Are you feeling alright, Dr. Whiting?"

My skin was tight like I had spent all afternoon in the sun. I licked my lips and closed my eyes to get my breathing under control. I was not going to have a panic attack in front of this man.

"I skipped lunch. Just a little light-headed."

"We can reconvene tomorrow, if that would make it easier?"

The afternoon sun was on my back. It was another two hours until nightfall. There were no shadows creeping along the walls. I hadn't believed any of that for so long.

"I'm fine. I'll just get some water on our way up." I held the medical file over my chest like a shield. I could do this.

Mr. Stuart didn't seem interested in small talk, and I

didn't have the skill for it, making the elevator ride dead quiet. Every time I peeked from the report, I caught him staring. It wasn't a cold aloof stare but a warm curiosity. The kind you'd expect from an effective priest or Chairman. How could he be either?

The elevator opened and the hall elongated, my vision tunneled, and my breathing grew shallow. Or it may have stopped altogether. This was going to require a little more preparation. I leaned against the wall and pretended to read the file.

"Let me go get you some water."

Mr. Stuart disappeared down the hall and I took a seat in a waiting room. There were problems I solved from the safety of a laboratory. Because I couldn't treat patients directly. Because hospitals made me sick. I closed my eyes and interlaced my fingers. There was no crying. All I heard was the muted music of the waiting room and the assuring whispers of loved ones with family at the hospital. Death wasn't haunting the air. The air wasn't painfully cold. I opened my eyes.

The information card in the medical file blurred, but I squinted and took another slow forced inhale. Male, Caucasian, patient since 1995, under transfusion regimen since 2007 for extreme case of anemia, and had dialysis treatment four times in the last six months for hepatitis. I couldn't find his name anywhere in the file, just the set of numbers, and my hands shook too hard to turn the pages.

"Here you are."

James Stuart was sitting next to me, holding a paper cup of water. I hadn't even heard him take a seat. I thanked him and sipped the water.

"Why don't we do this another time? I didn't realize you'd be so uncomfortable. I apologize."

There was something about the way he had said the words. They sounded assuring but there was also the hint of "I overestimated you." I'd be damned if I didn't meet his expectations.

"The patient room is just down the hall?" I finished the water. "It looks like he's due for dialysis soon. Let's go see him."

"Are you sure?"

I stood.

"Let me go tell him you're coming. That way there will be no surprises. Just give me two minutes."

There was a lovely view of King's College from the window. I glanced down at the small chapel where I had met Mr. Stuart. The research clinic had been built around the small chapel. I couldn't help but wonder if it were a historical building. Which reminded me of home. Three minutes had passed, and I wasn't sure I'd make it through the next five.

I took a deep breath and made my way down the hall. The floor had ten patient rooms. I stood outside the third room on the left and listened for any conversation. The room was quiet. Quiet was good. I knocked and heard Mr. Stuart say come in.

The room wasn't a patient room, but an examination room. The only person standing in it was James Stuart. His black suit stood in stark contrast to the bright white of the room, but it made his blue eyes more stunning to stare at in confusion. I waited for him to speak. And waited.

"Where is patient 8267?" I finally asked.

"I am patient 8267."

I blurted a laugh. "Is this some kind of joke?"

"No." He smiled. It was a little too confident, maybe smug.

"Patient 8267 is an eighty-six-year-old man."

"I think you have the date of birth wrong."

"Can you give me a second?"

I turned my back to him and pulled out my phone and Googled photos of James Stuart, Chairman of the Board, Hastings Clinic. A dozen pictures came up. And I'd be damned if it wasn't the good-looking priest. The pictures could've been posted at any time, including earlier today. But two of them were from the newspaper. Those would be harder to fake. When I had joined Stanford, someone sent me chimpanzee stool samples to run labs on. It wasn't unusual to haze a new member of staff, but this was elaborate. I turned back around.

"You're patient 8267, huh? You don't look very unhealthy." I dropped the tome of a medical file on to the counter.

He leaned against the exam table and the tissue paper crinkled. "Looks can be deceiving."

This guy was relentless and charming. There was no way he ran this clinic. I searched his shirt for easy to tear away Velcro.

"Do you really think I have nothing better to do?" I ripped open the medical file. "See, right here. Date of birth June thirteenth, 1934." I stabbed the file repeatedly, amazed I was still holding eye contact. This was progress. I was not good with confrontation.

He looked to where I was pointing. "It says June 1834."

"That's a typo."

"No it isn't."

I wanted to break into hysterics, but his reply wasn't flippant. It was sincere. That had to be the refined British accent. I reread the data sheet again, but the date of birth hadn't changed. I had assumed the typo. But it couldn't be correct, it made no sense, people age, people die. It was illogical.

There were no security cameras in the examination room. Only the bright fluorescent lights above, and I was sure they tilted down to get a closer view. My throat tightened.

"This is the point where you hand me an X-ray of a two-headed dog." I said.

"Do such things exist?"

"Yes." I shook my head. "I mean, no."

"Do you believe in miracles, Dr. Whiting?"

"Only ones I can prove." And I had given up my home in search of one.

"How about monsters?"

"Depends on your definition of monster. Can you be a little more specific?" Was I alone in a room with a criminal? He was five-foot-ten and roughly one hundred sixty pounds. Average build, not physically intimidating, but there was something uncomfortable about the eerie calm he exuded. I scanned the room for possible objects to fashion into a weapon. He didn't move, like a corpse.

"The medical file is real. You can see Mathieu's notes. It would take a fair amount of time to doctor that kind of proof."

The first problem I couldn't solve was why I didn't walk away. That was what normal people did. Walk away from the absurd. It was as if his smooth operator voice and perfectly balanced good looks kept me transfixed. And I wasn't that type of woman. Really, I wasn't. That was the first clue.

I skimmed the file again. The file could've been created in the last couple of weeks. Maybe this was what Tousain had been up to? That didn't explain the police investigation. I could prove he wasn't the real James Stuart.

"If you were under such a rigorous transfusion schedule, you'd have a sallow complexion."

"Are you saying I have nice skin?"

My mouth fell open.

He winked. "The sooner you do a blood draw, the sooner you'll have your proof, and we can move on."

Had he read my thoughts? Why would I even consider that a legitimate request? The hair at the back of my neck stiffened. Proof. Proof of what?

"Can I see you forearm?" I blurted.

He removed a cufflink and rolled his sleeve in three quick turns. His skin was pale, not unusual for a Brit.

"You don't have any scars from regular transfusions, nor a stint for dialysis."

"I heal very fast."

I huffed. "That's convenient."

"Have you never experienced something you couldn't quite explain away, doctor? Why don't you do the blood draw? I'm used to the prick of a needle."

I looked out the window, half expecting to see straw-colored hills, but I was nowhere near Stanford, or their foothills. The sweeping Gothic architecture of Cambridge upped the bone-chill factor, and weighed me down with indecision.

"Come on, my shirt sleeve is already rolled up. Let's get to work."

I rifled through the drawers and cabinets, looking for a solution. I grabbed a stethoscope, pulled out bandages, gauze, and medical tape from another. Because it felt like the right thing to do. It had been so long since I'd done a blood draw, I wasn't completely sure I was remembering the steps right.

I sensed him enjoying every choice.

The upper cabinet had Vacutainer kits. I pulled a packet out and stared at the contents—the hub, three vacuum tubes, and a beveled hypodermic needle. I snapped on a pair of latex gloves and ignored the tremors that had returned. I lined the items in a neat row in order of process. No one volunteered for blood draws. I would show him I could follow through. Two could play chicken.

I assembled the blood draw needle. I tied the rubber tourniquet around his lower bicep, trying not to notice how elegantly the muscle wrapped his arm. He was testing my sense of humor. I wasn't swabbing the median cubital vein of a man over a century old.

No way in hell.

I aimed the needle, but it bobbed from left to right in frenetic pulses.

"Do you need another minute?" He stared into my hesitation with a hint of a dare.

I slipped the needle into his vein, and crimson flooded the tube. Relief swept over my skin like someone opening a window. I didn't look up to see if he was okay, secretly hoping it hurt a little. I pulled the full tube and snapped on another, wiping beads of sweat from my upper lip.

The second tube filled, and I popped the third into place, and placed the second full tube on the counter next to the first. The first tube of blood was no longer crimson, but black.

Black as crude oil.

"That's real funny. You replaced the heparin with a coloring agent."

"I'm not even sure what that is. And how would I know you would grab that particular kit?"

"You would do it for all the kits. That's why you picked this room."

"I've always found obstinacy charming. Shall we go to the next room and try again?"

There was something about his expression. It wasn't earnest. There was no hint of joy or humor. It was resignation. Like I wasn't being quick enough.

I checked the second tube of blood in my hand, lifted it to the light, and watched it blacken. The coloring agent would work immediately, there would be no delay. My mind floated out of my head, levitated above me, bouncing like a balloon against the ceiling. This couldn't be happening. James looked like a healthy thirty-year-old. I examined his face for any sign of age, or disease, and realized the third tube of blood had been collected.

As if on autopilot, I folded gauze, tore a piece of medical tape, removed the needle, swabbed and watched the puncture wound disappear before I could bandage it. I shook my head. How was any of this happening? And why?

I paced the room looking for a biohazard bin. *Follow procedure.*

I disposed the kit, labeled the tubes, and resumed reality.

"When were you born?" I asked. Proud I looked him in the eye. And that was when I saw it. A spark flashed across his arctic blue irises, like someone running through an abandoned house with a flashlight.

This was no ordinary man.

"June thirteenth, eighteen hundred and thirty four. The fourth year of King William the Fourth's reign." He said the words slowly and clearly, and I noticed his accent was fainter than everyone else's. Unique, almost untraceable, and it made me want to listen. The room dropped in temperature, a terrible meat-locker temperature. "But that isn't the question you really want to ask."

Confused and stunned, I looked out the window and noticed the gargoyles perched on the arches of a nearby building. The sky clouded over as if he'd beckoned them to drive the point home. All that was needed was a clap of thunder and some rain to set the scene.

No matter how hard I tried to avoid looking at him, my eyes kept pulling back. The icy blue of his eyes, the emptiness they held, and yet he seemed full of knowledge.

The forbidden kind.

"What are you?" I whispered.

"I've been alive so long, I've forgotten what I am. Most days, I believe I'm just a man like any other. But then I remember what has come and gone while I've watched. While I've watched and never changed."

I pulled my lab coat around me nice and tight, not for warmth, but to keep my insides from spilling onto the floor.

He stood, and I was paralyzed with not wanting to hear any more of his words. He bowed his head toward me, his eyes darting back and forth like a metronome, ensnaring me. This was what we called "bonding" in the medical profession. It was a look you had to master if you wanted to be a good physician. It was a technique utilized to brace a loved one for terrible news. A technique I had never mastered. And one I had avoided since childhood.

"I believe the correct term," he said in that mesmerizing ancient voice, "is vampire."

I DIDN'T REMEMBER TAKING a seat, wasn't even sure how long

I'd been sitting. I held my forehead with my right hand, held the ice pack to the back of my neck with my left, and stared at the tiled floor between my knees. I definitely didn't remember blacking out.

He had said that word—vampire. The walls had shrunk, and all the doors in my mind had slammed shut. What had happened at Stanford, Gayle's death, why I had left my quiet safe job, and the one man I had come to find for answers was now missing, and now, a 184-year-old man stood in front of me. Everything had snapped and unraveled.

I pulled away the ice pack and placed my elbows on my knees, just in case. There were mysteries in science, things that didn't always add up. There were lethal odds that were beaten with prayers, fad diets, yoga, and bogus supplements. Even begging a God, an unkind invisible one, occasionally worked. There were miracles, but I hadn't come looking for any of those. I had come for answers.

The tips of James's shoes were to my left. He had gotten me into the chair, and found the ice pack, but what I appreciated most was his silence.

The ice pack had a small Star of Life printed on it. The single snake wrapped around a wooden staff within a blue star. My father had explained the myth, the duplicity of the symbol—life and death. That's why I had become a doctor, to prolong the former and prevent the later. And when I had to let go of Gayle's hand three months ago, I swore to find out why she had passed and I had lived. Again. Once was a miracle. Twice was something else.

I opened my mouth, but no words came out.

"You want to know what comes next?" he said.

I looked up, tried to look into his eyes, and stared at my feet. There wasn't an adequate first question.

"Why am I here, Mr. Stuart?"

In truth, that was the last question I wanted answered.

"You have a unique skill set, Dr. Whiting. And I have a unique circumstance. One I would like to replicate without killing."

"You want to make others?" I didn't mean to sound incredulous. But we were talking about creating an anomaly or a plague or a disease. Actually, I didn't know what we were discussing.

"No. Not really. I want you to find a way to replicate my blood."

"For what purpose?"

"To help."

"You're being evasive. I can't help if you don't tell me what I need to know."

"I'll tell you everything you need to know, to succeed."

I shook my head again, or perhaps I had never stopped. "Why me?"

"To be honest, circumstance. I have something you want, and you have skills I need."

I finally looked at him. There was his impeccable grin. The one that was disarming, innocent and guilty, and engaging. This had to be one of the keys to his longevity.

"And what is that I want, Mr. Stuart?"

"The medical files from Sturgis County Hospital, all thirty-one."

I squeezed the ice pack between my hands. This was what it was like to be a lab rat.

"And if I fail?"

"Are you really attempting to sell yourself so short? You were ready to repudiate a citation found in a published report written by a prestigious colleague. Someone you admired. Someone whose footsteps you wished to follow."

My nerves sputtered. "Did you kill him?"

He laughed, not with condescension. The laugh hugged me with warmth and kindness, making me instantly uncomfortable. "That would make an odd bridge to build in our relationship, to kill your competition."

"He wasn't my—"

"No. I'm not a monster."

"Can I leave?"

"Do you want to?"

I stood. Impressed, I was steady on my feet. More impressed, when I made it down the hall. Invigorated when I didn't fall down the stairs. The relief I felt as the fresh air touched my face was immeasurable. I just needed to keep walking. My backpack was at my desk, less than a quarter mile away. I didn't need to make eye contact with anyone, move ahead, pass go, get out of crazy jail free.

I was twenty feet from my building when I saw Mr. Stuart sitting on a bench. His long legs stretched before him, his head tipped back, facing the sun.

How was it that he could be out in the sun? Had I really asked that question? What was wrong with me?

"Dr. Whiting, do you really want to walk away from the key to your past all over semantics?"

"Semantics? You just told me that there are monsters. Real ones. The person I came to talk to is missing. I think it would be the logical thing to do."

"Logical? Even after what happened to your lab partner at Stanford?" He folded his hands and placed them in his lap. "I'm sure you have questions. More now than ever."

My chest burned. I didn't think it possible to hate someone so deeply in such a short amount of time.

"Who do you think you are?" I asked.

He didn't answer right away, which worried me because if he really was over a century old, his thoughts would have the weight of history behind them. He inhaled deeply. "Someone who understands your sense of loss. Your sense of guilt. To be left alone surrounded by death. I'm sorry for your suffering. But I believe I'm going to change your life. I think we both deserve some change."

"I don't want to change. And I didn't ask for this."

"No. But you did ask for the medical files of those thirty-one children. All who died, all but one. Whatever happened in that hospital, whatever happened to that little girl, you can't bury under a medical degree or a title, Doctor."

"Nothing happened."

He shrugged. "Semantics."

5

GROUNDED

I had made it to my gate. Almost boarded the United Airlines flight to La Guardia. I made one fundamental mistake. On packing my bags in the hotel, I had grabbed the local paper.

Nested between a story about a Cambridge man having bleach squirted in his face and a school renovation was an article about a grave robbing. The robbing had been the fourth one in six months. There were also two missing persons over the last three months, leaving police scrambling for answers and a growing public concern there was an epidemic of crime in the area.

It was an article that could be found in dozens of other newspapers. But there was that interesting word choice —epidemic.

What if Tousain had created a serum? What if he wanted to grant everlasting life to others? How far would he go to test his theory? There was no reason to rob graves, but worse things had been done in the name of science. The man had spent the last ten years researching and studying a concept he'd named universal immunity. He studied rare cases of survival against contagions. Which was why he had acquired the Sturgis files. But if he had a patient who could outlive time, there could be no better universal immunity.

I watched them close the door to the gate. The plane pulled away and taxied down the long runway. My flight officially missed, I wandered the large mall of the Queen's terminal of Heathrow. It was its own metropolis. There was a small grocery shop, plenty of charging stations, a massage clinic, the last remaining bookstore on the planet. Near one of the gates, a young mother hovered over her screaming toddler. The girl batted her mother's hands away and pulled at her ears.

Unable to listen to the child's pain, I walked up to the mother.

"Do you have any chewing gum?" I asked.

"What?" The young mother flashed me a sneer, revealing the depths of her exhaustion.

"Your daughter's ears haven't adjusted to the change in air pressure from flying." I pointed at the little girl's ears. "If she chews some gum, it will dislodge the fluid in her ears. It should cheer her right up."

The woman rummaged through a very large purse. She was almost in tears.

I unzipped the outer pocket of my backpack and handed her a packet of gum. "It's strawberry lime flavored."

The mother scrunched her eyebrows at me. As if I chose the flavor to lure small children from their parents. I liked fruit flavored gum.

"Do you want some, Emma?" the mother asked.

The girl snatched the treat. Between short gasps of air, the girl chewed the gum. She lifted her arms up and the mother picked her up. The mother patted the girl's back and mouthed thank you to me.

Crisis averted, I took a window seat and watched planes come and go. I watched mothers and wives and sons and fiancés come through the gates, watching their phones for messages. A few of them were lucky enough to be welcomed personally with a hug or a smile.

There was no one waiting for me at Stanford. No one had seen me off at my departure. I was alone. It was a self-prescribed state. I watched the large clock on the wall for hours. All that time spent parsing information and questions. Where would I go? Who would I call? Could I forgive myself? The most important—did I really have a choice?

I had fought hard to keep my position at Stanford, only to be shooed off by a lame OSHA case. Lost the only home I had ever liked. There was no way I could rebuild my career empty-handed. I would never find my way back to normal without answers. If I walked away, even from someone who didn't appear to need my help, I would be breaking the oath I took. If this was bottom, all that was left was up. I wanted to be welcomed. I needed to be needed. Someone sat next to me.

"You've been here a long time. When was the last time you ate?"

I turned and there was James, looking as fresh as the first pot of coffee.

I closed my eyes. "I don't know. This morning."

"You mean yesterday?"

The sun had broken the horizon an hour ago. I rubbed my face.

"Let's get you something to eat." He patted my knee.

"How did you get past security?"

"Bought a ticket."

"To where?"

He pulled the boarding pass from his inner jacket pocket. "Boston. Have you ever been?"

I shook my head.

"Me neither." He stared out the window, his eyes a little more glassy than usual. "Where do we go from here, Doctor?"

"I guess we need to start at the beginning."

He nodded. "Which one?"

Suddenly the airport was very quiet. People moved around us, like blood flowing to a wound. How many beginnings could a 184-year-old man have? By his looks, he could afford to reinvent himself every thirty years. If he had lived six lifetimes, I was woefully short on experience. My mother used to say people never changed. He may have had a history, but we had a future to figure out.

"The beginning that you would find most helpful," I said. "Because I want to help."

"I don't want you to help. I want you to troubleshoot."

"Semantics." I feigned a decent smile.

"What's your favorite meal? I'm sure we could find a good steak in this place."

"Breakfast. I like breakfast."

"Good, because I'm famished."

Jesus. He ate food?

"If I had a pound for every time I've seen that expression on a doctor's face—"

"How many doctors have you worked with?"

"I lost count decades ago."

"Huh." Shit.

"Let's go to Harrod's."

"There's a Harrod's in here?"

James pointed to the large marquee one hundred feet

from where we sat. Amazing the large touchstones you manage to not see when preoccupied.

"They serve food?"

"Oh yes."

I followed James and our silence like a well-trained service dog. He managed to get us the best table with an incredible view of the runway.

"How long has Tousain known about your condition?" I finally asked.

"I think he held suspicions for a long time. But I didn't confirm them until six months ago."

"But he's been authorizing your transfusions for years."

"He's been authorizing a process for years. Not my fault he never questioned it." James shrugged off the lie and I wondered how he had kept his teeth so white all these decades. The waiter brought us menus and coffee.

I didn't have my mind fully wrapped around what James Stuart was or how it all worked. Tousain had jumped that hurdle and was now missing. I glanced at the newspaper tucked in my backpack.

"Do you know what happened to Dr. Tousain?" I asked.

He peered over the menu. "I think what you really mean is am I responsible for his disappearance? And I guess, in an indirect way, I am."

I stared at the blurry menu. Oh, man. What was I getting myself into?

He placed his menu on the table. "I think he was becoming impatient with our secret, and was exploring possible side markets."

"He replicated your condition?"

"Wouldn't you try to bottle my condition?"

I shook my head. But I understood it was the second space race—longevity. Pharmaceutical companies made billions off the premise. The world wasn't big enough. There would be a severe biological counter balance to the notion.

"So you suspect he made a serum and has left to find a market for it?"

"He wouldn't be the first to make that attempt."

Right. He had cycled through a century of doctors.

"Are there more on staff who know?"

"I've found that if you want to keep something under wraps, it's best not to tell very many people. So 'we' is now up to three."

"Tousain, myself and...?"

"Nate Rothschild, the Director of the Blood Bank."

I didn't know what expression I made, but James let a small laugh escape. "I see you've met."

I rubbed my eyes. I wasn't sure I could work with someone that direct or mischievous. And painfully aware of both characteristics and his good looks. But he was a hematologist. "You said Tousain suspected for a while. How long do you think?"

"I'd say for the last eight years, when his focus changed from pathology to immunology. I had hired him in 1995, and although we had limited interaction, he hadn't seen me age very much."

"That was careless."

To my surprise, he accepted responsibility. The waiter returned and we placed our order. A full British breakfast. I braced myself for boiled meat because it was easier to distract my mind from the growing list of questions.

"What happened six months ago?"

"An unfortunate mishap. Sometimes I have the worst luck."

There was a new layer of coldness in his reply, so I didn't push. The question fell in one of those fuzzy interpersonal areas, an area where I didn't excel. And it was one I couldn't verify under a microscope.

We both watched a British Airways Airbus take off. I watched the detached politeness fall away from his face. It was replaced with what appeared to be longing.

"That never ceases to amaze me," he said.

A trapdoor opened in my mind. The world had evolved over his lifetime. Dramatically. Transportation alone had gone from horse carriage, to train, to automobile, to airplane, to self- driving cars. I palmed my unused boarding pass, folded it, and shoved it into my backpack. The waiter delivered our food. I don't think my eyes were prepared for the sumptuous feast. Even the plates looked edible.

"Whoa. I was expecting something much simpler." Like fried eggs and boiled meat with toast. But I was staring at two perfectly fried eggs, two browned sausages the size of fat Sharpie markers, five dressed cherry tomatoes, and two rounds of bread that resembled an English muffin. There was also a small tray of fresh fruit cut to precise perfection. And that was when my stomach made an abrupt u-turn from comatose to starving.

"What are you looking for?" James asked.

"Ketchup."

He asked the waiter for the ketchup. I think I jumped at the sight of the Heinz glass bottle. We thanked the waiter and I buried my eggs under a blanket of red.

"I don't think I've ever met someone that enthusiastic about ketchup."

Even when James grimaced, he appeared ageless. It would be an interesting product to bottle. "Are you sure he was able to replicate your..." I said as I checked over both shoulders, "blood?" I moaned after the food hit my tongue. Sometimes I forgot to eat, but I don't forget to savor.

"No." He handed me a napkin. "Please don't choke on your first day as my new doctor."

I ignored the jab. Food was fuel, and comfort. I popped a piece of chicken sausage into my mouth. "Even with all the surveillance?"

He spread a little jam on his toast. "The clinic isn't a prison."

"But the cameras. The network."

"We have some cutting edge research being conducted, millions of dollars worth of intellectual property. The level of security is standard and expected."

"Sure." I spun the lid off the pot of jam, slathered a thick layer on my toast, tore a piece, and tossed it into my mouth. "But how would you not know?" I stopped chewing the bitter toast and spat it into a napkin. "What is that?" I pointed to the pot of jam.

"Orange marmalade. You were raised by your father?"

"It tastes like sugar and ear wax. Yes, why?"

He pushed his half-eaten toast aside and grabbed another jam. "Try this, it's strawberry. What happened to your mother? If you don't mind me asking?"

I removed the lid of the jam, spreading it across the second round of bread. "She was cuckoo and then flew when I was ten. What is this by the way?"

"A crumpet."

I watched another plane take off. Instead of a sense of uncertainty, I felt a sense of flight. My sense of curiosity was starved of information. The level of noise in the restaurant was set at a polite hum, like an active beehive. I scanned the room. We didn't stand out. We looked like everyone else—weary travelers enjoying a good meal.

My eyes zeroed in on his with acute accuracy. "Why me?" I asked.

"Would it be enough to say that I believe in miracles?"

I think I made a pained face, and he changed his answer.

"Your name has been on the recruiting list three times. I would know, because I put it there. You have a passion for studying immunity. Rare immunity. You have an interesting eye for detail, but your age was a problem for the Board. I pushed harder this time. And Mathieu couldn't fight me as hard."

"I want access to his research."

"I can give you what I have, and that isn't much."

"Why?" I dropped my toast.

"He had installed his own server, which we caught too late."

The lingering taste of the marmalade wasn't even close to my bitter disappointment. Starting at ground zero was something I hadn't planned on, but it wasn't like I hadn't been there before. I tried to hide a massive yawn. "Sorry."

"I should get you back to your hotel. Let you get some rest."

"I don't have a hotel."

"I can get you back into the DeVere. Or set you up in a nice flat."

"Shit, my suitcase." Was on its way to LaGuardia.

"I'll have it taken care of."

My mind raced to keep up with the decision I was and wasn't making.

"So I don't see any of the Sturgis files until I figure out what Tousain has been up to?"

"Well, let's see how our first week goes."

"I guess it's not like I don't have time to figure this out."

My offhanded remark hit him like a slap, quick and smart. Across the table was a man who had survived decades, seen two centuries pass, had probably suffered many losses. He was fixed, irrevocable of change. Time was no longer a luxury for him, perhaps a curse.

"I'm sorry. I didn't mean to offend."

"It's alright. I don't offend easily."

I stood. Despite the fog in my head, the day looked full of promise. Something new, a gift not to be wasted. "Actually, can we go back to the clinic? I'd like to speak with Dr. Rothschild, if that's okay?"

James checked his watch. It was a unique piece. The watch didn't have a round face, but square with minimal fare, and a leather band that had been worn smooth. "He should be in by the time we get back into Cambridge."

It would take us less than ninety minutes to get back to the clinic, which meant Dr. Rothschild was a late night, late morning kind of person. I squinted at the planes lined up neatly on the tarmac. "Would you mind if we did another blood draw?"

"You mean the three tubes aren't enough?"

"You saved them?"

"Never waste a drop, I always say."

6

PUSHING UP DAISIES

"Can't say that I've ever seen anything like this." Detective Sergeant Victoria Moore's cigarette bobbed in her mouth, making DI Cooper consider snatching it from his trusted sergeant.

George shoved his hands in his pockets and kept his right hand occupied with the change from this morning's coffee. There were three dug-up graves, all within twenty meters of each other.

"It looks like Goldilocks couldn't find just the right coffin." Vic let out a thick plume of cigarette smoke and it hung in the warm summer morning air. George crossed the taped-off crime scene to see the view from the other side and to avoid savoring secondhand smoke.

"Ah shit. Sorry, boss." Vic extinguished her fag under the heel of her biker boot and placed the butt in her coat pocket.

"It's fine." It wasn't. He was climbing the big hill to becoming a nonsmoker, but he liked Vic's company. She didn't push to talk about anything personal. She kept things light. He needed light.

"Do we have anything on the occupants of the graves?"

Vic pulled out her phone. "One male and two females. They aren't related, so three singles. How depressing is that?" She quickly glanced at the graves and genuflected. Nothing frightened a police officer more than being buried alone. "But they were all interned in the last four months. The female was buried last week. And they weren't cremated. Which is costly."

"So someone has a designer fetish for graves?"

"That was a good one. Going to make a note of that." She thumb-typed on her mobile. "DI Cooper especially quick-witted this morning. Obvious he has a hard-on for the weird ones."

"Funny. Like your new haircut."

"You not liking the Matt Ritchie?" She fanned her fingers through her spiky red hair.

"Traitor."

"You're not even from Manchester." She attempted to subdue a yawn. "Are you sure you don't want to hand this off?"

"Are you afraid of a few corpses, Sergeant?"

"Hell no, it's just that it's seven in the morning. I'm afraid of not getting enough sleep. And I know you didn't leave the office before midnight."

The Tousain case was taking time to sort through. George shrugged. "Is there any CCTV?"

"Only from the street and parking lot. We might be able to see who came in, but not if they dug up these poor people."

"Let's get forensics to process the woman first. And let's call the families and find out if anything of value is missing."

"I thought the economy was going in the shitter, but this, this takes the cake. What if it's a prank?"

"I'd expect a little more theatre to it, wouldn't you?"

Vic squinted at her phone. "Weird."

"What?"

"Another complaint came in twenty minutes ago. From a crematorium."

George leaned over Vic's shoulder and read the station report. "That's a little strange."

"Someone breaking into a crematorium? Yeah, that's a little off the beaten path." She continued to scroll through the report. "There was a body molested. Bite marks. That's disgusting."

"Whose the SOCO at the scene?"

Vic pointed. George pulled out his phone and dialed.

"We're going to take on every complaint this morning?" she asked.

George smiled. He hadn't felt this excited in a long time, had been worried he never would. "It's only five miles away."

"Is this where you say something lame, like *the game is on*?"

"Afoot, Sergeant. And no, this is when I say *let's get cracking*." He crossed the lawn.

"Can we get a coffee first?" Vic called after him. "Maybe a scone? What's with the spring in your step? Ah, fuck me."

7

BLACK HOLE

The newspaper rested on my desk, neatly folded over my massive collection of reports. A reminder of the date I missed my flight home. The date to not regret.

Tap, tap, tap.

The gelatinous bag of black blood lay slumped on my worktable. Hypnotized by the contents, I stared at it, my mind analyzing results that added up to nothing.

Nothing but more questions, with more tests to run.

Sometimes I had to wait for complete solitude to test a theory. Like locking my lab door and watching his blood boil under the direct exposure of sunrise. It was quick and violent, and when the blood bag burst into ashes, I almost lost my oatmeal.

Tap, tap, tap.

His blood couldn't be examined under a microscope. It was like having the lens cap over a camera, pure blackness. If I added his blood to another's, it disappeared in a fraction of a second. His blood cells took on all the characteristics of the host blood cells. There were no curative properties.

They repaired nothing. Just held the hosts cells in limbo. To my right, a tray of tissue samples injected with his blood remained unchanged. There was no trace of James in any of my tests. He was an illusive ghost or a god.

His voice came out of nowhere. "What are you staring at?"

I jolted out of my chair, knocking my hand into the microscope. The sharp pain radiated past my elbow.

"Sorry, didn't mean to startle you," James said.

"Did you knock?"

"Several times. You had me worried."

That must've been the tapping noises. I attempted to flick the pain out of my hand, which made it worse. I tucked my hand under my armpit instead.

James sported a navy suit with dark green pinstripes, a hunter green silk shirt, and canary yellow silk tie. Given his real age, and the century in which he became a man, I couldn't help but wonder if his formality was more tied to his inability to be casual, or if he was a fashion whore.

In our forced working relationship, I had stopped wearing the uncomfortable pantsuits, and had switched back to jeans and baggy sweaters. Which seemed to irritate him.

He set two small black canisters in front of me.

"What are those?" I asked.

"Do you attend church?"

"That's a completely illegal employer question. And not relevant to my work."

"I'll take that as a no." He swiped one canister and slipped it into his inner breast pocket. He pointed to the remaining canister. "It's pepper spray."

"Pepper spray? Are you planning to attack me when I don't give you good news?" For most hours of the day, James was my prison warden not my patient. I wanted the Sturgis medical files. And with none of my tests working, I needed some assurance my past hadn't been stolen from me. This wasn't the assurance I was looking for.

"You've been putting in long nights. And you seem to adore public transit and walking."

"The current assault rate in Cambridge is 6.9 percent. Which is better than Palo Alto. The idea of trying to remember to drive on the wrong side of the road, coupled with my new research didn't seem like a good idea." I picked up the pepper spray. "What's in the other canister?"

"Holy water."

His assumption had been correct. The need for religion in my life had disappeared along with my father. "This is an effective deterrent?"

"It will buy you a few minutes. Sometimes that's all you need." He smiled. "To get away, catch someone's attention, find a stake."

"What does the holy water do?"

"Burns skin clear off, down to the bone. It's terribly painful to regenerate."

I could taste the lab's filtered air on my tongue. I willed my voice to stay level, matter-of-fact. I suddenly wanted to test the other canister. "You can regenerate skin?" My eyes drifted to the windowsill, hoping I'd cleaned all the ashes.

His gaze tracked mine. "Have you been conducting strange science experiments while I sleep?"

"Do you sleep?"

"Most days I read. Surf the internet for pertinent material, sometimes illicit material."

After a week of tests and interviews, I knew he was trying to get under my skin. It was frustrating it continued to work. I dragged my notebook across the worktable, waiting for my embarrassment to burn off.

"And how long does it take to heal or regenerate?" Work was always the best salve.

"Depends how extensive the damage is. Severe damage can take days, weeks even. Flesh wounds a few minutes to an hour."

"Stakes, really? What about silver bullets or...regular bullets?"

"Bullets are a deterrent. But again, tissue can be regenerated. So stakes are good. Through the heart, not the abdominal cavity. Wood or metal, doesn't matter. Or *fffhhuhtt*." He ran his index finger across his neck like a knife. "And then burn the body."

My eyes grew sticky like dehydrated fruit. People didn't run around staking people in the heart or cutting people's heads off, did they? Stanford was a lifetime away.

"Let me show you how this works." He grabbed the canister and sat close, almost touching shoulders, causing me to tense. "You push down this lever with your thumb and then press down."

"I know how it works," I stuttered. Jogging in the foothills at Stanford alone in the evenings meant carrying one. More for the mountain lions than stranger danger. He didn't get up, stayed seated next to me. I failed to get my resting heart rate back. It was content to race toward his dangerous secrets.

"Can I see any of the Sturgis files?"

He leaned back and crossed his arms. The charm of his smile was slick and evasive. "You don't understand. I need leverage."

"Leverage?"

"I need your help. If I hand over the Sturgis files, you'll lose interest."

"Lose interest? You're a biological anomaly, your disease could unlock infinite possibilities." If I could figure out how to separate his proteins. "You're a miracle. How could I lose interest?"

"You seem to forget, I care nothing *about* my disease. I just want it to end." The heat of his stare made the air feel electric. "I'm the one in search of a miracle. And you need to find it."

He'd survived world wars, influenza outbreaks, time, and people's desires. He was the ultimate research subject. There was no way to ferret out his secrets with lab tests alone. I'd have to get to know him, not under a lens, but as a person. Question by question, discussion after discussion. This was going to take forever. I didn't have that long.

"So you have transfusions done once, sometimes twice a week. Two to three pints. Has it always been so little?"

"Yes. And I have other arrangements."

My face strained to stay objective. The human body required the circulatory system to function. Otherwise muscles atrophied, bones became brittle, and organs failed. His body needed new blood to replace what his blood turned into—black sludge. A five-foot-ten male, who weighed one hundred sixty pounds, required ten to twelve pints of blood.

Every day.

"Live donors?" I asked. Proud my voice didn't crack.

He nodded.

"Do you draw from the same source?"

"I have multiple donors."

"How many donors?"

He pulled at his shirt cuff. "Six at the moment."

For some reason, I had a higher number in mind. "And they volunteer to let you do this?"

"They're well compensated."

"They're paid?" I forgot to mask my disapproval. He ran his tongue over his lips, and the temperature in the room rose to an interrogation level, but I continued. "Why multiple donors?"

"I can't have a monogamous relationship. It could prove to be..."

"Fatal?"

"Or eternal. It can go either way."

"How do you create another you?"

"Vampire. I'm a vampire, Dr. Whiting."

On instinct, I glanced at the security cameras. Which was stupid because he owned them. I had avoided saying the word. Afraid I'd break into a fit of laughter, because that's what happened when I practiced saying the word to the mirror. Now he looked like he wanted to burn the word across my forehead. There were worse words to have to say —cancer, casualty, coward.

"How do you create a vampire?" I asked.

"Through multiple blood exchanges."

Reassuring that the disease didn't happen through one bite, or one encounter, it was like a universal safety clause. "Multiple exchanges, like two? Three to five? Five to seven?"

"It's not that precise. Depends on the amount of blood exchanged, and the emotional attachment. And it takes time."

"You can't just make one in a hurry?"

He let out a hearty laugh, genuine in a frightening and exhilarating way. It filled every crevice of the lab with uncensored humanity. He rubbed his eyes and regained his composure. "No. You can't just make one willy-nilly. Or there would be a plague of us. There's a high failure rate."

What did that failure look like? I struggled to breathe. Our conversation should've only taken place in nightmares or on a movie screen.

"The chosen could bleed out. I could overindulge. There's the risk of exposure to disease. Although with rampant vaccination that's not so great a hazard any longer," he said.

I rubbed my neck, "Is it painful?"

"Yes and no."

"What do you mean?"

"The blood exchanges can be pleasurable. The painful part is realizing it can't be undone."

"Do you know any others?"

"We're not desirable to have around."

"You don't know of any others personally?"

"We don't have organized families. This isn't a special club or mafia. No secret handshake or special knock at the door. We're solitary creatures."

"That makes no sense."

"Why does that not make sense?"

"Wouldn't the whole point of creating another vampire be for companionship? To spend eternity not alone?"

"No, that's the whole point, Dr. Whiting. To spend eternity alone on the fringes."

"But that's cruel."

"Damnation isn't a cakewalk."

There it was again, the high-pitched hum that agitated my skin and made my ears ache. I had crossed the line into some indelicate personal area. His face became a solid mask of emptiness. He stood, buttoned his blazer, and left.

"Dammit." I looked down at my notes. Too close to give

up, I ran down the hall and caught him before he reached the elevator.

"I want to meet them," I blurted.

He stopped, but his anger hadn't subdued.

Checking to see everyone's lab doors were closed, I lowered my voice, "I'd like to meet your donors. It's strictly professional. I won't ask them anything personal. Just collect their medical history. And blood samples."

"No." He hit the down button. "It is not relevant to your research."

"It's part of your biology and completely relevant. I've already combed through everything you've given me."

The elevator door opened and he stepped in, giving me his normal unexpressive face. The door began to close, and the words flew out of my mouth.

"You don't need to be ashamed."

The last sliver of his discontent disappeared behind the elevator door, leaving me with a mouthful of regret.

8

A REASONABLE QUESTION

There were only a couple of other places I hated worse than hospitals. The first, cemeteries, and the second was police stations. Even though this one had an exceptional view of the Cricket Club of Cambridge, I fidgeted.

I checked my phone for the fifth time. Two weeks post-vampire revelation, Detective Inspector Cooper had asked me to come down for some follow-up questions. Actually, I think he phrased it as "pop in for a chat," which didn't sound all that bad. We had agreed on four thirty. At four thirty, I was asked to sit in a waiting room and not his office, and it was another twenty-five minutes before I saw him.

When he walked down the hall to greet me, there was a distinct problem with his left hip, which he tried to disguise by walking faster.

"Thank you for coming to the station, Dr. Whiting." He shook my hand, not bone crushing firm, but firm. "I'm terribly sorry to have you wait. I had an interview that ran much longer than expected. Sitting causes my sciatic nerve to flare up." He smiled. "Can I get you a cuppa tea?"

I think I reared my head back in wonder. This was what happened when I spent too much time locked in a lab playing with tissue samples, I forgot about humanity. I scanned the few desks I could see from the waiting area and noticed everyone using a mug and not disposable cups. But there were a couple of empty water bottles in Cooper's office.

"Water." I rubbed my eyes. "Water would be nice."

DI Cooper asked a workmate to grab a bottle of water for me as he walked me back to his small but tidy office.

"Please sit down." He leaned back in his chair, stretching. "Again, my apologies."

I sat, tucking my backpack between my legs and folding my hands on my lap. He waved someone into his office and handed me a bottle of Evian. I cracked open the bottle and took a sip. Funny thing, the pounding in my chest wasn't subsiding.

"Are you enjoying Cambridge?" he asked. He took a sip of whatever was in his coffee cup. It disagreed with him and he grimaced. "Cold tea." He palmed a sugar cube from a small chipped bowl sitting on his desk and tossed it into his mouth.

I looked out beyond the window framing his face and nodded. "The King's College tour was really nice. Europeans know how to do churches. But the library in Trinity College, that's something to write home about."

He had a disarming smile and patient eyes. Good qualities for a cop. "Have you gone punting yet?"

"Is that a...sport?" I turned my head to the right to ensure I heard him better.

His nice smiled deepened, causing little wrinkles in the corners of his eyes. "On the River Cam. The punts are the boats."

"With the big sticks?"

He laughed. "Yes, they're poles."

"I haven't gotten around to that." We slipped into an uncomfortable silence. I began to wonder if he was doing this on purpose or if I was spending too much time with a manipulative patient. "So you had some follow-up questions?"

"Right." He leaned forward and opened a folder. He rubbed his nose and crunched another sugar cube. "You said you were interviewed by Dr. Tousain in May?"

"Yes."

"This interview was conducted over Skype, yes?"

I nodded. "But it was a voice call, no video."

"And he made you an offer of employment on the third of June?"

"Yes."

"And that was over email." He fanned out some of the papers in his file and pulled one to the top.

"I sent your Sergeant a copy of the email." I twisted the water bottle open and took a bigger sip of water.

"But had you ever met Dr. Tousain personally?"

"Of course, I've met him." I took another sip of water, and was embarrassed when some dribbled down my chin.

He handed me a paper napkin from his desk drawer. "But Dr. Tousain never came out to Stanford to meet you?"

"He held a lecture there two years ago." I quickly blotted my chin and wadded the napkin into a tight ball.

"And that's when you met him?"

"Yes. There was a dinner party held for him and I attended."

"And did you correspond after that?"

"A little. He had some reports I wanted access to for some research."

"But the interview and the offer of employment were not done in person. Is that odd?"

"I wouldn't know. You'd have to ask his assistant."

"Are you sure you spoke to Dr. Tousain and not someone else on staff?"

"I'm sorry. I'm not following you. Are you saying I wasn't interviewed by Dr. Tousain?"

"No, not exactly." He palmed another sugar cube but put it back when he realized I was watching. "Terrible habit." He took a deep breath. "Here's the thing, Dr. Whiting, it looks like your work visa forms were filled out and dated back in March."

"That makes no sense," I said. My life had been turned upside down in March.

"That's what I thought as well. Why would Dr. Tousain request a work visa for an employee he hadn't even interviewed yet?"

I rubbed my neck. There were tactics for moments like this, lies were one thing, but cover-ups were another. It shouldn't have been a surprise James had lied or schemed or possibly set up my entire circumstance. My right foot struggled to stay attached to my leg.

"Had you ever submitted an application before May?"

"No."

"It's not something you'd have done and possibly forgotten?"

I leaned back. "No. I never forget things. And I didn't submit an application, they actively sought me out."

"I didn't mean to imply you did. It's not unusual for clinicians to apply for jobs they aren't interested in, in order to receive grants or renegotiate salaries."

I sat spine straight. "So I'm not forgetful, I'm scheming

for grant money?" And how did he know about these things?

"Sorry. I'm just trying to figure out why James Stuart had filed work visa papers for you in March." DI Cooper reread his notes again.

There was an awkward few seconds or minute where I just stared at his left ear. "I don't know." And I would be asking James the same question the minute I was out of the detective's office. "I thought you said Dr. Tousain had filed those papers?"

He looked down at his file. "Sorry, I meant James Stuart. It's been a long week." He smiled again, this time forced. "Which makes this even stranger, wouldn't you say? Are you sure Dr. Tousain was the man on the phone?"

"Yes. Positive." I stood. "Is that all, Detective?"

His brows squeezed together. "Are you happy at the Hastings Clinic?"

"How does that relate to your investigation?"

"I just want to make sure you're... comfortable."

"Comfortable?" What kind of question was that? I knew I made a terrible liar, but surely he didn't understand my complete circumstance. He was fishing.

"It's just that, I've come to notice something very strange about the Hastings Clinic."

A small alarm buzzed in the back of my head. There was something else the detective wasn't telling me. "Such as?"

"There seems to be an awful lot of missing or deceased employees over the last fifteen years."

I cleared my throat. "People die all the time. Surely, you know that." A part of me resented the game he was playing, another part of me wanted to call his bluff.

"But three deaths and two unexplained disappearances in such a short span, seems suspect. No?"

"I wouldn't know. But my guess is it has you concerned about my safety. Were they all Americans? Or females? Or right-handed?"

He rubbed his bottom lip with his teeth, making those nice eyes more attractive. "No. But they all hail from the same department—Research."

It would be a relief to just blurt it out. Say it to another rational human being. My employer was a vampire. I was in a foreign country, and had swam into territory far beyond my medical training. I had no friends, no one to confide in. And the only person I had conversed with this long besides DI Cooper was almost two centuries old. But that nice smile of DI Cooper's would become patronizing the minute I uttered those words. And technically, I had a patient to protect, and a confidentiality not to break.

"The real secret to numbers and statistics is they can be interpreted many ways. They're useful to win either side of an argument. To tell a story. Sometimes there is no pattern to a set of numbers or statistics. So unless you have proof that I'm in some kind of danger, I kind of resent the scare tactic."

THERE IT WAS, that awful feeling. George had crossed the line. He usually regarded that line with a sick enthusiasm. When the world became a not so clearly bordered civil place, people cracked a little, especially liars. He loved that most about his profession, catching people off-guard. It was very strange for him to quickly course correct for the doctor's sake. There wasn't a time when he had ever concluded an interview by asking a subject if they were happy. He didn't feel good about poking around Dr. Whiting's clearly defined borders.

George couldn't conclude Dr. Whiting was lying, but he did think she was hiding something. And she was trying really hard to cover up her fear. Which was where the awful feeling stemmed, and it lingered in his stomach after she left. After hemming and hawing for a couple of minutes, he ran out of the station looking for her. Never had he done this.

She was easy to find. The jet-black hair set her apart. He called out to her and she turned. There were traces of cold confusion and fiery frustration in her stare. Admittedly, she was a bit of an enigma. The high, proud cheekbones and the rich chestnut brown eyes weren't a match to her father. A basic search had turned up information about her publishing credentials, linking her to her published father who had been a professor at Stanford University. The man looked like any professor, from Stanford to Cambridge, to Swansea or Liverpool—the ever-present Caucasian male.

"Did you *forget* something, Detective?" Her thick eyebrows were encroaching on her high forehead. Her almond-shaped eyes pierced the point.

He raised his hands in surrender. Strange, he didn't think he was ready for that. "I really didn't mean to imply you were making up anything."

"No, you were implying I didn't understand my situation."

So she believed there was a situation. But it wasn't time to pursue that yet.

"How about I make it up and take you to dinner?"

She crossed her arms over her chest. "Is that allowed?"

There was a small divot between her eyes when she was offended. There was a growing part of him that felt an obligation to iron it smooth.

"You're not a suspect, Dr. Whiting. I'm just offering to

show you a different side of Cambridge. The side where people are friendly and welcoming. Not insulting."

Her body relaxed, a little. She looked over her shoulder in the direction of the clinic.

"I can pick you up from work. Completely platonic." Why had he said that?

She rubbed her chin. "Okay. I'm free tomorrow."

"Seven o'clock?"

She nodded and looked at her phone.

"Do you need a lift back?" he asked.

"I could use the walk."

From the security records, he knew the woman broke up her day with a five to ten mile run every afternoon, so a walk was far from needed. She wanted to be alone. There were times when he resented cataloguing behavior, but it was his job to intuit things.

"Then I'll see you tomorrow at seven. I'll pick you up at the west entrance, by the oak trees."

"How did you know there were oak trees there?"

He tapped the side of his nose.

"Right, see you tomorrow, Detective."

Her father had taught American History. From colonization through the Civil War, but his specialty was Native American history. That was the closest he had come to a guess about her mother, whom he had found no record of, but he hadn't dug very deep.

There was a wave of eyes pretending not to notice him when he walked back to his office. There were also several smirks on clear display. He hadn't put a lot of thought into chasing Dr. Whiting, and had failed to cover his tracks. Never a smart thing to do in a room full of detectives.

"Calm down," he warned. "You're all worse than a knitting circle."

Two sergeants began to mimic knitting, and he promptly gave them two fingers.

Vic followed him into his office and handed him a report. "Coroner's report on the body found at the crematorium. The mortician says it was a new client who had been delivered the evening prior. So he hadn't begun his process." She shook like someone had dumped worms down the back of her shirt. "Mortician's timeline has been confirmed by another employee. Anyway, Martin says it looks like someone drained the body of blood."

"Does he know how?"

"Aside from the other bite marks, there were two puncture marks on the neck, so through the carotid artery."

"With a device?"

Vic rubbed her bottom lip.

"What did Martin say?" George asked.

"Teeth."

"Are you kidding me? Like a snake or something?"

She threw her hands up. "Martin also found bite marks on one of the males recovered from the cemetery ransack. He was the most recently deceased."

"So the crimes are connected." He rubbed his thumb against his index finger, his trigger finger. He turned toward the window. "What kind of wacko does that?"

"Martin will have the cemetery victims done later today, maybe tomorrow. Like I suggested earlier, we could always pass it off. The victims were already dead anyway. And it gives me the jitters." George was listening, but didn't respond. "A doctor and a detective, isn't that a bit cliché, Sherlock?" Her tone laced with excitement.

"She's not that kind of doctor, Watson." And she must've taken a brisk walk because he couldn't find her at the end of the block.

"Whacha mean?"

"Not a physician. She's a pathologist, an expert on disease." He scratched his chest, the tip of his nail grazing a scar. "Where are we on the clinic?" he asked.

"Turner and Hsu are going through the archives now. But it's going to take a couple days. I didn't realize it had been there so long."

"Yeah, one-hundred-twelve years. But it really hadn't made a whole lot of press until Stuart took over." His body had tensed with resentment, but he ignored it.

"Better tread carefully. You can't make this about you and him. Is that why you chased down the American? To make sure we looked nice?"

George shrugged. The warning wasn't lost. Given his personal ties to the clinic, and that this was his first major case since the accident, he couldn't afford to jeopardize the investigation.

"There hasn't been any activity on Tousain's accounts. Even if he had a stash of cash, he would've made a slip by now. I feel like we're chasing a ghost." He looked at Vic.

"What?" she asked. She could read him like a book.

"Can you run a background check on Dr. Whiting?"

She pouted and looked up at him with puppy eyes. "I thought she wasn't in that column?"

"I don't think she is. But her life was in Stanford. She's a very particular kind of woman."

"Is that code for peculiar?"

"No." Vic shot him the calm-down-boss look. "She uproots from her stronghold after one interview with someone she's never really met and relocates half a world away. She rarely ventures out of that clinic. It doesn't quite add up."

"She's being held hostage?"

"Dunno. Dunno the first thing about her really."

"So she is in the person of interest column. You're such a buzzkill, boss."

"How'd ya mean?"

"Everyone knows you're crushing on the American. I mean c'mon, she's fit. And no one likes a damsel in distress."

"She's distressed about something."

"Did you ask her out?"

He glanced over the case files. "I have more questions."

"She comin' back here to answer these questions?"

George didn't look up.

"And what's your ex going to think 'bout that?"

"She's not going to think a bloody thing, because it's nothing."

"They work at the same place. In the same bloody building, in the same flipping department." She tilted her head back, revealing the edges of the tattoo below her collarbone. "You want to add her to the board to throw the scent off. To convince your work mates everything is on the up and up. But I'm not that stupid. You've never so much as followed a weeping widow out of this building."

"That's not true."

"Or you want to light a fire under Padma." She snatched Dr. Whiting's file off his desk. "Although I'd pay top dollar to watch that match up."

"You have a wild imagination."

"One that includes you chasing a hot American into a fire."

"Go off and have a cold shower, pet."

"Take more than that to get the American off my mind." She winked and headed out of his office. "You and your exotic taste. You forgot to take your meds. You're limping again."

He fanned through the case file, ignored Vic's quip, and pulled the employee photo of Dr. Whiting. Pain radiated up his left leg as he stood. Skipping treatment wasn't an option yet. After six months, he had hoped it would trickle down to nothing. Nate had wanted to get drinks anyway. He fetched two pills from his top pocket and swallowed. With much hesitation, he added Whiting's picture to the case board, his fingers lingering on the photo.

Nothing was going to happen.

9

AGENDA

I t took me less than fifteen minutes to get back to the clinic. Odd, since it had taken me twenty-two minutes to stroll to the police station. Finding James's office took me much longer. Probably because I was trying to get to the upper floor without being noticed, a difficult task when you are DEFCON 1 pissed.

After checking the third corner, I realized a corner office would be too obvious for James. Where could a chairman hide? I checked the lobby directory and hauled ass for the biggest boardroom. In the center of the floor was a room surrounded by alternating walls of glass and the richest, deepest toned wood.

"Bingo."

James sat in the room surrounded by ten other graying suits. I pulled my clenched fists from my pockets and tore off my sauna hot coat, which must've looked like me waving a red flag. He eyed me and made a quick side comment to the woman sitting next to him. She promptly sat up and I whipped open the door.

"Who the hell—" but before I could finish, the other

meeting attendees stood up and filed out the door. I waited for the last person to leave, grinding filings loose.

"What is troubling you, Dr. Whiting?" James asked. He leaned back in the chair and pressed the seam in his trousers.

"You filled out visa papers for me back in March?"

"Ah, I see. Have the police been troubling you?"

"Screw you. I get to ask the questions. Why?" I was going to shake out of my skin.

"I knew you would be available."

I almost jumped across the table. But he stood, elegant and confident. Traits I'd never possess.

"Before you make the wrong conclusion, I knew it would be hard to get you here. You had spent seventeen years at Stanford. It's where you grew up. You rarely went anywhere. And I was running out of time. It still took me four months to get you. Four months I regret waiting."

My sight blurred for a couple of seconds.

"Did you...did you arrange—" My voice caught.

He leaned forward. "Did I arrange for your lab partner to die?" He spread his fingers across the table. "Is that what you came here to ask? If I had your only friend murdered?"

There was something about the way he articulated the last word. It was full of passion. An emotion I hid in my work. I had never shown Gayle any affection, only professional respect, until she had gasped her last breath. I still remember how warm her hand had felt. How cold and fearless she looked as she stared down death. Something smacked the window hard, and I shrieked.

A bird had flown into the window. I slammed my hand over my mouth. I couldn't afford to be meek. Not anymore.

"Sorry, it happens," he said.

I cleared my throat. "Did you manufacture my circumstance?"

"No. If DI Cooper was a proper man, he'd have shown you the date. I filed for the visa on the twenty-fourth of March. Ten days after the passing of Dr. Daniels."

"How do I know you didn't hire someone to sabotage the lab?"

"You know there was no sabotage. You went through a six-week investigation. Your colleagues threw you under the bus. Because they couldn't reconcile her death with your survival."

"Don't act like you know what I went through."

"I know something close to it."

Oh no. This wasn't about me. "Have you ever killed anyone?"

"You don't want the answer to that question."

I nodded my head. "Yes, I do."

"Why does it matter now?"

"I need to understand who I'm involved with."

He cleared the table of papers. "You already do." His phone buzzed. "And you're running out of time."

"What?"

"If DI Cooper is half as good a detective as I suspect he is, he's not going to let up." He checked his watch. "These things have a way of getting too large to manage. So you have thirty days, perhaps less, before I need to disappear."

"Disappear?" I wiped the sweat from my upper lip. "We just started."

"You just started. I've been at this for quite sometime, remember?"

"And what happens if I don't have anything in less than thirty days?"

"I'm out of your life and you lose your files."

Frozen between my anger and my inability to turn off the panic growing in my head, I couldn't move. I just watched him. Watched him gather papers, place them to the side, straighten his cuff, rub his brow. He knew I was watching. He knew I was paralyzed with indecision. I didn't know how to play this game. My head was filled with wet cotton.

"You need to breathe," he said.

I opened my mouth and gasped. An ugly drowning inhale. How did he know I had been holding my breath?

He opened a window. I tasted the crisp air and my desire to run.

"If you want to know if I'm a dangerous man, the answer is yes. But it's been yes for almost two centuries now. If you want to know if I'm capable of taking your life and getting away with it, the answer is most certainly yes. But I haven't and I've had ample opportunity."

Despite the breathing, my chest burned. I still couldn't find the courage to run. I was so out of practice.

"It's never been my intention to be a killer, Abby. It's never been my intention to have this life or ruin yours or anyone else's. I need you to focus."

"I want to meet the donors," I blurted.

"Fine."

"Tomorrow. All of them." If I was going down, I was going down swinging.

"I'll pick you up at four."

"They can't come here?"

"Absolutely not."

"Fine."

10

PISTONS

The black Jaguar XKR smelled of new leather and James. The polished grain of the console reminded me of the notes of sandalwood and tobacco in his cologne. It was a bouquet that followed me everywhere, and harassed my moral compass. I placed my hand on my foot to stop it from shaking.

"Are you nervous?" James asked.

"No." I kept my gaze out the window, taking in the view, tracking our route. There were apparitions flying around my imagination that I needed to get a hold of—virgin brides, silk clad sirens, depraved men. As much as I needed to interview James's donors, I wasn't prepared for them to exist in the real world.

The only music was the purring of the engine. Liquid money pumped through the pistons, making that luxurious drone. Through every turn, I continued to look in the wrong direction. There was no way I could ever learn to drive on the wrong side of the road. I glimpsed at his watch. I couldn't help it. The ten thousand dollar accessory was captivating. I had Googled the Tag Hauer Monaco timepiece after our second interview.

"What's so funny?" he asked.

"Your watch costs more than my first car. You drive a car most people don't even imagine test-driving. I don't get it. It's like being Count Dracula isn't enough."

"It isn't."

His reply was meant to be haughty and aloof, but I caught the undercurrent of melancholy. I think.

"I couldn't arrange for all my companions to meet you today," he said. "They've never met one another, so I've spaced the interviews to allow for that. I expect their anonymity and confidentiality kept."

I snapped my mouth shut. He knew I didn't need to be reminded about confidentiality, but I was getting better about not responding to every jab. He had probably made a difficult father. A question I hadn't the courage to broach yet. The parcels of green lush land became larger, the trees denser, and the estates grander.

"Not all of them are excited to meet you," he continued. "They know you're my doctor. Not what type of doctor."

I shot him an accusatory look, suspecting he was already rigging outcomes.

"I don't want you to scare them. I still need them," he admitted. He tipped his chin up slightly. "There she is, Heritage House."

Our final destination, a three-story Edwardian mansion, stood a mile ahead. We drove up a steep peat gravel driveway lit up by footlights ensuring visitors viewed the full majesty of the estate. The precise rectangular stonework framing the exterior had weathered into varying shades of gray.

He opened my door and I took in the scent of crabapple

and citrus. Espaliered lemon trees formed an elegant border around the parking lot with large walnut trees forming a dark canopy above. My father maintained a modest orchard in our backyard. There wasn't a fruit he couldn't get to flourish. I rubbed the pain from my throat.

I had prepared for something more hazardous than a classic English estate—a seedy motel or a dark underground club. Definitely expected something more private than a place open to the public like some historical tourist attraction.

He retrieved my backpack from the trunk, and slid it over his shoulder like he'd known me forever. No one had ever offered to carry it for me. It was such a paternal gesture.

"What is that?" James pointed to a small leather satchel in the trunk.

"I brought a medical bag."

He closed the trunk, locked the car, and headed to the entrance, leaving my medical bag behind.

"I might need that." I trailed after him, pointing to the car.

"You asked to meet them. And that is what you're doing here today. No poking, no prodding, no measuring. Just asking and listening."

"But I..." I pulled on my backpack, slipping it from his shoulder.

"Or we can go back to the lab." His grip on my backpack tightened.

I groaned. This wasn't the time to push. "Fine. But you can't interfere with the interviews." I released my hold on the backpack.

"I wouldn't dream of it." He slid my security blanket over his shoulder and I winced with embarrassment. The backpack had faded to an inky gray, and slung over his black woolen jacket, it looked like an arson victim.

The larger than life oak doors opened. Filtered through a domed stained-glass ceiling, the foyer shimmered in the soft afternoon sun. My eyes danced over the expanse of black and white Italian tiles covering the floor in a mosaic pattern. This house, no, this epic estate was like walking onto a set for a historical movie. Instead of feeling overwhelmed and unworthy, I let the beauty soothe my nerves. If I was going to fail today, I couldn't have asked for a better stage.

The clap of heels pulled my attention away from the floor. A woman with silver fox hair and an engaging smile approached. The woman had to be in her early fifties. A cream-colored wrap dress hugged her voluptuous curves. She wore her age with confidence, without the shield of abundant jewelry or any heavy makeup to compensate for lost youth.

"Hello, Jamie." She wrapped her arms around his chest and kissed him on each cheek.

"Lovely to see you, Helen. This is Abby. My new companion."

I blushed. I needed a thicker sense of humor. The woman's green eyes twinkled. There was something familiar about her smile. It was disarming, warm and genuine. Nothing like James's.

"Dr. Whiting, this is Helen Robson, the proprietor of Heritage House."

Proprietor? Was this a bed and breakfast? I really needed to pick up a British/American dictionary.

"I've heard so much about you." Helen gave me the warmest hug I'd received from a stranger in all my life. Unprepared for it, my chin collided into her shoulder. "I thought we could go up to the gallery for a drink." She laced her arm around James's and waited for my reply.

Gallery? Perhaps this was a museum. "Sure."

The polished wood banister reflected our phantom figures as we climbed a staircase too grand for my Nike running shoes. All the warmth from the foyer evaporated when we entered the gallery.

Leather chairs, worn smooth from decades of occupation, filled the room in parallel arrangements. White uniformed waiting staff peppered the room delivering and taking drinks, newspapers, cigars, small trays of food. A group of three older gentlemen, nursing brown drinks and pink newspapers, glanced up from their conversation to acknowledge us. The audience of banker types, local politicians, and socialites sprinkled throughout the room gave me an instant sense of unease. The room inhaled and exhaled power.

The complete opposite of the dark lascivious lair I had envisioned.

Helen escorted us to a sofa and chairs near a set of windows, facing the back of the property. Tall hedges formed a geometric design, and I was thrilled there was enough light to make out the pattern.

"What's your tincture, Dr. Whiting?" Helen asked.

"She's more of a caffeine addict," James said, and sat in a leather wingback chair.

I crinkled my nose at his reply. He knew me like an open book and I couldn't pry him open with a degree in medicine from Stanford. It was infuriating. I took a seat across from Helen, perpendicular to James.

"We could have a French press brought out for you if you like." A uniformed waiter stood behind Helen.

"I'll have whatever you're having." I wanted to be a good guest. I needed to fit in.

"Gin and tonic," James said to the waiter.

"Make that three," Helen said.

Dammit.

"You don't drink?" Helen asked.

I wanted to be polite and lie, but I sensed I didn't need to around Helen. "Not usually."

"Would you prefer coffee?" Helen asked.

I pulled a folded paper from my pocket. "I'd like to begin the interviews, if that's alright." I had five interviews, five hours, and a list of occupations with no names.

Helen looked to James.

"Your first interview won't be here for another half hour." His tone was firm, reasserting his control of the situation.

Helen cut through our stare off. "Tommy, bring us a bottle of champagne and a tray of sandwiches."

I refolded the paper and tucked it away. "So what is this place?" I asked Helen, ignoring James with all of my might.

THE RETIRED Royal army officer walked with a slight limp when he entered the small office. I noticed his right pant leg didn't cling as closely as his left. He wore a prosthetic leg, which attached mid thigh, but his six-foot-four height and two-forty build kept my eyes on his chest.

The man filled the room with a level of testosterone I'd never encountered, not even with James. The shock of gray hair at his temples and crow's feet that appeared when he attempted to smile did nothing to soften his appearance. The sharp angles of his jaw line commanded attention, loyalty, fear and respect. A man followed onto any battle-field without question.

Spartacus.

To be honest, I hadn't considered a male companion. And if I had, it wouldn't be this type of man. I reached for my water and spoke my name into the glass, amplifying the croak in my voice. He didn't acknowledge my intimidation, just kept his eyes locked out on the wall behind my left shoulder.

"How long have you known Mr. Stuart?" It didn't feel right wasting this man's time, so I jumped in, feet to flame.

Impressed, he took a seat at the window. He extended his legs, pulling up his slacks to reveal the titanium prosthe-sis. "I've known Father Stuart for eight years."

I expected the direct reply, but the content of the answer was startling. It caused me to pause before firing the next question. James had admitted in a prior interview he used the former occupation to find companions over the decades. For some reason, people found the profession disarming and trustworthy. Even I had fallen for it.

"But you've only been a companion for the last three months?"

He nodded.

"When did you retire from the military?"

"Three and half years ago."

The man rubbed at his leg, and I noticed a simple gold wedding band. The retirement had to coincide with the injuries. "Post Traumatic Stress Disorder?" I asked.

He lifted his gunmetal gray gaze. The posture he exuded was still calm, but not warm or kind, possibly defensive. He looked back at the wall and nodded.

"Are you being treated for PTSD?"

"I take medication." He spun his wedding band with his thumb.

"And what do you do now?"

"I run a private security practice."

Translation for military contractor. There was no way a man like this gave up war.

"How long have you been married?"

"Twenty-four years in August." He sat up taller, like a flame had lit within his chest, but his eyes kept it guarded. He continued to spin his wedding band.

"Why do you meet Mr. Stuart here?"

"He needs blood, and I let him have mine."

All of his answers were matter-of-fact, not to be questioned. I wanted to consult my notes, but it would've reeked of pretense. He knew the follow-up question.

"And what do you get out of it?"

"I get to be normal."

I wasn't sure I'd heard him correctly. There couldn't be anything normal about letting someone sink their teeth into you, to suck blood out of your body.

"I know it sounds strange. But it's the truth," he said. "I can sleep soundly. I can eat a meal. I can hold a conversation with my wife. Make her happy. I can take my sons to a football match. Participate in their lives. Instead of spending time in my head, with a barrel of gasoline and a box of matches."

We both heard me swallow.

"Do they know?" I continued. It's amazing the amount of armor a doctor's title will grant you.

"About Father Stuart? No. They think I'm seeing a therapist. My time with him is therapeutic."

I grabbed my water glass and downed its contents. The

next questions were well outside my comfort cul-de-sac. I remembered to offer him water, which was declined.

"Are you alright?"

I nodded and leaned forward, setting my elbows on the desk. My mouth rehearsed the next question before I uttered it.

"Is your relationship with Mr. Stuart sexual?"

"I'm not a homosexual." His reply was spoken with such force it felt like a shove.

I was careful with the next words, not wanting to cut the wrong wire. "It has nothing to do with sexual orientation, Colonel."

He opened his mouth and licked his bottom lip. He also crossed his legs. Although he looked directly at me, I felt his gaze travel through me to some other place. A private place.

"My relationship with James is intimate."

11

BRIEF ENCOUNTER

J ames scanned the river. The full moon reflected against the glass-like surface. He tasted the bitter of juniper and the salt of his disdain. There was a time when he had considered this view of the River Cam its most under-appreciated. Its most romantic. Now it only held his despair. Too many decades, no, too many lives had passed since he had watched the sunrise dance along its surface. Even the late afternoon's rays could not compete with that muted memory.

He heard the snap of branches, the rustling of leaves. His body tensed and he resented the Pavlov reaction. How many more years would pass until he felt nothing for her? *Charlotte.*

She sat next to him. "Why are you always so sentimental?" she asked.

"This is where I wished I had left your body."

She laughed, placing her hand atop of his. "I don't understand why it always has to be this difficult." He allowed her to entwine their fingers. They weren't really her fingers anyway.

Each time, she found a young, lithe body to take over. Each time, she tried to seduce him with threats. Each time, it had worked. Albeit temporarily. "Why you can't be happy."

"I am content. Your company doesn't improve that." He placed a light kiss on her hand.

"But your life would be so droll without me. You like the challenge."

He turned to face her. Carefully removed a strand of hair from her mouth, leaned in and whispered, "Why don't we take off our clothes?" Her mouth parted slightly, a hint of smile appearing at the corners of her plump lips. "Tie a few stones to our feet, and drown?"

She turned away and cast her disapproval at the river.

"Come, come, we've over stayed our welcome, don't you think?" He snatched her hand and squeezed hard.

"Careful, you might break a few bones. It might even register." She leaned in. Her hard nipple brushed against his fingers.

"I'm tired, Charlotte. This has to end."

"It always does. Never well for you. You can't accept the inevitable outcome. I will have every part of you. Body and soul, no exceptions."

"There is only one outcome for us." He released his hold of her and looked back at the river. He had to tread carefully. She could always smell his hope. There was no hope now. He had definitely buried that in the river.

"The American is an interesting addition," she said.

"Don't," he snapped.

"All these years, playing. All this wasted effort. Do you really believe science is going to save you?"

"I'm well beyond salvation."

"Then come and enjoy our private hell together. It

would be wonderful. I know how to make you feel alive. So much better than what we've had to endure thus far."

He smiled at her. "You have no idea."

She leaned her head on his shoulder. "Do you remember how we walked the River? Hand in hand, laughing at the sun?"

He leaned his cheek against the top of her head. "No."

"Surely, you do."

"I'm sure I would remember such a pleasantry."

She pointed across the bank. "We made love under that tree."

He drew in the cardamom scent of her hair. "Did we?"

Her big brown eyes stared up into his. Despite them not being her original pair, they still held his misery. "I'm close," she said. "Close to breaking you. The last one is within my grasp."

He kissed the crest of her forehead. "You break that last straw at your peril." He slinked away from her. "The sun is setting. You better go." He stood and reached for her hand. She took it and sighed.

"When will you learn? I do all of this out of love and devotion." On tiptoe, she kissed him. His lips didn't react.

"When will you learn? That I do all of this out of love as well." He sniffed her mouth. "The cardamom seeds don't hide the stench of death on your breath." She sneered her displeasure and walked to the path. The sway of her hips was a marvel. It didn't matter what body she occupied, the hips always swayed in that manner.

As if she sensed his malice, she turned and smiled at him. "I love seeing you this way." Her eyes glistened.

He wanted to wrap his hands around her throat and squeeze. But it was borrowed and wouldn't do.

12

RUNNING ON EMPTY

After five hours of interviews, my exhaustion was like a lead coat. The interview with the Colonel had inflicted the most damage. The dinner plate Helen had sent up at eight o'clock sat on the corner of the desk untouched, covered with a napkin, my appetite buried within the pages of my notebook.

Most of the companions had leapt at the chance to clear themselves under the cloak of doctor-patient privilege. Three of them had given me their name five minutes into the interview. A part of me understood their need to share the secret. But the reason I'd chosen pathology was to not learn about the lives attached to any of the names. I didn't need to compare my life to a stranger's, good or bad or very empty.

I had interviewed three women and two men. They ranged in appearance, sharing no common feature. Not knowing what to expect, I knew it would be improbable for a common trait to surface immediately. Tidbits of information had caused me to pause during the interviews, floated through my head like moths. Every time I grasped one, it dusted my mind with more questions. I was getting nowhere fast.

One male and one female companion physically beat James before he drew their blood. Both claimed it was done at his request. Aside from the vampire's bite James inflicted, he never harmed any of them. Sex wasn't always requisite either. James had spent hours holding the sixty-six-year-old retired flight attendant. Marjorie Haven enjoyed the sense memories that returned to her when James took her blood: the smell of her husband's cologne, the scent of brewing coffee in the galley, or the downy softness of her third son, the son she'd lost to SIDS.

The only common denominator was James. For all of them, his bite didn't register against the euphoria of being a live donor. They desired his company, needed him to feel whole again. The interviews proved him the perfect listener, the perfect lover, the perfect friend. He absolved them of their pain and darkness.

The complete opposite of the way I saw him.

I couldn't help but suspect that this was his way of giving me a hard lesson in curiosity. If I could only examine their blood for some common biological trait, I'd have more than just intimate confessions. All caused agitation, but no illumination. I was never leaving square one.

There was a knock on the door, and James popped in his head. I felt exposed with all of my new knowledge. Like clockwork, he smiled. That timeless knowing smile I resented.

"Ready to go home?" he asked.

I zipped my backpack, trying to shove my loneliness deep within it.

He led me down the hall. The luster of the wood paneling caught the light, making the wallpaper luxurious. I

reached out to feel the wine-colored velvet. The peachy softness reminded me of summer, but not for long. I fixated on
all the doors we had passed, all sixteen. The matching ivory
knobs tempted prying.

"Why are there so many rooms up here?" I asked.

"This floor was originally the servant quarters."

Smart for a mansion to be converted into a social club,
instead of withering to shards of paint, wood, and plaster.

I followed James down a smaller hall then down a set of
stairs I didn't remember climbing. When we got to the
bottom, I realized we had entered the foyer from a different
direction than before.

"Huh," I murmured.

I had a strong sense of direction and rarely got lost. In
the foyer, I stopped and turned to correct my internal
compass. The clever design of the house bothered and
amused me. The layers of secrets it held. It was the perfect
home for James. We had entered the foyer without notice
from the second floor where the open gallery was. How
sneaky. I eyed James with suspicion as we left the mansion.
The soft glow of the evening made him more handsome and
hazardous.

"Do you have any questions for me?" he asked.

I was done with questions. The cool summer night air
dampened the fire growing in my gut, and I walked to his
car determined to sleep instead of diagnose my uneasiness.

The conversation we shared on the drive back to the
DeVere Hotel was dense in its non-existence. Again, I kept
my attention out the window, tracking the shapes of things,
and ignoring the shapes of hands and mouths in my mind.

"You skipped your dinner. Want to go grab a bite?" he
asked.

I shook my head, but my stomach growled. The traitor.

"We can stop and pick you up something."

"No, I'm tired."

He allowed silence to engulf the ride back to town, which I pretended to not notice or to be thankful for. He pulled the car into the parking lot of the hotel, instead of up onto the driveway, pinning me under his scrutiny.

"Are you okay?" he asked.

"Yep."

He leaned over, and I bumped the back of my head against the window.

"You don't want to talk?"

"Nope." I popped the door open and hopped out of the car. But he'd placed my backpack in the trunk, so I couldn't make a casual run for it. He always had me cornered.

He slid out of the car, opened the trunk, and lifted my prized accessory. I reached for it and he slipped it onto my shoulder, tender like a parent on the first day of school. He buttoned up my jacket, and tucked a stray strand of hair behind my ear.

"You sure you don't want a little company?" he asked, the moonlight reflecting the dare on his lips.

I finally looked him in the eye, heart pounding in my throat, palms heating up with sweat. We were so different, and I always believed I stood on lower ground. His knowledge, his history, his experience outpaced my limited view of the world, but given everything I'd heard from the companions, I was sure my moral ground sat higher.

"Do you have any family?" I asked. Proud I shoveled it just as hard.

Everything stilled, the only sound was my breathing and my heart pounding in my fists.

His eyes grew glassy and remorseful, cutting right through my spitefulness. "I had a wife and three children."

He sniffed the air and my faltering indignation. "Many life-times ago."

"No other family or relatives?"

He ran his tongue over his teeth and shook his head. "I don't think so. I'm sure they've all passed on."

The small hairs on my arms were standing tall. Did I have the courage to press? He had allowed me to dig for hours, probably because he knew it would be a dead end.

"You have a heart murmur," he said. "Did you know that?"

My eyes stung. He could've dug that up from my medical file. The one he was holding hostage.

"I don't have a heart beat. No pulse. I don't even have to breathe, Dr. Whiting. Do you know how strange it is when your body makes no noise? It allows me to hear things I wouldn't ordinarily notice. Like your regret."

Bile slithered up my throat. I watched him climb back into his car and drive away, leaving my wounded pride whipping in the breeze.

13

FIRST CONTACT

The scent of unfamiliar welcomed me back to my hotel room—industrial laundry detergent, a freshly vacuumed carpet, and starched curtains. My suitcase sat in the corner, daring me to pack.

I shed my clothes and folded them into a pile on the bathroom counter. I'd spent the evening swimming in silk and wool, prints and plaids, wonder and wonderful. The temptation to toss my new clothes into the garbage grew as big as the theories I wanted to burn. Every interview with James ended this way. There was new information to dissect, there were new wounds to lick, and the Sturgis files disappeared from view.

Under the hot spray of water, I hoped the tightness in my chest would wash off, but it didn't budge. My vision blurred and the taste of salt seared my tongue. I was drowning in emotions I couldn't label.

It was exhaustion. It was spending all my time in make believe. It was dealing with facts I couldn't validate. The towel glowed a brighter white against my lobster red skin. My dark hair parted in the middle out of habit. I had never paid more than twenty-five dollars to have it cut. And I had never bothered to care. On the dresser, there were five items in my make-up bag demoting it to common toiletries. My newest lipstick, I bought two years ago, was still in near mint condition.

I pulled open the slender top drawer of the dresser. When I had unpacked that first night, I intentionally laid out the drawer to mimic the one I had at Stanford. The same drawer revealed the thorn of my irritation. Cotton panties, all white, and seven matching bras; a tray filled with three pairs of earrings, all from my father, a pearl necklace that belonged to my paternal grandmother who had died before I was born; and a lime green band for my Fitbit.

The drawer had never contained anything of interest. No love letters, no bag of weed, no photos of old boyfriends, no lingerie, no vibrator. Nothing of notice. I slammed the drawer shut, the dresser hit the wall with a bang, and my cell phone dropped to the floor.

Home. I wanted home so badly. Even though it would've been just as empty, it would've been my controlled kind of empty. I snatched the phone from the floor and noticed the time. I was eight hours ahead. I could still get ahold of him. My heart swelled with hope.

I slipped into my pajamas, which consisted of an old Radiohead t-shirt and pink and lime green boxer shorts. While I waited for the call to be approved, I brushed and braided my hair. Sam's cool cat voice came on the line. My body loosened, and I fell to the floor sitting Indian style. The way we sat together as children, planning our next escapade while Dad worked.

"See the Queen yet?" he asked.

"I'm in Cambridge, lame brain, not London."

"What's it like?"

"Different. Weather's been all over the place." I couldn't remember a clear afternoon with sunshine. I couldn't remember stepping outside in the afternoon.

"Do anything interesting yet, or has it been work, work, work?"

I rubbed my quivering bottom lip. "I toured a really old library." *And I met a vampire.* I covered my mouth, just in case it slipped.

"Can you do me a favor?" he asked.

"Anything."

"Send me some stuff."

"Stuff?"

"Leaves, brochures, ticket stubs, stuff from where you are."

"Leaves?"

"I just want to know what it's really like. The stuff will make it real."

Sam had a habit of collecting trinkets from places. Rocks, bottle caps, ticket stubs, postcards, felonies. This was the first time I'd gone somewhere he hadn't torn through.

"Sure. I can do that." I yanked my jeans from the corner and fished through my pockets for the Trinity College tour ticket stub. It had been so long since I sent him anything. I was such a selfish sister. "There's a funny grasshopper clock."

"What?"

"It's at the center of town. A mechanical clock. It has a creepy grasshopper thing on it. She eats the seconds."

"Aren't all clocks mechanical? How do you know it's a girl?"

"It's made out of gold. All beautiful, scary things are female. You'd totally dig it."

"I didn't think you'd go," he said.

"Why's that?"

"You hate change, Abs. Not like you to shake things up. I'm proud of you."

The compliment made me want another shower. I wanted everything unchanged, even if it meant never knowing. My search for the past and the truth was costing too much, and my isolation was now a heavy handicap. I carved a large divot into the carpet.

"How's it with you?" I asked.

"The usual. Three square meals a day, TV is shit, and I'll be ready to try out prize fighting when I get outta here."

I laughed, harder than usual. The image of Sam winning a fistfight was almost harder to fathom than my new circumstance.

"Looks like they might move up my hearing."

"When? I'll book a flight." There was a way back. A way out. A way home. I felt the tension in my chest uncoil.

"Don't do that. You don't always need to be here."

"I want to be there, Sam."

My eyes burned with regret. I could hack off a limb for being snide to him all those times.

"Nothing's going to go wrong." The confidence in his voice pushed me farther away. "I'd rather see you at Christmas anyway."

Christmas was five months away. My life wouldn't even be the same thirty days from now. I tried muffling my sob.

"Abs? What's going on?"

A moan escaped, low and wounded.

"God dammit, tell me what's going on. Did someone give you shit about your age?"

There was nothing he could do, but stir the pot he was pickling in.

I took a deep breath. "No. I'm tired. And I'm alone. And I

haven't seen the sun since I've been here." I couldn't even see the floor. "I miss you is all."

The silence swelled as Sam tried to think of something funny to say. This was foreign territory. "Why don't you ask someone out for a drink or something?"

Because he drinks blood. And despite his company, he makes me feel incredibly lonely. I should've kept the date with Detective Cooper. This was a mistake. I didn't need to worry Sam. "Keep me posted on the hearing, 'kay?"

"Yeah, yeah. Send me some stuff."

"I love you."

"Love you too."

I thought I had taken a deep breath, but I set loose the words I had wanted to say. "Sam, there are monsters. Real ones. I've made a big mistake. The man who hired me is missing. I think he's dead. And I don't know what I'm doing. Oh God, what the hell have I done?"

But the line had already gone dead.

THE ELEPHANT WEIGHT of sleep began to smother. My skin was ablaze and I shoved off the comforter. I dangled a foot over the edge of the mattress, searching for cool air but the thick heat of exhaustion paired with an Ambien refused to let up. I rolled onto my side, stuck both feet out from under the covers, and cracked an eyelid. The window seemed too far.

Why was it already open?

Going to sleep with an open window, in a hotel where I didn't know the neighborhood, let alone the country, was not an idea I would've even considered. The scent of moist pavement floated in and tickled my nose. The good news was my room was on the second floor. Could I be killed on the second floor? I stared at the window and wondered if I truly cared. But my imagination pushed oxygen and adrenaline to other parts of my body.

The digital clock read 4:12 a.m. and cast a blue glow across the small room. Clothes were still piled on the floor. My backpack was still slumped in the corner. Nothing was out of the ordinary.

But I hadn't opened the window.

I squeezed my eyes shut and just listened. One slight motion registered. It sounded like a crisp shirt rubbing against itself, or a ragged inhalation of breath. *Something out of the ordinary.*

In the left corner of the room, by the door, I saw the outline of his figure. I stood, wrapped my comforter around my body, and braced for someone extraordinary.

James didn't move as I approached. I reached for the light switch but he gently brushed my fingers away. The softness of his touch brought on a strange security. I stood in front of him and saw the signs of injury and deprivation, but his eyes were still cold blue.

His tailored shirt was slashed open. I traced the scratches across his chest. He didn't move. His left brow felt rough with dried blood or dirt. The musky scent of sweat and earth filled the space between us.

"What happened?" I asked.

"I'm dirty." He looked hopeless.

I dropped the comforter and all my inhibitions, opened the bathroom door, and started the shower. The golden glow of the nightlight and the soft sound of spraying water were hypnotizing. What had happened to him? The steam from the shower descended, caressing my skin, leaving a trail of wet kisses across my arms.

The scent of sandalwood and soil entered the bathroom.

I tipped my head back to draw in more of him and forced my eyes open. He had removed his shirt and worked on his trousers.

I reached inside the shower, gauging the heat. The soothing stream bounced off my fingers. The rhythm of the water drew my eyelids back down. I stood, engulfed by the moment, almost asleep. He entered the shower as quietly as he'd snuck into my room. Why had he picked my room? He laced his fingers with mine and held my hand to his chest. I wanted to be angry, but he was hurt.

"I'm going to take a look at you, but I need to turn on the light."

His fingers unfurled from mine in a slow release. The steam had grown thick and buffered the harsh light. I pulled my hair into a ponytail and stepped into the shower. My t-shirt soaked up water and clung to my body, greedy and earnest. I didn't have the strength to care.

His body resembled a creamy slab of marble, carved with admiration for the human form. His erect shoulders were broad and tapered down to his hips. His muscles seemed fashioned to highlight their precision of design. They hugged his skeletal form. Rodin never had a finer model. Red slashes crossed his chest, smearing his perfection.

Streams of red and brown cascaded down his slick body, pooling at the drain. I took the washcloth and cleaned the dirt and dried blood off of his back. He didn't flinch or make a sound, stood firm in his silence. I wondered if he had always looked this beautiful, or if he had been a softer man a century before. I also wondered where my fear had gone.

James turned and the water spilled down his back, washing away my work. Not a hair graced his chest. I blotted the gashes, watched them heal and fade under my touch.

Water drops bounced off his shoulders onto my face. Again, I didn't care.

He sank to his knees and wrapped his arms around my waist. He tilted his head back, the hot water cutting into his matted hair. I washed the dirt and blood out, careful not to pull a golden strand. His hair felt like silk. The foam slithered from his head, down the middle of his back, over his backside. The soap and water rinsed away both the grime and crime.

His hand traveled down the back of my thigh to my knee. He pulled forward until I kneeled over his lap. In my mind, I protested, but my legs wrapped around his waist without second thought.

"Forgive me." His words and mouth hovered over mine.

My eyes fixed onto his, I was afraid if I closed them, he would disappear. His arctic stare held me captive. I wanted to uncover the secret world behind the blue of his eyes. Desperately wanted. My hips pitched against his and I felt the power he held over me. Flames fanned across my thighs, up my abdomen, across my breasts. The only barrier to his erection was my boxer shorts.

His hand gently stroked my right breast, sending a shock of sensual electricity through my veins. My head kicked back, exposing my neck. His grip at the back of my head tightened. A low growl built in his chest and he punctured my neck with his fangs as a peal of thunder shook the window hard.

I shot up in my bed, covered in sweat. My mind tried wildly to piece together what I'd imagined, conjured, witnessed. I rubbed at the fire surrounding my neck. No pain. No injury. I didn't dare touch the fire below my navel.

Another crash of thunder and I blew out the remnants of my dream in a loud gust. My hand trembled as I clicked on the bedside lamp. I pulled my knees to my chest, forcing my muscles to bend back to my will. No one stood in the left corner of the room. I watched the clock turn from 4:11 to 4:12 a.m. The window was closed.

"It would never happen." I swore to the walls of my room and waited an eternity for the next clap of thunder.

14

TWO BIRDS

H elen's greenhouse was large enough to be mistaken for a guesthouse. Not a hobby shack for an amateur, but enough room for botanical adoration that didn't border on obsession. The blackened steel frame reminded me of a large birdcage, and I wandered through the rows of colorful blooms like a bird in search of nectar.

None of the flowers were especially heavy with perfume. They tinted the air enough to make time feel slow and easy. Helen explained each plant, the genus, the species, the time it took to nurse it into bloom. Some of the flowers I knew— African violets, bearded irises, and wild orchids—but most I'd never seen before.

"I'm so glad you called," Helen said.

"I couldn't pass up an invitation to come back." I had found a handwritten note from Helen tucked within my interview notes. There was something gracious and myste- rious about the invitation, and I was determined to prove my curiosity wasn't a lethal pathogen. "I rarely have weekend plans." I needed to get out and make friends, even if James already had dibs on Helen.

Despite the grandeur and beauty of Heritage House, a chord of belonging resonated deep into my bones, and for once, I wasn't going to rationalize the feeling away. Perhaps it was the way Helen treated me, not as a child, nor a daughter, nor someone far younger than she, but as an equal. There was a softness to her. Her hazel eyes didn't seem to cast judgment. Or pity.

"I wish the weather were better. It's splendid on a sunny day."

"I imagine." I wanted warmth and sunlight so badly, and Helen made a great substitute.

It was especially cold, bitter with wind and threatening rain. I had to admit it made the longing for home worse. I was a morning person, a sun person. The sweet humidity of the greenhouse made me feel like a whole person. I felt safe and untouchable.

Helen kept a small table, flecked with chipped white paint, near the prettiest and most unique flowers of the greenhouse.

"I hope you're hungry?" Helen asked.

"Starving. I haven't been good about meals lately."

"Jamie said you were rigorous about work. You can't forget to look after yourself. I thought we'd have lunch in here. Do you take tea?"

I nodded and took a seat across from her.

Helen offered milk and sugar. I took the milk and passed on the sugar. She palmed two sugar cubes and sucked on them between sips of her tea, almost like Detective Cooper. I exercised restraint and didn't ask if that was a custom.

Tommy, the waiter from drinks last night, brought in a large tray. He set down a wooden board filled with hard-boiled eggs, cheese, sliced apples, dried fruit, nuts, and a large meat pie.

I rubbed my hands together. "You don't mess around." I cut into the pie first, and marveled at its contents. This was straight out of an Austen novel.

A roll of thunder rumbled in the distance and the patter of rain served as our soundtrack.

"The end of summer always this rainy?" I asked.

"Usually, there's a quick afternoon shower every once in awhile, nothing this fierce. Dreadful to relocate here with this as your welcome."

A large dark purple flower hovered above a row of plants, like a huge phantom butterfly. The strange flower had a plume of delicate whiskers draping inches below its petals.

"What kind of flower is that?"

"Tacca chantrieri. The black bat flower or cat's whiskers."

Unable to resist, I set down my fork and stood to get a closer look. I went to touch the whiskers when Helen cut in a warning.

"Careful, the nectar is toxic."

I yanked my hand back. "I've never seen anything like it." Still entranced. "It's strangely beautiful."

"Most dangerous things are." Helen's tone had grown cautious.

"You mean like James?"

She took a plate and filled it with a slice of meat pie and some dried apricots. I found her loyalty to James admirable. And wondered how she came about it, then she answered my question.

"I mean his past. His Achilles heel—Charlotte."

There was a surge of excitement and slight caution from the pit of my stomach. "Was she his wife?"

"No, she's his curse. As long as James is around, Charlotte follows. Which is why I left you the invitation. Because he always fails to begin the conversation with her."

I stared at the tray of food, and really hoped our conversation wasn't going to ruin my appetite. It all looked too wonderful to ignore. I bit into the pie and almost began to cry. I sipped my tea. "Is she a vampire?" I studied the crystallized dew on the flower, and bit into an apple slice.

"That would make her much easier to get rid of." There was a darker note in her voice and it had struck an alarm. I really couldn't take on another paranormal dimension. Or client. Or reality.

I took another bite of pie and casually asked, "Who is she? A forgotten companion?"

"His maker."

"But you said she wasn't a vampire." I jammed half a hard-boiled egg into my mouth.

"Charlotte is a revenant. Somewhat the same but not. He feeds off the living, and she the dead. But she's responsible for who he is. What he is."

This was like discussing anti-matter, or politics, or emotions, none my area of expertise. "A revenant? Like a ghost?" I quickly finished my egg.

"She inhabits a human form, but they're no longer living. Don't you believe in seeing the dead?"

Had Helen really sent the invitation to baptize me in the supernatural? The last ghost I had ever met took small children by the hand in the middle of the night. And it had been a figment of my fevered imagination. I stared at the food. It would be rude and dismissive to continue to enjoy it. I shook my head.

"You don't believe in God?" Helen gently continued.

Volumes of data supported the fact that patients with faith were happier, lived longer, survived traumatic events better. "I didn't believe in vampires until eight days ago. I'm a little slow on the uptake." I palmed an apricot. It was hard to limit the credit to a benevolent blob of nothing, when science had accomplished so much. "Can we table the God discussion?"

Helen smiled, conceding the request. The apricot tasted like a warm orchard. She reached behind and pulled out a book. The book was small but dense, reminding me of a prayer book. She held it out and I eyed it with poorly veiled suspicion.

Undeterred, Helen opened the book to a marked page. "Revenants can be traced back to the middle ages."

She slid the book under my nose. The pungent aroma of old superstition wafted from the pages. There were several illustrations of a beautiful woman entwined with a serpent, half her face veiled with a skeleton's mask. The thick muscled serpent wrapped between legs, around waist, over breasts. The beast's head nestled around her neck. I took the book. I didn't want to be rude.

"She's a demon spirit born of desire. Desire for love, power, revenge. She takes root in your lesser self. Digs around for a weakness to cling to, until she embeds herself into your soul. And drains you of everything."

I turned the thin pages and continued to skim. Siren, harpie, witch, enchantress—in my hands the book was full of terminology I wasn't in the habit of proving. And despite my current patient, I wasn't ready to expand my practice.

"Unfortunately, James is the object of her desire," Helen continued.

"Why?" I knew he was an attractive man, but he had avoided attachment at all cost.

"That I don't know, but as long as he has been undead, she has followed and left a trail of death behind." Helen paused and seemed careful with her words. "He can walk the earth for an eternity. But she cannot without a body."

"She's a spirit with no body?" I struggled to keep the skeptic out of my voice.

"Once she finds a host, she'll waste no time getting James back into her life. Back under her control."

"A host. Someone human but dead?"

"Yes."

"Seems risky to choose a regular human body. Why not find another vampire?"

"Vampires have no life, no soul, no weakness to cling to."

"No blood," I murmured while flipping through pages.

Helen reached across the table and squeezed my hand. "Everything they have is borrowed, including their time here."

Something thick and uncomfortable wound its way into the middle of my chest. It almost felt like pity. Where would James end up after his time here? Would he pay for the borrowed time? And how would he pay? Then I remembered he would disintegrate into a pile of ash and blow across the lawn of irrelevance just like the rest of us.

"She will not give up until he belongs to her. Forever. She has taken everyone from him. Once she destroys his bloodline, he will have nothing left to anchor him."

"Anchor him to what?"

"His humanity. He'll forever be hers."

"But he has no soul." It was a harmless jab, but Helen's eyes grew wide and took on sheen. I rubbed the nervous tic from my eyelid. "I don't get how this has anything to do with me. I'm just a means to an end." I put down the book, picked up my tea, and walked to the glass walls. White oleanders swayed in the wind like frenetic hula dancers.

"To what end? James is sharing his secrets with a complete stranger. A clear sign of desperation or weakness. Which means Charlotte is back. She will be stronger and more determined. We're all in danger."

Again, there was no edge or threat with Helen. The woman could deliver apocalyptic news with delicate politeness. She'd make an excellent doctor. I paced and catalogued flower colors. "Is that hemlock?" I pointed to a tall shrub with clusters of white flowers like baby's breath.

She nodded.

"Please tell me you're not a witch."

"I am not a witch."

I wasn't sure if Helen was humoring me or being sarcastic. "How long have you known James?"

"Long enough to know you mean something special to him." There was just a hint of and-I-don't-know-why in her reply. Not envy on Helen's part, just a resignation that I belonged in some group that was different from the others.

I hated being different.

"I was wondering if I could use that office upstairs again?" I asked.

She stood and placed her napkin over her plate. "You want to speak with his companions again?"

Helen wasn't stupid. It's why she was so damn likable.

She wove her arm into the crook of mine and we strolled down another aisle in the greenhouse. It was painfully nice. "And you don't want me to tell Jamie?" she asked.

"I'd prefer to tell him after I have what I need."

"What do you need? You've already spoken to them. And you didn't look like you enjoyed it."

We stopped in front of a row of zebra striped calla lilies. I couldn't help but grimace. "Horrible flower."

"You've had a mishap with one?"

I paused for a heartbeat. It wouldn't hurt to share a childhood story that had nothing to do with Sturgis. It wouldn't hurt to have Helen like me, really like me.

"My aunt had them in her garden. It was spring, and the plants had those red clusters of berries on them. Sam and I thought it would be fun to pelt each other with them." The warmth of Helen's grip on my arm was soothing. "The oxalic acid from the berries had burned our fingers, blistering our skin. I don't think I've ever screamed so loud. My father nearly had a heart attack."

Helen touched the green flower. "Charlotte fed those berries to his children."

"What?" My throat tightened. "Why would she do that?" The pain, the bleeding, it would only take a handful to kill a toddler. It would be the equivalent of swallowing shards of glass mixed in acid.

"She did it to break him."

Darkness slithered in from outside into the small space between us. The frame of the greenhouse groaned against the harsh pressure. My past, the past I had carefully locked and buried in a box abandoned in Sturgis, had reared its ugly face. The face of death. So many children. So much death. They coughed and cried blood, the warmth of their blood spattering my cold tight cheeks. The greenhouse became suffocating. Like the hazmat suit back at Stanford.

Helen held onto me tighter. "Are you okay?"

"I need to sit down." I was hyperventilating. There were children crying in my head. Their cold small fingers wrapped around my hand. Their eyes pleading for comfort.

Helen shoved plants and pots from a bench, and helped

me sit. I sunk my head between my knees and forced air through my tight, dry lips. She brought me a glass of water, and once the awful rasp disappeared from my breathing, I drank. To be honest, I didn't want to ask, but my curiosity never failed. I looked up at Helen with watering eyes. "Did it?"

"Did it what?" Helen asked.

"Did it break him?" Because dying children had broken me a long time ago.

Helen took my hands. "This nightmare has been going on for far too long. Too many have paid for his mistake. Too many lives have been lost. That's why you need to kill him. It's the only way to stop her."

I yanked my hands away. The words were clear, Helen had not slurred, but my clinician mind examined her steely gaze for a flaw.

There wasn't one.

I had clearly misinterpreted her regard for James. How was I supposed to help humankind, if I couldn't even read their intentions?

"Charlotte didn't just kill his three children. She's killed many children. And she won't stop. It's why you're here. It's why things are different this time. Because she's close to succeeding."

The ground rumbled with thunder. I had spent my life helping the dying, curing the diseased. "I'm not a killer." The clouded words barely made it past my lips.

"I would do it, but we've known each other too long. Jamie would see it coming. Charlotte would come after me and..." There was a unique note of desperation in her voice.

I stood, relieved the ground didn't give out. There was no way I was going to entertain her idea. It was better to ignore the request entirely. "I need to see his companions again." I retook Helen's hands. "Can you help me with that?"

"Why?"

"I need their blood."

Because there was no way in hell I was going to kill him.

Helen slid her hands from mine and looked out of the greenhouse toward Heritage House. "Sometimes a cure can't be found under a microscope." She gave me a sad look of disappointment. "He's tried to use science for a century now, and it's never saved him. If you're a technician like Tousain, James will continue to watch those he loves die. Sometimes the disease is the patient. I thought you were in the business of saving people."

"I am."

Helen waited for more words, but that's all I had.

15

ELECTRICITY

The fluorescent lights in the lab throbbed as I examined another slide under the microscope. I had spent twelve hours processing the blood samples I'd collected over the weekend. The sun was soon setting and I was starving. My only sustenance had been from packets of saltine crackers spread with peanut butter and jelly, and five coffees. I grabbed a travel-size toothbrush and toothpaste and went to battle the stale film in my mouth before calling it quits.

"You need to eat better and get more sleep," I reprimanded the girl in the mirror foaming with toothpaste. I splashed cold water over my face and considered what takeout to pick up on the way back to my sterile hotel room. I made a mental note to contact Helen about apartment recommendations, because the comfort of housekeeping and room service at the hotel was dangerously addictive.

I stepped out of the restroom and felt a delicate current of electricity. Afraid I was imagining it, I froze and gauged my suspicion. The vibrating atoms registered along my cheeks and arms, tickling the fine hairs. I rolled my shoulders back and braced. James really didn't want to mess with me on an empty stomach.

He sat in my chair at my desk with his back to the door. I attempted to assess what emotion he was trying to mask by reading through the medical files on my desk. Thank God I was smart enough to give each of his companions pseudonyms. Paranoia was healthy. I closed my eyes, took a deep breath and entered my lab.

"Are you making any headway, Dr. Whiting?" he asked, his back still to me. Crumbs from crackers salted the edge of my desk. "You've been quiet. And busy." He tossed the file and spun around, his eyes holding the amusement of a playground bully.

"I like busy." I collected slides from the counter and laid them onto a stainless steel tray for refrigeration. He helped himself to one of my crackers. I winced a little when I heard him crunch.

"Do you always keep so much garbage on your desk?" He went to swipe the pile of leaves, bottle caps, and ticket stubs into the garbage.

"Don't. That's not garbage." My voice had cracked. It wasn't garbage to Sam.

He pointed to a matchbook. "Looks like you enjoyed another visit to Heritage House." He took a spoonful of jam, spread it on a cracker, and tossed it into his mouth, then fanned out the medical files on my desk. My chest tightened. He was a cat toying with a pissy mouse.

I shut off my microscope.

"I didn't know you were taking on additional patients," he said.

"You're my only patient."

He sprang out of my chair and reached for the tray of slides.

This was how my big brother used to torment me. How he would snatch my favorite stuffed animal and either dangle it above my head out of reach, or fling it out the window for me to fetch. My eyes lobbed from the tray to James's open palms, and I remembered how I had once kicked Sam so hard he had toppled over my bed and sprained his wrist. Sam had stopped being a tease after that. I handed James the tray.

"This looks different, definitely not samples from me. Which makes me guess that you have a set of new patients." His lips mouthed numbers: one, two, three, four. "Five new patients."

I stared at the smile of an angry man.

He opened the refrigerator under the counter. I expected him to toss the tray in, or slam the door shut. He did neither, which worried me more.

"I wanted to see if your companions shared any common traits. They're a part of your routine, just like the transfusions. They hadn't been examined."

He walked into my personal space, leaned down, and licked his lips, tasting the stale air between us. I needed to freshen it.

"I'm going to find a biological connection between them. A reason you prefer their blood to others." I pushed past him and shuffled the reports together, making a neat pile. "It can't be random. Otherwise the transfusions would be enough." I turned to face him, prepared to defend my degree in medicine, immunology, and pathology.

"You want to know what the connection is between them?" He didn't wait for my answer. "I enjoy fucking them."

My fists tightened with resentment. "Charming. You may feed from them, but you don't own every drop of their blood. They wanted to help." I bit the inside of my cheek to keep from calling him an asshole.

"Do you always go behind a patient's back? Break their trust?"

"I don't have to ask *your* permission to test *their* blood. It's my job to help you. They all consented. I haven't covered anything up. Your anger is unjustified, and frankly, slightly infantile. You don't have a cell to stand on in the trust department." I lifted the files and hugged them over my chest, knowing it was a paper-thin shield.

There was a look of sick surprise on his face. "Did you log their names anywhere?" His jaw tightened, causing a harsh pop. The hairs at the nape of my neck snapped to attention.

"I would never give anyone their names. They're anonymous case numbers. I had to figure out why Tousain never followed up on your companions."

"Because I never told him about them."

"What?" My confidence nosedived.

"I've never told *anyone* about my companions."

Static whipped up my spine. I winced and stood painfully tall. If this was what Helen was referring to, I no longer wanted to be treated differently than the other doctors James had employed.

"What is the matter with you?" he asked.

I slammed the files onto the counter and held on to steady myself. The high pitch of his anger rattled my eardrums. I thought they were going to explode. He walked up behind me. "Don't touch me. Just stop whatever you're doing."

"What are you talking about?"

The electric current eased out of the room, and I took in

trembling breaths of air. He leaned over and tried to catch my eyes.

"Every time you get upset, you turn on some electric pain thing."

He grabbed my arms to help keep me upright. "I don't know what you mean," he said.

I shook him off. My body was reeling in pain and throbbing with confusion. Never sure when he told the truth or when it was entombed within a lie, I snapped.

"Get. Out," I shouted.

"Is that what you want?"

He appeared wounded, but I remembered I was dealing with a monster.

"Yes."

To my shocked surprise, he complied.

GOOD GUESSES

D I Cooper hoped like hell the tingling sensation in his legs had nothing to do with the sun setting. This happened every time after dialysis, this peculiar discomfort. Like his body wasn't his, that somehow it belonged to some foreign entity.

This was the total bullshit he fed himself to cope with the fact that he was on dialysis for the rest of his fucking life. At the age of thirty-three.

He removed his jacket, and sat on a bench outside the clinic under an umbrella of oak trees older than the building he stared at with contempt. He leaned back, closed his eyes, and debated the merits of manning up to his condition while cataloguing his symptoms. His heart rate was normal, his vision remained clear, and no nausea. All good. Nothing to worry about.

Someone walked past, almost knocking his jacket off the bench. Quick to pick a fight, he opened his mouth to make a smart remark when he recognized his assaulter. Dr. Abby Whiting stomped down the path, whispering curt words to no one in particular.

Fifty meters from where he sat, she stopped, dropped a bag of crisps to the ground, and emitted little grunts of foul language as she pulverized the bag into a hundred shards of white. He watched the flecks of crisps shoot out from the bag, as if the entire episode was playing in slow motion. Part of him reveled in her blatant act of destruction, while the other attempted to process why he could see every detail. Was this the new perspective a near death experience brought?

She picked up the decimated bag and tossed it in the rubbish bin. How very American. She huffed and released one last brilliant and shocking expletive. "Fuck it."

George blurted a grateful laugh of solidarity.

Her head snapped up. Her stare was horizon flat. Excitement surged under his skin. If she was going for intimidation, it was working against her. He stifled his laugh and presented a smile instead. There was something about her shock and anger he found attractive. It was a shameful form of instant gratification.

"Detective Cooper?" she asked. Her defensive stare had lowered to a polite squint.

"Hello, Dr. Whiting."

"Sorry. I didn't recognize you."

A hint of a blush shaded its way up her cheeks as she walked toward him.

"I'm out of uniform," he joked.

He moved his jacket, signaling for her to come join him on the bench. Odd, he was usually quick to avoid company at the clinic.

"So now you're running an undercover operation?" She sat the appropriate distance from a police officer and placed her backpack down.

"Not really."

She leaned in and took a closer look at his face. He knew this look.

"Are you feeling okay?" she asked.

That small divot between her brows he had noticed on their first meeting returned, but it was deeper this time.

"I always look a little flushed after treatment." Had he just said that?

"Treatment?"

He pointed to his inner arm.

"Dialysis?" She leaned back and gave him her full scrutiny. "Accident?"

"That's an impressive first guess." For a woman who had questionable interpersonal skills, she was astute.

"You don't fit the profile of a kidney failure patient. What happened?"

"I had rhabdomyolysis after a car accident."

"That's terrible." She almost put her hand to her mouth, but refrained. "When?"

"Five months ago."

"I'm sorry." She had moved in closer. "Is that where the scar on the chin came from?"

He ran his fingers along the scar. "No. That's ancient."

"Well, shit." She slumped into the bench, lost in thought. Probably recreating the trauma in her mind, probably with better accuracy than his recollection. The divot in her forehead grew deeper. He felt lightheaded, and needed to redirect her attention.

"Bad day?" he asked.

She looked at him with confusion, and he pointed to the trail of demolished crisps.

"Difficult patient." Her eyes faintly traced the scar that went along the left side of his mouth and disappeared under his chin. She smiled when she finally noticed he had been watching. "So both kidneys were damaged?"

"Lost one."

Her eyes grew wide. "Damn."

He laughed. It was nice to talk to someone about it. Openly. Without fear. "It could've been worse." He shrugged. "I actually thought it was. I heard this awful snap when the car rolled. I thought for sure my spine had been..."

She stared at the ground, lost in medical speculation again. "That must've been terrifying. Do you have any family members who could...?"

"I don't think I'm at that point yet." And he didn't have any family left. The one kidney would have to last until he found a donor.

"Huh." She nodded. "Good. Good." She was looking for the exit door to their conversation. "So you come here for dialysis? Isn't that a conflict of interest?"

"I'm not investigating the entire clinic. And it's just a few blocks from work."

"Right."

"Who's your physician?"

"Are you going to go snooping, Dr. Whiting?"

"That wouldn't be legal. Just wanted to make sure..." She paused, as if she was suddenly caught admitting to something. Maybe she didn't hate him? Then why had she cancelled their dinner?

"Nate Rothschild."

"Nate? Rothschild?" The divot returned with a slight sneer.

"Careful with your criticism. He's an old friend."

"Really? From where?" She appeared genuinely concerned.

"School. It wasn't a school for nice kids," he admitted.

"He's nothing like you."

He scratched the side of his head. "No." Nothing alike, but somehow it worked. "He has an odd sense of humor. Not everyone gets him."

She looked up at their shared work floor and slowly nodded. "Would you like something to drink? Maybe some juice?" she asked.

"No. I just wanted some fresh air." He lifted the metal travel canister. "And Nate always sends me off with some concoction."

"Concoction?"

He sniffed the lid. "Beet juice and carrot juice, and ginger, and ginseng, and whatever else he fancies. This month it's juicing, next month it'll be ground elephant tusks." Her eyes widened. They were more light brown than he'd remembered. Warm caramel. "I'm kidding."

"Oh." She took a deep, slow breath.

He did the same. "I'm fine, Dr. Whiting. You look like you need the night off anyway."

"Are you sure? I don't mind sitting with you."

"I'm sure." He nodded.

She stood and discreetly waved goodbye. After a few paces, she turned back to him. "Are you free tomorrow night? For that dinner you owe me?"

She had cancelled, making her joke the closest she'd come to flirting. "Sure." He didn't even consult his phone. Odd. "Does seven work?"

She nodded. "Did you catch him?"

"Sorry?"

"The bad guy. The day of the crash."

How did she know he was in pursuit that night? He shook his head. "I don't think so."

"That sucks."

He smiled. "Yeah, it does." What was worse, he couldn't remember if he was pursuing or being pursued. He just knew he had woken up with a broken body and a broken heart. And there was only one person to blame. "If you have any real trouble with your patient, feel free to give him my card." He winked.

He watched her walk to the parking lot, trying hard to ignore the guess that had popped into his head. Seven. He could hear seven. With much hesitation, he slowly turned his gaze back to the crisp demolition site. There, in a rabid frenzy, were seven crows snacking on the shards of potato.

The warmth from his body drained and he slipped on his jacket, eyes closed, telling his suspicious mind it was another lucky guess.

17

HOT AND SPICY

Twenty minutes had passed before George reached for his phone. He had checked it several times for a text or missed call already. He didn't think Dr. Whiting would be late for their date. But she had cancelled before. And this evening wasn't a date, even though he had shaved, but skipped the cologne. He had changed his shirt, but he had a desk drawer full of clean ones, and it had been a long day in that white shirt.

Who was he kidding? George wasn't the friendly tourist-information-center kind of guy. He wasn't a casual dater either. Perhaps this was payback for holding her up at the station? Abby Whiting didn't seem like the vengeful type, not even in a poking fun kind of way. No, she had forgotten, because *Doctor* Abby Whiting was a workaholic.

He weighed the phone and his options in the palm of his hand. There was enough paperwork to go back to at the office. Surely, there was a match to watch at the pub. He thumbed the screen and heard the quick pitter-patter of someone running. Abby raced down the footpath like a late pensioner hailing a bus—one arm in her coat, the other flailing behind her for the other sleeve.

"Sorry, sorry, sorry." She came to an abrupt stop. "I lost track of time." She got the other arm in before he could help, which left him feeling slightly disappointed.

"It happens." George casually slipped his phone back in his pocket. Why was he smiling so hard? "We don't have a reservation to make."

"We don't? Oh good." She took a deep breath and exhaled with relief.

She was so peculiar and captivating. Maybe it was the honesty. "Are you up for pub food?" he asked.

Her smile grew. "Is that code for fried food?"

George laughed. "Only if you want it to be."

He watched her eyes, drowning with caution. "Uh, sure."

That was a definite polite no.

"How about Indian?"

She leaned back and then gave a resounding yes that nearly bowled her over.

Indian food was the perfect food for a non-date date. It was coat-your-tongue spicy and capable of staining a good shirt. Perfect. This wasn't a date. But what was the strange feeling swimming around his chest?

"It isn't very far, we can walk," he said.

"Great." She turned and looked back at her office building.

"Did you leave the light on?"

She huffed. "The lights go off automatically at one thirty."

He had no reason not to believe her, which meant she knew the lights went off at that late hour. Workaholic didn't seem the right adjective. Obsessive seemed more apt.

"South or north?" she asked.

"South Indian."

"Cool. How long have you worked in Cambridge?" she asked.

He noticed the moon. It was a bright yellow and only half full. "Almost eight years." He then noticed a muddied matchbook with someone named Lucy's phone number in it. Five yards away, and under a bush. He shook it off.

"Almost eight? You must really like it here."

"How do you mean?"

"You offered to take a perfect stranger out to show off your town. Like a proud parent."

She wasn't perfect or a stranger, but she had lingered in the back of his mind all day. "It's quiet but not too quiet. There are always new faces because of the university. The crime rate is low, but interesting." He pointed to his right, marking their next turn. "College towns have plenty of attractions or distractions—art, music, theater, lectures. If you're into that." He came to a sudden stop. "It's very much like Stanford, I would guess."

"I guess so."

"Here we are."

She peered into the dimly lit windows cut into the door. "This is a pub."

"It's a pub owned by a South Indian family." He pulled open the door. The scent of curry, coriander, and garam masala yanked them inside.

George cut a path through the noisy and crowded bar to the tables in the back. Relief shook off all the itchiness of doubt when he found two empty seats. He knew it was a calculated risk bringing her here. But this wasn't a date, so there really wasn't anything at risk.

She sat. "I would've never, never guessed this was an Indian place."

"Helps to be in the know."

"I guess I need to look into dark windows more carefully."

A waitress brought them menus. George ordered a pint, and Abby asked for a mineral water. Which probably meant she was returning to work after their dinner. Definitely not a date. Or worse, she didn't drink. He watched her eyes scan the menu.

"The chips here are top notch."

"Are they?"

Her gaze didn't leave the menu. Perhaps a fried potato was offensive to the fit Californian? Or she had expected this to be a date. He told himself to stop thinking about it.

The waitress returned with their drinks. "Alright loves, what suits your fancy?" she asked.

Abby peered above the menu. "You order first, I'm still debating."

"I'll have the lamb curry with a side of chips." He examined his half empty pint glass with surprise. "And another pint."

Abby pressed her lips together. "I'd like to try the fried okra to start. And I'll go with the Chana Masala, spicy." Abby handed her the menu. "And a side of chips with raita."

The waitress tucked the menus under her arms. "I can't remember the last time a woman came in and ordered a proper meal."

George waited the appropriate amount of time to see if Abby had been offended by the waitress's sticky commentary. "Are you a vegetarian?"

"No, why?"

"Nothing you ordered had meat."

"Oh. I wasn't feeling like meat. I'm not biggest fan of lamb or goat. Or meat right now."

She pulled a small container from her pocket. Squeezed a ball of clear liquid onto her hands and rubbed.

He pointed at the small container. "I thought there was nothing beneficial about hand sanitizer?" he quipped. "Or is there something you know that I don't?"

"It's still a decent preventative." She lifted the container. "And if you culture germs all day, it's a little hard to get them out of your head."

George held out his hand, palm up. She squirted the cold gel into his hand. He rubbed the antiseptic over his hands, the sharp smell punching his nostrils. He held up his beer. "Cheers."

"Oh." She lifted her bottle of mineral water and clinked his glass. "Cheers."

She squinted her eyes at the bar as if she were trying to get something into focus. "So you don't have any family in Cambridge?"

George forced beer past the lump in his throat. "None that I know of."

"That's a strange answer."

He shrugged. "I had a rather strange upbringing. Very Dickens like."

"I didn't think debtor's prisons existed any longer. And I haven't seen any street urchins." Her eyes sparkled when she allowed a laugh. "But I don't walk the streets that often either."

"They are safe. Relatively speaking."

"Even with the surge of dead or missing doctors?"

His stomach tensed.

"Sorry. That was mean." She shook her head. "Do you have any other interesting cases?"

He rubbed the back of his neck. "Someone is disturbing the recently dead."

"What?" She put down her bubbly water.

"Apparently, someone is attacking the recently deceased."

"Attacking? Like hitting or digging up and stealing parts?"

George finished his pint. How was he supposed to explain this? "More like desecrating."

"That's awful. And kinda gross." She took a sip of her water. "More than once?"

He nodded, but she didn't really seem interested in his answer. Perhaps she was trying to picture what a desecrated body looked like. "Why did you ask about stolen parts?" And was old blood a part to her?

"It's an old anatomy class joke. Modern medicine began in the cemetery." She lifted her mineral water.

The waitress delivered the fried okra and chips. The chip portions were on the generous side. Abby dove into both without hesitation. This was like hanging out with his work mates. No formality. Just relaxed. He hadn't expected to feel easy around the awkward woman. Clearly, dead bodies didn't steal her appetite.

George felt his phone vibrate in his pocket. "How old were you when you entered medical school?"

"You haven't dug that up yet, DI Cooper?"

"Okay, how old were you in this anatomy class?"

"Sixteen."

He leaned forward. "Sixteen? You weren't intimidated?"

"I had been sneaking into lectures at Stanford since I was thirteen, so no. I was used to everyone being older and bigger and taller."

"Thirteen? Your dad didn't mind?"

"Are you kidding? It beat paying a sitter."

"You knew at the ripe old age of thirteen you wanted to study medicine?"

"I think I knew sooner than that. I just started ruling other things out at thirteen. Like I definitely did not want to study quantum physics or go anywhere near the business school."

"When did you pinpoint pathology?"

"Twenty."

His phone vibrated again, but he ignored it. Abby had launched into an argument about the rise of resistance to antibiotics, which initially sounded dire and depressing, but she believed they were on the verge of an evolution in immunotherapy. Something about nanotechnology being paired with genetic and stem cell therapy.

He didn't understand all of it, but reveled in watching the level of her passion and enthusiasm. For some reason, he thought those were her most heavily guarded emotions. But when she spoke of her work, there was no curtain. She loved it.

His phone vibrated again. He pulled his phone out of his pocket. "Sorry."

"No worries."

Vic had left two messages. Strange. He checked his texts. She had sent a text before making the phone calls. All it said was FOUND SOMETHING. CALL ME.

He debated whether that was a positive or a negative. Positive that it didn't say found another disturbed dead body. Negative in that Vic only bothered him with information relevant to the cases they were working.

The waitress placed their dinner on the table. Abby had finished the okra and was close to finishing the chips. He had no idea where any of those calories went, not that he was counting. The idea of leaving her to finish her dinner alone didn't sit well, and Vic was competent enough to follow a lead.

The waitress lifted the empty plate of okra. "I guess you liked it okay?" she asked with a smile.

"Were they fried with curry leaves?" Abby asked.

The waitress beamed with pride. "Not everyone gets that. You've got a smart tongue."

George didn't even know curry was a leaf. What else could she taste?

"Work?" She tipped her chin at his phone.

"It can wait." He dug into his curry. They were half way through their meals when his phone vibrated again.

"It's okay," she said. "You can get that, really. I would feel terrible if you didn't."

He picked up.

"Hey boss, I need you to meet me at the archives," Vic said.

"Archives?"

"What's all that noise in the background? Ah shit, you're out on your date."

He closed his eyes. It wasn't a date. He grunted into the phone and noticed Abby was racing through the rest of her meal. He reached out and touched her hand, signaling for her to slow down.

She put her fork down.

"What did you find?" he asked Vic.

"Something that doesn't make sense. Or can't be possible. So I need a second pair of eyes. Tell you what, I'll see if they'll let me take copies and I'll meet you back at the station in the morning."

Tomorrow? Because Vic was betting this was a date. And was looking forward to possible entanglements and gossip.

"I can be there in an hour."

"You're an idiot. That American is totally—"

He hung up and looked across the table at Abby, and then at his plate. Abby picked at the remaining chips on her plate, his was still half full.

"New lead?" she asked.

"Not sure."

"Do you always work at night?"

"Depends on the case. Probably give up a few nights a week when the case load is high."

"Must make it hard to maintain a relationship?"

That was a strange question coming from a woman who didn't talk personal. "I guess so."

"Is that what happened between you and Padma?"

Curry seared his esophagus. "How did you know about Padma?"

She pointed to the corkboard behind the bar. "There's a picture of the two of you." She smiled, the kind of smile a cop would give a low-level burglar who'd been caught climbing out of a broken window.

"Well that wasn't very smart," he admitted.

"But this isn't a date. So you have nothing to worry about." She lifted her mineral water.

"Welcome to Cambridge. Have you ever considered police work?"

She laughed. And his appetite suddenly disappeared. He'd made a terrible mistake. He had underestimated his interest in her. Lying had become too common a practice over the last few months.

"It's okay. I had my sights set on a university professor anyway." She casually shrugged. "Free access to the libraries and all the attractions."

"Don't judge a book by his cover. I just arrested one last week for sex trafficking."

"Holy shit. Really?"

Why did it hurt him to laugh now?

Their walk back to the clinic was clinical. He pointed out various storefronts and other obvious places of interest. The entire time knowing full well she could read signs and pick up a tour guide. If he were going to be nailed into a platonic coffin, he might as well go all out.

"I hope you've enjoyed your taste of Cambridge," he said as they approached her office building. "Nine-thirty seems awfully late even for a dedicated clinician."

"Death waits for no one." The way she uttered the words sounded almost flippant.

"Right." They were at the awkward goodbye stage of the evening.

"Sorry, I didn't mean to be morose or gloomy."

"Can I ask you a question, off the record, professional to professional?"

"Of course."

"There isn't a medical condition that would provoke someone to want or crave blood? From a dead body?"

The blood drained from her face. Her mouth fell open and for a split second, he worried she was going to pass out.

"Are you serious?" she blurted.

"Sorry. It's just this case. It doesn't make any sense. Like there isn't a medical use for blood from the deceased, right?"

He heard her take a long, deep breath. There was sharp bitter taste on his tongue as well.

"From a dead person?" She shook her head and shut her eyes. "Huh. Well, I don't think so. I can do some poking around. But that sounds like a question for the psych department."

"Right." She was visibly shaken and relieved.

"Anyway, thanks for the tour," she said. "The dinner was fantastic. I would've never found that place."

She leaned forward. And he went in for the polite kiss on the cheek. The way someone would greet a relative. Somehow it landed just to the side of her mouth, causing her to lurch back in surprise and embarrassment.

"Sorry. I was going for the double cheek kiss." He had forgotten Americans didn't do that. "That's how we greet people here."

Her eyes and mouth opened simultaneously. "Oh. I was going for a hug. We hug where I come from."

"Fantastic. Good to know. So Rome or home?" he asked.

She shrugged. "Rome. Sure. Why not."

"I'm going to your left cheek first."

"Okay." She turned her face to the right and then left. "Good night, detective."

"Good night, doctor."

He waved and watched her return to her building. The minute she left his sight, he shook his head. "Bugger. Bugger. Bugger." He had never, ever not once, in his thirty-three years, fucked up a goodnight kiss.

18

MATTER OF RECORD

"How was your platonic tonic?" Vic asked. She kept her attention focused on her computer screen. Which was a relief, because he could mask the disappointment in his voice but not his eyes.

"Good."

She copped a quick glance. "Ouch. That bad?" With a knowing when to quit smirk, she clicked her mouse and the printer began spitting papers.

"What did you find?" he asked.

"I'm not sure." She pulled the printouts and cascaded them across her desk.

The news articles were from various papers—a few local, two from the university medical journal and another he didn't recognize. All had photos and the articles revolved around one place.

"Hastings?"

She nodded. "But here's the thing." She pointed to one figure in each photo. "It doesn't make sense."

James Stuart had made a few appearances in the paper. It would be difficult not to, being the Chairman of a cutting-edge medical clinic. Vic then pointed to the dates of the archived articles.

She had laid the photos in chronological order, the latest from this year and the oldest from an article forty years prior.

"Are these real?"

"Yeah. I double-checked against the county archive at the university."

"That can't be." George's vision tunneled as his gaze zeroed in on the man in each photo. James Stuart was thirty-two, not fifty-two.

Vic slipped her hands into her trousers and leaned back, examining the photos. This was what she did when she chewed through facts, linking them in a neat row. He imagined she had done this several times over the last couple of hours. No wonder she had called so many times.

"How is that possible?" he asked. He suddenly felt warm and loosened his tie.

"Dunno." She placed her thumb into her mouth and began to chew her nail.

That was never a good sign. "What?" he asked.

The sigh she released held a bit of a groan. She pulled a large, black journal from the top of her filing cabinet. It was an old dusty journal, the insignia of King's College embedded into the cover.

She handed it to him as if it were a live bomb.

"Page two twenty-eight."

George didn't understand the caution she was exercising. He studied the side of the tome. It was a medical journal. The kind maintained for papers published by the college. The journal was for the year 1918.

No. Bloody. Way.

He checked the date again and looked up at her. She

stared at the photos on her desk. He flipped to the page she had indicated.

The article was about genetics, but that wasn't what caught his eye. At the bottom right of the page was a small photograph of a group of men. In the back row was a familiar figure.

No.

George pulled the book closer. It wasn't the clearest black and white photo, but he saw what Vic had wanted him to see. A sharp pain shot up the back of his left leg and his head felt squeezed of logic.

"Did you forget your meds today?" She rolled her desk chair next to him. "Here, sit down."

"This makes no sense." He stared at the photo and read the caption. He wasn't James Stuart in this picture, but a Stuart Henry. What the bloody hell?

Vic disappeared into his office and returned with a cup of water and a couple of his pills.

He took them without complaint.

"Are they related?" he asked. Because he had to start with something that made sense, there was no way the photos were of the same man. It was literally impossible.

She opened her bottom drawer, pulled out the bottle of brandy, and poured some into his empty cup and her coffee.

"I can't find a record of either person."

He drank the brandy, savoring the heat as it trailed down his throat, across his chest, and pooled in his stomach. "You checked church and state records?"

"Everything. Every combination of the aliases. There are Stuarts and Henrys and James. Even St. James. None of these men has an official birth record. Or death record, unless they were buried as John Does." She refilled her cup and his. "I don't get it."

He scanned the photos and articles again. Each a different time, he had a different name, a simple name, nothing noteworthy, but the men all looked the same. All had one thing in common—they appeared timeless. His dinner suddenly protested.

"You alright? Where'd you go out anyway?"

"The Jewel."

"On a first date? What the bloody hell?"

He set down his cup. "How about we pick this up in the morning? With fresh eyes?"

She nodded. "The Jewel." She stood up and gathered all her papers. "You have a cock death wish."

"It's fine. She enjoyed herself."

"Yeah, but you didn't."

"It wasn't about that."

"So, is she still in that column?" She pointed to the case board.

"Everyone is in that column."

"Even Nate?" Her smile was as big as a thin cat with a fat canary.

He pinched his eyes shut. The meds were not working, if at all, anymore.

"Okay, okay." Vic's tone conceded and soothed in equal measure. "Let's bugger off home." She grabbed her satchel. "Did you at least kiss her?"

He lifted his hand and waved her off.

"Christ. You're bombing out on a massive scale. I told you not to wait this long." She cut the lights and they walked down the hall. "Padma is a cunt. And you need to get her out of your system. Playing good copper with the bad American isn't helping you an ounce."

George pulled the door open, welcoming the hit of cold,

fresh air. For some reason, he couldn't get the softness of her skin off his lips. "She isn't a bad American," he said.

"Then stop treating her as if she's the plague." Vic pulled a packet of fags from her coat pocket and lit up. "Think of her as an opportunity to flush your system out. Get the blood flowing. Because you've got too much bad juice locked up in you." She motioned to the lower half of his body.

"You are the crassest bitch I've ever met."

"No, I'm not," she purred. "That's Nate."

19

BIRD'S EYE VIEW

George always enjoyed the pursuit of suspects. There were times when his life was so infused with the conversations of strangers, he wondered if he were capable of living without them. He regarded some suspects with curiosity and some with disdain.

James Stuart was both.

Stuart was never anywhere expected or convenient. Didn't matter how many times George called his office, he was never there. Because that wasn't where Stuart wanted him to look. The man understood first impressions. He was a classic sociopath. After much frustration, and a quick guzzling of one of Nate's beet juice concoctions, George walked across the minty lawn and followed a path up a small knoll. And as if on cue, there sat Stuart on a bench, feeding birds.

George shook his head. The man understood how to set a scene. And George was determined to end his long acting career.

"Mr. Stuart. I've been looking for you."

"I am found."

"Communing with nature." And God only knew what else.

He smiled. "You should join me." He held out the bag of birdseed.

There was something about his grace and control. George found it admirable and unnerving. He also resented how Stuart looked five years younger but behaved decades older. Which wasn't possible. It just didn't add up. George accepted and pocketed the bag of birdseed.

"Not a fan of birds?"

"Don't have time for such diversions."

"Have you found Mathieu?"

George sat next to his prime suspect. He took in the view and wondered why the young, affluent Chairman of the Hastings Clinic would waste time feeding birds. "No, we haven't."

"That's a shame. I guess he'll never be found."

"How do you mean?"

"I read an article once that said the first forty-eight hours were the most critical in a missing persons case. And we don't even know when those hours began. You have made no arrests. You've barely questioned my staff. It's been almost five weeks. "

"You haven't really made yourself available to me."

Stuart brushed seeds from his dark tweed pants. "It's not easy taking care of all this. And without Mathieu to take on the press." He shook his head. "I've had to spread myself more thin than usual."

George followed Stuart's gaze, which seemed to drift back to one building. It was smaller than the others, only two stories, and more modern than the other classic Cambridge ancient fare.

"Why was Dr. Tousain accepting large financial transfers

from MacCombe Bio?"

Stuart smiled. It was that million-pound playboy smile. The smile that dazzled the society page and the one that ate at George's broken ego. "That would be a question for MacCombe Bio. I could ask my assistant to get you some contact info." How could Padma not fall for the charm? And the money, and the power, and the guaranteed media following?

Stuart's gaze returned to the building. Two employees walked out, patting their sweaty faces with small white towels with the Hastings Clinic logo. George figured he had been reading one too many company press releases to recognize the emblem from so far.

George spotted what held Stuart's attention. The third window had a direct view of Abby running on a treadmill. Her treadmill didn't face out toward the windows. Instead, it faced a wall. George assessed the distance from the bench to the building. His farsightedness had much improved since the car accident.

"Are you watching your employees exercise, Mr. Stuart?"

"No, just the one."

George felt his control on the interview slip and his gut tightened. He couldn't arrest the man for watching the employee gym. James was jabbing an old wound. A wound with plenty of scar tissue.

"The American. Whiting, is it?" George bluffed.

"You have astounding vision, DI Cooper. She told me you took her to the Jewel. Interesting choice."

Punch landed. George inhaled slow and deep.

"She's an interesting bird," Stuart continued. "I can't understand why she doesn't want a view when she clocks in that kind of distance."

How long had Stuart been watching his precious bird?

Did Abby know she was being held in a gilded cage? George grabbed a handful of birdseed and tossed it to the ground.

"Maybe she needs to stay focused. How many miles?"

"Twelve to fifteen, four times a week. Californians do appreciate their exercise."

He had her pegged for a runner but not that kind of distance. "So you admit to watching her often?"

"I come to feed the birds. She just happens to go run in the late afternoon." Stuart turned to face George, but George resisted the urge to make the conversation casual and kept his eyes and body locked on Abby. "At first, I couldn't understand why she didn't want a view. I mean, she sometimes spends two hours on that machine." George felt Stuart's scrutiny, probing for a reaction, relishing the turning of tables. "But she has these epiphanies toward the end of her exercise. That's when I know she's on to something." Stuart released a sigh. "It's amazing, to watch such talent."

"Why did you have her visa paperwork filled out so early?"

Stuart didn't flinch. "Is it a crime to be proactive? I didn't want Mathieu to continue to drag his feet."

"But I thought he had made the offer."

"Yes, after many hours of deliberation and arm twisting."

Had he twisted Tousain's arm off? "He didn't want her here?"

"She's a lot farther along than he ever was at her age. She was a threat. A younger, newer threat." Stuart checked his watch.

"Am I keeping you from something?"

"No. She's making incredible time today. Her last few miles are always her fastest. Completely brilliant."

George's eyes returned to the long row of windows. She

had picked up her pace. Her eyes were trained on the white wall. There was no amount of imagination in his reserve to spend well over an hour staring at a blank wall. What else could she endure? He checked his watch. It was getting close to his appointment.

"That level of dedication and focus is admirable." George squinted. She was running faster.

"That's one way of looking at it."

"How do you look at it?"

"I keep wondering what she's running from."

The nicotine tick returned, making George's lower left lid twitch at the very wrong moment. "We looked into MacCombe Bio. Interesting thing. It's a shell company. Another company you seem to own. Did you know that?"

James tapped his chin, feigning surprise. He shook his head. "It gets hard to keep track of it all. Sometimes it's a massive undertaking. How do you keep track of so many cases, suspects, and interviews?"

"Is this when you make your disappearance, Mr. Stuart? Or whomever you are?"

"I'm sorry, have I offended you? Because I'm unclear as to what you're asking?"

George wasn't really sure how to phrase it. He had gone on a fishing trip and wanted to test the water. It was too soon to call the man in with little to no evidence of wrongdoing without a body. He handed Stuart the bag of birdseed. "I'll be in touch."

George stood and began to walk back to the employee gym.

"How are your treatments coming along, Detective?"

"Very well, thank you."

"And how are things with Padma?"

George stopped cold. "Terminal, thanks."

CHEMISTRY

I caught my cell phone as it vibrated its way off the counter. It was James's ninth call. All of his messages were the same, so my guilt about not picking up had diminished after his third attempt. There were two more chemical reports to print. I had to present a clean report, irrefutable proof.

The medical history I'd collected on his companions had been run through a series of formulas to extrapolate patterns. Cholesterol levels ran the gamut, no blood type commonality, one diabetic, four family cancer histories, two heart disease candidates, and no concerning genetic disorder markers. Medically, they were a random pool of people, except they all felt happier and more complete after giving him their blood. But how did he feel after taking it?

Once I stopped looking at biology, and remembered my chemically-induced-food-coma, I found something. All of his companions suffered from depression. Clinically diagnosed depression. All were on medication to treat their symptoms. Although two of them had omitted the information in their medical history forms, their blood didn't hide their antidepressants. That was his mysterious aphrodisiac. The chemistry was almost comical if it weren't so sad.

There was a quick knock on my door. A sharply dressed but flustered Nate entered. He pinched the bridge of his nose between his thumb and index finger. His unshaven face added another level to his exasperation. He cleared his throat and rubbed his coarse chin.

"Listen, I know James can be difficult to work with. Nasty when provoked. But to not return his calls for almost twenty-four hours seems a tad unprofessional. Not to mention childish."

The tips of my ears burned. "Sorry. I was onto something and had to wrap up some tests."

"Onto something?" he asked.

"Not sure what it means yet, but it's something new."

He quickly glanced at the report in my hands. "May I?"

"I don't think he wants me to disclose what I'm working on."

Nate's left brow peaked. "Is this about his other blood sources?"

James had said he had never told Tousain about his companions, but that didn't mean the man who maintained his transfusion schedule didn't know. But I held the reports closer.

"There is no way he can live off two to three pints every couple of weeks. I didn't flunk basic maths."

I handed him the chem reports and noticed his complexion had taken on a less rosier hue. There was also a sour note hiding under his posh cologne. There was a netting of broken capillaries under his nose. I wasn't an expert, but my guess was drugs were no longer recreational for Dr. Rothschild. Was this how James was holding him hostage?

"Antidepressants?" There was a hitch of skepticism in his voice.

"Not all of the donors take medication regularly, but when I mapped out their use and dosage over the last six months with his selection process, there's a pattern. At least a preference." I pulled up a plotting map on my computer.

He leaned over my shoulder. "Interesting." He gently cleared his throat. "James mentioned you had a physical reaction to his anger. Has that occurred before?"

I took a step back, stunned James would share the incident. What else was James sharing? Nate's eyes dug around, examining me for the impartial truth. I suddenly felt nine years old, different, alone, and unsure.

"No," I said.

He didn't blink, continued to stare into my pupils. This wasn't going well.

"It's just that I've been verbally eviscerated by James. It's not pleasant, occasionally erotic, but it's never been physically painful. Maybe you have some other sensitivity?"

"No," I said in two distinct syllables.

"You don't have to be all tetchy."

I resisted the urge to look up the adjective and shrugged. "Maybe it has something to do with his level of stress? I'm sure it's not unique to me."

All I heard was the click of slides as I placed them on the storage tray. I couldn't look at Nate any longer for fear that he would continue to dig. Dig all the way back to my childhood.

"Do you think he seeks them out for this one purpose?" he asked.

"I'm not sure, but it is a connection between five very different people. It'll be interesting if the same trait appears in his next ones."

"Next ones?"

"He doesn't keep the same donors for very long."

Nate paled. "What do you mean?"

"He fears attachment, and he doesn't want to risk passing the disease."

"Right." He resumed reading the report and rubbed his nose with his index finger. "And you've confirmed the depression in all of his live…" He gestured, unable to say the word.

"One donor is a former officer of the Royal Army. He had multiple tours through Afghanistan and Iraq, and suffers from PTSD. One had a successful realty business, but that went under." I grabbed my notes. "And another lost an infant through SIDS twenty-five years ago. I'm sure I'll find similar stories from the others."

"You can find that in anyone off the street. Don't you read the Sunday papers?"

I stared at him, surprised by his quick misgivings of my report. I doubted he knew anyone with those kinds of stories given his occupation, and his air of superiority.

"You don't believe me?" he asked.

"How many veterans do you know?"

"I'm a veteran." He leaned towards me. "Why do you look so surprised?"

"You don't look the type."

"We don't all look like G.I. Joe. We come in all shapes and sizes. I was a medic. It was a surefire way to undercut any hopes the pater had of me ending up behind a desk swindling pensioners."

"Or give him a good scare."

Nate laughed. "I gave up on that a long time ago. He's a heartless tosser."

"Is that why he sent you off to boarding school?"

"How'd you know about that?"

Shit, how was I supposed to bring up whether or not Detective Cooper was on an organ transplant list?

My phone rang, interrupting our uncomfortable exchange of assumptions.

"Please answer that," he said. "For every message he leaves you, I get three." There was no humor in his request. He set my report down and made for the door. "The woman who lost the infant, is she older?"

"Yes." I stared at my phone. "Why doesn't James just come up?"

"You told him to leave."

"I really don't think he finds me that intimidating."

"You have to invite him back."

I gave Nate a quizzical look, and my phone buzzed again.

"If you ask a vampire to leave, they have to be invited back. It's one of their rules of engagement."

"I thought that was superstition." I picked up my phone. "It wasn't in his file anywhere."

"Where was she from?"

"Who?"

"The SIDS case."

"Birmingham."

He nodded goodbye and I answered the phone.

"Look out your window," James said.

Startled by the request, I couldn't help but follow through. James stood in the back courtyard, holding a brown bag with something heavy inside. He opened the bag and pulled out a cylinder-shaped object wrapped in foil.

"I think it's called a burrito."

I couldn't help but smile.

.   .   .

THE WARMTH of summer had finally descended in Cambridge. The blue that had been hidden under a thick slab of gray for weeks stayed until well past eight o'clock now. My body sung at the fresh air.

James handed me the brown bag.

"I didn't think there was any Mexican food in this country." I pulled the warm burrito to my nose and inhaled. Deeply. "How did you know?"

"A quick review of your credit card history."

I held the burrito frozen in shock.

"I'm kidding. I figured anyone this far from home would want comfort food. Shall we sit?"

We sat on a bench under a large weeping willow.

I bit into the burrito, my eyes watering. "Where did you get this?" I asked and a chunk of rice flew out of my mouth onto his jacket.

He laughed and flicked the rice away. "I asked someone at Heritage House to make it."

I took another mouthful of comfort.

"Perhaps I should consider adding a burrito bar in the cafeteria?"

"I'd love you forever."

I wanted to catch the words and shove them back in my mouth.

"Tsk, tsk, Abby. You're getting awfully close to being sentimental."

My stupid mouth, I needed to rein it in. I shoved more burrito in.

"What's the prognosis?" he asked. "Am I dying?"

He smiled, clearly pleased by the success of his apology. I handed him the chem report, and wiped my mouth with the hem of my lab coat.

He opened the file and scanned the report. "You're telling me I'm depressed?"

"I don't know. Are you?"

His brows lifted but not in a threatening way. "I'm rich. I'm forever at my peak. I have the luxury of time, why would I be depressed?"

I leaned my head back, allowing the food to sit and warm my soul, and thought about an answer. What would I do with all the time in the world? All goals could be attained. But not shared. Fortune could be accumulated, lost, and regained. Evolution could be observed and recorded. But I would remain an outsider, an anomaly pretending to belong. That would be depressing as hell. Answering his question honestly would be a bad idea. A very bad idea.

"Ah, the sweet slow passage of time," he said.

Could he really read my thoughts?

"I haven't always been an active member of society," he pinched the crease in his trousers. "I go into periods of hiding, otherwise people start to notice."

"Hiding? Like forced exile?"

"More like hibernation."

"How?"

"I stop feeding, and at some point, I fall asleep."

I put the burrito down. "Where?"

He gave me that icy blue gaze. The gaze that said there was no way in hell he'd share that secret.

"How long does it take?" I asked.

"The first time, it took three weeks."

He looked across the courtyard at the clinic. His eyes seem to trace the lines of the buildings, but they were remote like he had remembered lost attributes.

"Have you ever watched someone fight an addiction?" he asked.

"No." I felt a little horrible for lying.

"I paid for my own funeral, once."

My voice strained for a response, and I finally gave up. I hate funerals.

"I had tried not feeding before, but the hunger overrides everything. Rational thought, morality. Faith. I knew locking myself away wouldn't be enough, I always found a way out. I needed the inescapable. So I had myself buried."

"Alive?" The question was out of my mouth, too late to catch. But my hand had attempted. He smiled at the gesture.

"I heard the entire service. It was short and simple, but lovely." He looked down at his hands. They were palms up, holding an imaginary book. Pieces of my resolve flaked away from the cage wrapped around my heart.

"I ordered a custom-made coffin. A fine piece, made of oak, had locks attached. Inside and out. I spent all the energy I had left trying to scrape through the lid." He turned his hands and I stared at his manicured nails. "Sleep finally came. In those last moments, I thought I'd feel something besides the hunger, but it screamed until the very last second."

I shoved the burrito aside. "And you slept for how long?"

"Fifteen years, four months and three days. But I miscalculated."

"What do you mean?"

"After I woke, I killed six people feeding in twenty-four hours. It took me several days to remember who I was, what I was."

James held me captive with his cold blue eyes, and they denied nothing. He wanted me to have the uncensored truth. A precious commodity between the two of us.

"You thought you'd sleep forever?" I asked.

"It was naïve and shameful, but I hoped I would perish. The disease doesn't feed off of blood alone. No one wants to die, truly. That's why we have so many options. Why we have medicine. It's why you study me. To extend the warranty a day longer, a decade longer."

"That's not why I study you." I wanted to give him hope, just like any other patient.

"I underestimated my desire to live," he said. "That's what the disease feeds on. Desire. But I no longer want to kill to stay alive. I don't fear the darkness. I fear coming out of it, and who has vanished after I do." A trio of black ravens burst from the willow tree and cut across the sky. "I know you've worked hard these last two days. But I've been alive too long to be depressed about it. I'm well past that."

With the cruel speed of lightning, all of my tests meant nothing.

The companions were more than just a fix, more than just some chemical imbalance, more than medicine. They were his comfort and I'd missed it, because of my own self-imposed loneliness. All the years I had avoided building relationships just backfired. The nights spent in libraries, labs, and study halls. The days spent buried in work. All of my conversations had been rehearsed for like-minded professionals. My closest relationship was with a brother I couldn't visit. My last heartfelt words were to a dying lab partner, whose children's names I had memorized but had never met.

"What do you get out of feeding?" I asked.

"I get to feel alive. To hear my heart beat. Sometimes I get a memory from them." His eyes glassed over. "A lovely recollection, pure and unedited emotion. And it's beautiful.

To be alive is different than living. You understand that, right? One is to exist and the other is to feel connected."

I wanted to touch him, to see if the experience could be relayed in some way. Something within me wanted to be set free.

"How did you get out?" I asked.

"Someone dug me out."

"What happened to the person?" But I already knew. They were dead.

Every muscle in his body snapped tight like a horse bucking flies. I forced my shoulders to go lax. I wanted to show him I wasn't afraid, not afraid to walk down every dark alley of his memory.

"I've buried her so many times, but Charlotte never stays buried."

Spots of black danced around the edges of my vision. He had said her name. She was real. A reality I hadn't wanted to consider. Helen was right. No one could have James without death. His eyes were full of contempt, but not for me, and I began to understand the waltz.

"You must really hate yourself," I whispered.

"You have no idea. Or perhaps you do."

What did he mean?

He leaned in and kissed me.

The warmth of his lips surprised but didn't shock me into stopping the kiss. The kiss lingered in a tender way, like we both understood his confession deserved absolution. His pain deserved compassion.

He brushed a stray hair from my cheek. "It's time for me to go now."

"Where?" I asked.

"Hello, Detective."

I turned. There at the end of the path stood Detective

Cooper and another police officer, a woman with cropped red hair. The sneer on her face expressed the disappointment George had clearly masked with cold detachment. In two heartbeats, I had moved from a place of innocence to one of guilt.

21

THE SWISS INQUISITION

Vic followed George down the hall. "Are you sure you're okay?"

"Yeah, why?" He gave her a good shove off with a scowl. She held her hands up.

George yanked open the door to interview room three. He nodded at Vic when she took her seat. She started the recorder.

"This is Detective Sergeant Moore. Time is sixteen twenty. In the room are Detective Inspective Cooper and James Stuart, Chairman of the Board of the Hastings Clinic. Mr. Stuart has agreed to an interview and has been warned of his rights. Mr. Stuart has agreed to an initial round of questions before his counsel arrives. Is that correct, Mr. Stuart?"

"Yes, Detective Sergeant. Is Victoria your mother's name?" Stuart asked.

"How'd you know that?"

George shot Vic a quick are-you-mental glance. Vic readjusted her jacket and looked down at her hands. He heard her heart rate pick up. Or it could've been his, but he felt fine. Stuart tilted his head slightly, jutting his chin forward. There was a hint of curiosity mixed with benign respect in his thoughtful gaze. The man knew how to play his cards.

"Mr. Stuart, I visited you a couple afternoons ago, on the second of August, and asked you about MacCombe Bio. I would like to ask some more questions, if that's alright?"

"Fire away," Stuart crossed one leg over the other like he was settling in for an interview with *The Sun*.

Good.

George tiled three papers across the small interview table. Stuart followed his movements with keen interest. "We checked the business registry for MacCombe Bio. Although your name isn't tied to the company, it looks like your legal team had a British Virgin Islands registry agent form the LLC. It can legally conduct business in the UK, but there is no physical office for the entity. Is that typical?"

"It is if you do not want to report your business to the British government. And it's also all legal."

"True. But it's also how some individuals hide questionable financial transactions."

"Agreed, but one that is perfectly within my rights. I'm not money laundering or drug trafficking. I don't believe you want to get into the mechanics of running offshore accounts or shell entities? That could take days." Stuart leaned back in his chair, folding his hands in his lap. "You want to know why MacCombe Bio sent Mathieu a payment of one hundred thousand pounds the week before his disappearance?"

George looked at the financial statements. The print was miniscule. How had he read through every line item so quickly? Vic leaned forward and scanned the payment transaction report. Her brows wrinkled with wonder.

Stuart continued, un-phased. "My guess is it was for a patent of some kind."

"As his employer, why wouldn't you pay him through the clinic? Wouldn't you want all intellectual property to be registered to that legal entity? It seems a little careless to allow one person such freedom."

"Very good argument. One I've made with Mathieu on several occasions. But sometimes registering patents should not be associated with the clinic, especially if those patents are for processes or applications that may have a high failure rate. Mathieu wanted the freedom to conduct his research and I wanted to give him the room to fail without compromising our investors. But I'll have to ask my comptroller at MacCombe to find out the specifics for that transaction."

Stuart wasn't even close to breaking a sweat. In fact, George wasn't completely sure the man had a heartbeat. But that might've been due to the high starch content of his collar. George continued to look for signs of it anyway and caught Stuart eyeing the coffee stain on the right cuff of his own shirt. George turned his hand, covering the blemish and resenting himself for the tell.

"So you admit to owning both entities?" George asked.

"Yes. I don't believe there is anything clandestine happening here. I'll be more than happy to provide you with the documentation you need. But I fail to see how this relates to Mathieu's disappearance? Unless you're suggesting I paid him to disappear?"

"No. I don't suggest. I just conduct investigations. But if you're amenable to helping me fill in the blanks?"

"Absolutely amenable, Detective. I'd do anything to help you."

There was something about the way Stuart had said the

words, not as a threat, more like a vow. George pulled the last two papers from his case file. "Then if you could have your comptroller explain why Dr. Mathieu Tousain received over a half million pounds over the last five months, I'd be grateful."

Vic choked on her tea.

Stuart reached for his pocket square and George lurched forward, a rush of partner protection pulsing through his veins.

Stuart carefully pulled the square as if raising a white flag and handed it to Vic. Vic accepted the peace treaty and kicked George under the table. George unclenched his jaw. The momentary tension had been diffused. Stuart pulled the financial statements across the table.

"Well, that's a fair amount of go-away money," Stuart said the words with amusement.

"Are you admitting to paying him off, Mr. Stuart?" Vic followed.

"Not at all. That wouldn't make a lot of financial sense. I've invested millions in Mathieu over the last fifteen years."

The room quieted. The man had admitted to investing in Tousain for fifteen years. Fifteen years. George examined Stuart's face for any fifteen-year-old wrinkles. Even George had crow's feet creeping into his own gaze. George had spent hours looking through the pictures Vic had found in the archives. His mother used to tell him about the pretty beasties—handsome men who would be young forever. But she was a heroine addict who enjoyed partying until the wee hours of the morning. She had held onto her youth permanently by dying young.

"Fifteen years is a long time to believe in someone," George said. "That takes a lot of faith. I'm not even the same person I was fifteen years ago."

"You joined the Royal Army, yes?"

Why wouldn't Stuart have done his homework? If the man had lived a century, surely he had learned information was the greatest weapon. Nothing in his body language advertised alarm. He was too brilliant. A higher functioning being? Weight lightened from George's shoulders. He hadn't met an adversary like this, ever. "Yes. Six years."

"Afghanistan must've been difficult," Stuart said.

"Did Padma tell you that?" George waved it off. Because it wasn't relevant. "It was a life-changing experience." The scent of opium drying in the afternoon wafted into the room. George almost reached for Vic's cold tea.

"Is that what convinced you to choose police work? I must say it's an excellent fit. But I wonder if you miss the excitement of military engagement?"

"Military engagement? I guess you mean war? There is nothing exciting about killing strangers." George rubbed his index finger.

"So you have shot someone?"

There was a knock at the door. The youngest desk sergeant entered the room. George wiped his palms on his thighs. He heard Vic let out her breath.

"Constable Hsu has entered the room," Vic said into the recorder.

"Mr. Stuart's counsel has arrived," Hsu said.

Stuart waved off the constable. "Tell them I'll be out shortly."

They all watched Hsu leave. George felt Vic's foot against his own, pressing him to make the next move. What was the next move?

"I will have my comptroller get the details for all of those transactions. Do you have any other questions for me?"

Stuart held his hand in front of his mouth and rubbed his fingers.

"One more." George stood. "Who are you?"

"Pardon?"

"I can't seem to find any record of you Mr. Stuart. So I'm wondering if the name is just another shell to hide who you really are? I mean, you can't be more than thirty-five, forty years old? So you took up funding medical research in your twenties?"

Stuart laughed. It was a warm, boastful laugh full of confidence and strength. There wasn't even a whiff of a bluff in it. George held his ground.

"Detective Inspector Cooper, you are a credit to your profession." He stood and buttoned his blazer. "I'm not a British subject. But if I were, you would make me a proud citizen. I was born in Zurich. I can have those papers provided to you as well."

"Zurich?" This man had the most well-crafted passing game George had ever seen.

"Wie gaats dur?" Vic asked. George wanted to kiss her.

"Guet, merci. Und Ine?" Stuart replied.

"Mir gaats nod so guet."

"Hats da es Spitaal noochi."

"Your Swiss German is decent," Vic said.

"Yours is passable." Stuart winked at Vic. George wondered why Vic's cheeks were flushing pink. Nothing ever shook her.

"Tell you what. The clinic is hosting a gala next Friday, one of those tedious black tie champagne events. Why don't you both come? As my special guests. It might be the best way to explain what all that money goes to. Nate will be there, so it's not like you won't know anyone there."

Vic shot George a don't-shove-him-off warning.

"What time?" George asked.

"Champagne starts at five, dinner at seven."

"Where?"

"Heritage House."

George swallowed the bile in his throat. "We'd be happy to."

"And please, feel free to bring a plus one."

George slipped his hands into his trousers and leaned back. Vic did the same as they watched Stuart leave the police station with his legal team in tow. Once they all poured down the steps and spilled into their black, expensive cars, Vic slapped George on the back.

"Half a million quid? When did you dig that up?"

"Last night."

"That was fuckin' brilliant."

George released all his tied up nerves in slow, deep exhale. "What the hell are we chasing?"

"Dunno, pet. But we better have a game plan."

"I get the funny feeling that's what he's expecting."

"It's like he has your number. Even has the same hand gestures."

"What do you mean?"

"He mirrored every one of your hand gestures. Even did that funny finger rubbing thing." She rubbed her thumb along her index finger. "You do it to calm your worry. *Your itchy trigger finger.*"

"I don't have an itchy trigger finger."

"I didn't say you did." She gave him a concerned look, like he was losing his grip. "Seriously, play back the video recording. He waited two beats, but he did it."

George rubbed the bridge of his nose. Constable Hsu knocked on the open interview room door. "There's someone here for you, Cooper."

"Who?"

"The doctor. The American one."

Vic's brows perked up, which George ignored.

"You can show her to my office."

Vic followed three cautious steps behind. Which silly, he wasn't going after the doctor. The doctor was innocent. Of a crime.

They almost collided when he got to his office door.

"Please let me explain," Abby said to him. Her face was silhouetted in red and her hair was down. The hair tie was around her left wrist. Her hair smelled of shampoo that held the scent of apple blossoms.

"Dr. Whiting, this is my partner, Detective Sergeant Moore. Vic, this is Dr. Whiting."

"Nice to meet you," Abby blurted. But she didn't move out of the way.

George slipped past her into his office, careful not to make contact. "There is nothing to explain." His voice was calm, even friendly. His stomach was roiling.

"Don't do this, please," she said. The words tripped from her lips. She was flustered. "It isn't...it isn't what you think, what you saw."

"I saw you kissing your employer."

Her body grew stiff as a board. "But it meant nothing. And he's not my employer."

He placed the Stuart case file on his desk. "That's a shame." He itched his ear lobe. "Because if you're going to be intimate with someone, in public, it should mean something. Whether he's your employer or not."

She let out a small groan and closed her eyes. They had grown glassy and she wanted to cover it up. "Of course it should." She shook her head. "Mean something. But it didn't mean what you think."

"Abby, it's fine." He sat. "You are free to do whatever you like in your personal life." He gave her his best neutral victim-of-a-crime smile.

She laughed. It was a pained one. She propped her mouth open by keeping her tongue pressed against her upper left molars. "Right. So are you charging him for anything? For Tousain going missing, I mean?"

"I'm sorry, I can't disclose any particulars at the moment."

She nodded. "Sure." She stared at her feet. "Just for the record." Her eyes were locked on the floor. "Our dinner date that wasn't a date." She pressed her lips together. "It was nice. Better than any real date I've had in a really long time." She nodded, turned quick as a whip, and walked out of his office, wiping the corners of her eyes. Vic leaned out of her way.

George grabbed the Stuart case file, ignoring the glare emanating from his partner.

He logged onto his computer. Vic hadn't moved. He glanced at her, lifting his shoulders to his ears. "What?"

"That. Was. Shitty."

"I didn't say anything mean to her."

"You didn't have to. She was a sweaty mess and fidgeting all over the place. And instead of making her comfortable, you rubbed her face in it." Vic planted her hand on her hip. "What the fuck? She hoofed it all the way from her office to apologize to you. She didn't even attempt to cover it up."

"Didn't attempt to cover what up?" George didn't think his voice could hit that register.

"She didn't say she wasn't kissing Stuart. She said that it wasn't what you thought. And I have to agree, it probably wasn't."

"What's your point?"

"She isn't Padma."

He slammed his fist on his desk. "This has nothing to do with her."

"Oh mate, that's where you've lost the plot. This has everything to do with Padma fucking James Stuart the night of your accident. She was discharged two days later and couldn't even be bothered to visit you until after she got a fucking manicure. And don't act like you didn't notice."

George folded his arms over his chest. His vision was cutting out and the heat wafting off his skin was untenable. He closed his eyes. Every time he attempted to remember all the details of that night, he hit a wall. There were only the facts that had been fed to him and nothing more. "I don't want to have this conversation right now." When he looked at Vic, she was two shades paler.

"Fine. I'm going for a smoke."

"Good."

She turned back around. "Actually, I'm going to call it night, if you don't mind."

"Fine."

"And I don't think I'm up for some swank-ass party either. Neither are you."

"I'll take that under consideration."

22

COCKTAILS

George scanned the large ballroom with an eerie sense of déjà vu. Strange, he had visited Heritage House on more than one occasion over the last seven years. Always tracking down the person of interest, while successfully avoiding any conversation with its proprietor. But the familiar sense of the room wasn't from one of those visits.

No, it was something entirely different.

The last time he had been at a large event for the Hastings Clinic, he had come as Padma's plus one. She was the eager new hire, and he was eager to end that evening in her bed. That afternoon tea party had been successful on all counts.

George pulled at his tie, loosening it just enough to air out the disappointment of arriving sans plus one. The only woman he'd be remotely interested in accompanying was no longer speaking to him. And Vic hadn't answered any of his texts. After spending two days going through the twenty-five neatly delivered boxes from Stuart, with every line item and transaction accounted for, he resented being back at square one. There was no sign of either Padma or Mr. Stuart. Well, there was a plus.

He saw a hand shoot up at the back of the large room. It was Nate. There was one last tree to possibly shake loose of information.

Everyone he had interviewed associated with the clinic had nothing but accolades for the place and its staff. He couldn't even find a recent case of misconduct, much less disenfranchised employee resentment.

He'd even received a poorly rehearsed "don't go sniffing around the grand madam of Cambridge without probable cause" lecture from his Chief. The Chief's nephew happened to have received a cutting-edge treatment for Hodgkin's lymphoma. James Stuart had his casual, benevolent hand in every coffer.

If there were one thing George could count on, it was that Nate never had anything good to say about anyone. Full stop. Nate cut through the crowd.

"Are you here to arrest someone?" There was a hint of "already sauced" and "vehemently looking for action" in Nate's tone.

"I was invited by the Chairman." George raised his voice a little too loudly and the conversation around him lowered to a whisper.

"Really?" Nate waved off the prestige of the personal invite as if it were a fly. "There's a bar at the back." Nate politely pulled George through the crowd of beaded gowns and black suits.

"You liking your new boss?" George asked.

Nate arched his perfectly plucked brow. "New boss? Oh, you mean James? He's not my boss. My boss skipped town, remember? Where are you on that?"

"Nowhere I had expected."

Nate stopped short of the bar and his shoulders drooped. "Fuck me."

Vic lifted her pint glass at them and blew a wet kiss to Nate.

Nate turned on George. "Did you bring her as your plus one?"

George locked up his laugh. It was enough to see his partner enjoying herself at Nate's expense. "She got the personal invite as well."

The circumstance of both his and Vic's presence sunk in. "Oh." Nate's brows were mid-forehead. "Do tell." He shimmied next to Vic and ordered two whiskeys.

He handed George one and took a refined sip of his own. "Did he kill that prick?"

George felt his confidence give a little. Nate was never bothered by the most extraordinary of circumstances. Everything was part and parcel of life – wives cheating, husbands beating, murder, child suicide bombers. It was all normal fodder for Nate's consumption. It's why he had excelled in the most horrific of situations. Unlike the rest of the population, those moments never served as a warning to Nate's mortality.

"Should he have killed your boss?" George asked.

"Yes." They clinked glasses. "I heard he once spent a year trying to see how many interns he could get to cry in front of their own spouses. Like he recorded it in a journal somewhere."

Vic leaned into the conversation. "He doesn't have any interns."

"Exactly." Nate finished his drink and ordered another.

"Hardly grounds for murder." George sipped his whiskey. It went down smooth without a wisp of complaint. Top shelf for sure.

"I would've killed him for his expense account." Nate took a generous gulp of his newly arrived drink. "What a bore."

"Tousain? Or murder?" George asked.

Nate closed his eyes. "All of it." His hardly innocent green eyes popped open. "So I was thinking, perhaps a gay lifestyle would be more interesting?"

George groaned. Nate loved to pick a fight with Vic.

"Think of the Sunday scandal."

"Do you ever consider anything else?" Vic asked. "And it's really not a choice, you posh tosser."

"Oh come on, really? That's so 2008. Don't ruin the only thing that is accidentally attractive about you, Sergeant. Everything we do is choice. That's how our synapses are wired. Picking up a glass. Driving to work. Having a three-some with the headmaster's twin girls." Nate left a splash of whiskey in his glass. "Even deciding to wear a secondhand knockoff Armani pantsuit to this party. That was a choice. A terrible choice, but a choice nonetheless."

"It's not secondhand." The tips of Vic's ears turned bright red.

"But it is a knockoff."

If George didn't veer the conversation soon, they would be fist to cuffs in two minutes.

"I have some interesting pictures I'd like you to look at." George elbowed Nate.

Nate placed his empty glass in Vic's hands. "Please be a dead body." Nate feigned applause.

Nate glanced at the photos and then looked up at George and gave a pout. "I wanted dead bodies. Not pictures of James Stuart."

"So you agree that it's Stuart?" George asked. God, he needed a cigarette desperately.

Nate took the small photos from George. "Well, that one isn't very clear. But it looks like him." Nate licked his lips.

George unfolded the bottom edge of each picture, showing Nate the date each photo was taken.

"Hmph, white people. Am I right?" Nate replied.

"How do you mean?"

"Well, if those dates are correct, then those are three people who look a lot a like. And when you consider that they're all white males, well..." Nate shrugged.

Vic flashed him a cursory warning glance. George placed the photos back in his pocket and finished his drink.

"You're not seriously entertaining the idea that they're the same person?" Nate never hid his laugh.

"Piss off."

"Oh, I love it when you get all working class. So back to my dilemma." Nate took Vic's half-full pint glass "If we were to say possibly get loaded tonight, and find a beautiful conservative female to take upstairs, do you think we could give my gay baptism a go?"

George spotted Abby making her way through the crowded room. Her eyes were wide and her smile wider with terror. She uncomfortably shook hands as her companion introduced her to everyone in her wake. George stood on tiptoe to get a better sight of her handler. It was Helen.

"Christ, no," George whispered.

"I didn't think you'd be so offended," Nate said.

"What?" But George's attention quickly swung back to Abby.

"What spectacle are you watching?" Nate looked past George's shoulder. "Oh. So you were listening."

"What are you talking about?"

"You, me, beautiful conservative, upstairs." Nate pointed

to the ceiling. "Although I think it would take a serious narcotic to get the American upstairs. But I'm counting on the depth and length of our friendship to make this work."

"No." George wanted to choke Nate. "Piss off."

Nate turned to Vic, placed his hand on his chest, mocking offense. "I've trespassed?"

Vic blew air from her cheeks. "It's complicated."

"George never likes simple." Nate waved down the bartender. "Do you have any black coffee?"

"Bloody hell," Vic said under her breath.

"When did this start? I didn't even know they knew each other. I guess Americans are really easy. Where did I go wrong?"

"Nothing... has started." George needed to cut Nate off at the pass. "She was a person of interest in relation to the case."

"Please tell me she killed him. It would make her *infinitely* more interesting."

"Yes. She flew in the day before her first day of work, strangled him, and dumped his body in the river."

Nate thanked the bartender for the coffee. "That was the best story I've heard all year. I'm stiff just thinking about it."

Vic stepped between the two friends. "He's bored," she said to George. "Don't entertain him."

Nate tapped Vic on the shoulder. "I'd like to file a complaint. The detective is giving me multiple stab wounds with that glare, Sergeant." He batted his long supple eyelashes at her. "If he pops that cork, I'll give him the Aston Martin. Hand to God." Nate raised his hand and smiled at his oldest friend.

"Bugger off," George hissed.

"Don't be so tetchy." Nate smiled.

"What the fuck does that mean?" Vic asked.

"Crabby," Nate said.

"Who uses that word?"

"Really old people," Nate and George said in unison.

"I see the mischievous three musketeers are back in the saddle again?"

The voice had the lyrical quality of only one person they all knew. Nate's smile blossomed, Vic's knuckles cracked, and George's organs tensed.

"Padma." Nate stood. "You look lovely." He kissed her on both cheeks, and quickly returned to his coffee. Strange, Nate always enjoyed the distraction of Padma's company.

"Coffee? This early in the evening?" Padma asked. "That must mean Vic's wit is extra sharp tonight."

Vic's stare quickly drifted to the crowd. Padma turned, scanned the room, and smiled at Dr. Whiting. She was always so intuitive.

"I'm happy to see you here," Padma said to George. "I was wondering if we could talk privately?"

Vic cut in, "Actually, I was hoping we'd catch up on the case. I found something of interest in one of the boxes. Who wants to eat a fancy plate of cold food anyway?"

George wasn't sure if Vic was making it up to keep Padma away, but they weren't in grade school. He'd avoided Padma long enough. "Why don't we go over the case in the morning?"

Nate giggled.

Vic leaned over to Nate. "You do realize you're the third wheel, right?"

"You do realize you can have that taken care of?" Nate tapped his upper lip. "And at least I'm part of the ride."

"It was an enjoyable ride," Padma interjected. She smiled at George. "Wouldn't mind having another go at it."

"You mean you're all done with the other attractions?" Vic asked.

Padma looked down, embarrassed.

"Vic," George cautioned his partner.

Nate turned back to the bar and drained his coffee.

23

BLACK AND WHITE

I followed Helen the way a child followed a parent through an airport. One of her uniformed waiters walked by with a tray of crystal glasses filled with lemonade. I snatched a glass and drank, holding the glass to my mouth to limit the amount I had to talk to other guests.

When Padma had passed on the invitation for the clinic event, she had said it was a black and white affair. Of course I took her literally. I paired my black trousers with a white cashmere sweater and finally donned my grandmother's pearls. In the room Helen was parading me through, I was woefully underdressed. I traded an empty glass of lemonade for another, the waiter flashing me a look of disapproval. Embarrassment made me thirsty.

Upset, I scanned the room for the second-year intern. Padma was walking toward the back. She was wrapped in purple silk—a stand-out color in a sea of black sequins and stiff white collars. She was the belle of the ball and I was going to be mistaken for the waitstaff. I searched for my beacon, but James was nowhere to be found. Weird, since he was the host and a hog for attention. It had been over a week since the interview at the police station and the innocent kiss we shared.

I continued to burn curses into the back of Padma's head. She suddenly turned, scanned the room, and flashed me a smile. Dammit. I waved hello and received three waves back. I squinted and noticed Nate, Detective Inspector Cooper, and his partner Detective Sergeant Moore standing at the bar. I finished the second lemonade.

The tension in my neck and shoulders melted. Who knew lemonade could be so relaxing? When life serves you lemons... I suddenly had a different view of the party. The clinic was celebrating the launch of a new cell repair therapy. It wasn't even my department, and I got an invite. This event was not designed to make me feel small, unwanted and disliked. And three people had just waved hello. There was a slim possibility I had friends or was liked in some way.

"I didn't know you knew George?" Helen smiled and led me toward the back of the room.

"Kind of." And after the misunderstanding, I was sure I would know him less now.

There was a little more energy in Helen's walk. Either she was determined to drop me off with my friends or she was anxious to speak with the Cambridge Police. My money was on the former.

I wasn't sure what I was going to say to either police officer, especially after all I had said in his office. He had drawn a clear line in the sand. We were professional acquaintances, nothing more. It had not been a date. And the kiss he had witnessed was nothing. Nothing important. The last time I had been kissed was by my lab partner. After we had isolated the glycoprotein of the Ebola virus, and we were both in hazmat suits.

Padma and DI Cooper made an attractive couple,

although a stiff one. Padma kept touching his arm, and he seemed to ignore the gestures by looking over her head at the wall behind her. She leaned closer and he shook his head. I almost felt sorry for her. My sweater was sweltering hot.

We were a few feet from the group, and Nate jumped from his chair first.

Fantastic. He was always prowling for entertainment.

"I thought you were a teetotaler?" Nate asked.

"A what?"

"Someone who doesn't drink alcohol." He pointed to the empty glass in my hand.

"This is lemonade."

"This is England. We don't do lemonade." He smiled.

"Oh." Oh, that explained why I felt so relaxed. Perhaps, drinking wasn't a bad idea. "What is this?"

Nate took my empty glass. "I think it's a vodka concoction. Would you like another?" His eyes lit up like the Northern Lights.

"Sure." My speech sounded a little different, maybe slurred. I had skipped dinner, hoping to find food at the party. "On second thought—" Nate was already talking to the bartender.

DI Cooper's partner stepped forward. "How are you, Dr. Whiting?"

"A little out of my element. Obviously." I pointed to my sweater. "And you, Detective Sergeant?"

"Please, call me Vic. The feeling is mutual. Not my idea of a cracking time."

I wasn't sure where I stood with the sergeant. After the public display of affection with James, I was pretty sure I was on her shit list, but this evening she seemed congenial. Or maybe it was pity for what I had said in the detective's office. She was also blocking my view of George and Padma. I found her protectiveness endearing. I would've given an arm for that kind of friendship.

"Good evening, Detective Inspector Cooper. Padma, you look beautiful." I stood on tiptoe and yelled over Vic's shoulder. It hadn't been a date anyway. I could be a good sport.

Nate placed another cool glass in my hand. I didn't taste an ounce of the alcohol, but it gave me all the false confidence I needed.

"How are you, George?" Helen asked. "Your recovery has been remarkable, wouldn't you say, Padma?"

The question seemed to pierce the balloon framing the lovely couple. Padma looked at her hands and George's jaw stiffened. It made me wonder if the accident had something to do with their relationship going south? Interesting. My admiration for Helen doubled.

"It's gone better than expected," George said. He didn't look at Helen. Strange. Helen was hard to ignore. There was her charm and her kindness and her style. Clearly, the detective didn't feel the same. I checked the room again for James. He was probably going to make some grand entrance. Style before substance, always.

"I hear there are several rooms upstairs." Nate gently nudged my elbow. "Do you want to get out of this penguin party and go explore?"

I didn't understand Nate's sudden interest. "There are sixteen bedrooms upstairs." Liquor loosened my lips.

"Sixteen? Have you been given a tour?" Nate asked me but his gaze was fixed on Helen.

I nodded and nearly tackled a server with a tray of hors d'oeuvres. "I haven't seen inside any of the rooms." I shoved two canapés in my mouth. "It's awfully warm in here."

"It's probably less crowded upstairs." Nate's eyes were locked and loaded.

"But heat rises."

"There are probably sixteen showers."

Was he hitting on me? And why was George clenching his fists?

"A shower would be so nice." I blinked heavily, I needed more food. "Listen," I slurred, "you're a doctor. I'm a doctor. We already have a pretty decent sense of each other's anatomies. And I just don't think there is enough meat on your bones to make it worth all the awkwardness at the office."

"I really like you, pet," Vic said.

"How about if we all go upstairs, and I watch the two of you..." Nate pointed at me then the sergeant. "Like each other some more."

"You really need to find a hobby. Or some self-worth. But the pout is priceless." Did I just wink at my co-worker? I placed my half-full glass on the bar, grabbed some almonds, and checked my watch. "Wasn't the announcement supposed to happen already?" I asked Nate.

"He is running behind," Helen said. "I was under the impression he was with you?" The question was a cold slap. Well, it had a sobering effect. I kept my gaze sharply turned from DI Cooper.

"I haven't seen him all week." I hated how defensive I sounded.

"But the two of you are inseparable," Padma said. The soft notes of her voice had all but evaporated. There was no way in hot hell perfectly put together Padma felt threatened by me.

Helen stood straighter like some silent alarm had gone off and she excused herself from our company.

Nate gave me a strange look of concern, one that attempted to telegraph some piece of critical information.

Padma whispered in George's ear, and they too excused themselves, leaving Nate, Vic and myself hopelessly staring into the crowd for a life preserver.

"Sixteen bedrooms? What do you think goes on in all those bedrooms?" Nate asked.

"Probably nothing interesting. Just sex, lies, betrayals and double crosses." Vic leaned on the bar and watched George and Padma disappear to the outer terrace.

"Maybe," I countered. "Or perhaps a little harmless fantasy. Or hopeful comfort." Their stares cooled my intoxicated tongue. "Probably nothing at all."

"Whatever happens, I'm sure it's unforgettable," Nate said.

"Or unforgivable," I said.

"Fuck, I need a smoke," Vic said.

I turned on the sergeant. "You do know those things will kill you?"

"Not fast enough." Nate smiled.

"Have you seen James...I mean Mr. Stuart this week?" I asked.

He shook his head. He shot me that look of concern again.

"Huh," I said. "When is dinner?"

I needed to sober up and find my patient.

"Let's go look for a snack. Helen tells me there is a massive kitchen downstairs."

I hadn't realized Nate was on familiar terms with Helen. There was a strange possessiveness tightening around my chest. Like I hadn't thought Nate decent enough to be on speaking terms with her.

Nate navigated the room with ease, slipping through a

hall that led in a direction I had never explored. Crap, he wasn't really going to try and trick me into a bedroom?

He pulled me into a dark corridor. My heart pounded in my throat.

"James hasn't come in for a transfusion this week."

Relief flew through my body and I uncurled my fists. "I wondered about that."

"He hasn't come in for over three weeks."

"What? Why didn't you say something?"

"I figured you were taking care of things."

"What?" I rubbed my eyes.

"He's become quite enamored of your company, so I just figured..."

"Well, you figured wrong. There is nothing going on. He's my patient."

"A patient with gilded bedrooms upstairs, all waiting for some action."

I shook off his taunt. "When was the last time?"

Nate slipped out his phone, entered his security codes, and scanned through screens I had never seen before. "Twenty days ago. No wait, twenty-two."

"Shit."

"What is it?"

"He's going missing."

"You mean gone missing."

"No, going to go missing. He's planning his disappearing act. Fuck. That's what this party is all about. It's all smoke and mirrors."

"Where are you going?" he asked.

"I need to find the Detective."

"George? You can't bring the police in on this. They're already suspicious."

I held my head in my hands. "Why did you let me drink?"

"How is any of this my fault?"

"How do you know George anyway?"

"Oh it's ancient. So is it George or the Detective?"

"What's the difference?"

"Never mind."

"Is there any chance you'd give me a ride back to the clinic?"

"And be seen leaving this soiree with you? Absolutely."

I rolled my eyes.

The crisp fall air was a welcome balm against my warm skin. I followed Nate to his car with a lingering trail of apprehension. Nate was all talk and no bite, but I couldn't shake off the discomfort. Like at any second, we would run into DI Cooper and Padma. But they would be happy and beautiful and reconciled, so I didn't need to feel guilty about a lift back to the office, for fuck's sake.

Nate held his keys out and the lights to his car flashed in reply. He opened the passenger door to a silver DB11 Aston Martin.

"Does everyone drive a Bond car in this town?" I asked.

Nate huffed a laugh. "Perk of the job."

"You're a hematologist, not a spy."

"I have no wife, no children, and I'm the *Director* of the Blood Bank, thank you very much." He motioned for me to climb into his car. "Actually, I'm probably well above the limit. Why don't you drive?"

"I can't drive."

"You've never driven a car?" The pitch of his voice jumped two octaves.

"Of course I have, just not here, yet."

He slid into the passenger seat and beamed a smile as wide as the Thames from inside his car.

Dammit.

Once inside the car, I scanned the dashboard for the key. Nate placed his thumb on a backlit circle and the car purred to life.

"Seriously?" I whispered. "I really don't want to scratch your one hundred thousand dollar car."

"Come on, nothing is really beautiful until it has a couple scars on it anyway. And if this had cost a one hundred thousand, I'd have three of them."

I kept my eyes on the road and my hands at ten and two. After I had spent the first fifteen minutes grinding gears, Nate's car finally understood who was boss. Nate had dozed off, his head bobbing with every bump in the road. Luckily, his fancy car had a kickass navigation system. There was no way I was going to hit anything or get lost.

The soft evening fog rolled off the river, giving me an odd sense of comfort. There was so much to appreciate about the Cambridge countryside. The quiet. The green expanse. The taste of fresh air. Refraining from running outside seemed like the lamest form of cowardice.

But after a century, I'm sure its charms had grown thin. Where was James going to hide? And why now? He had seemed delighted when George had escorted him to the police station. I sure wasn't going to let him go without a fight. The thin layer of fog reached across the road, caressing the windows, creating odd shadows. Shadows that, if I allowed my mind to imagine, appeared like specters waving for help.

I played with the levers around the steering wheel, hoping to find the windshield wipers.

There was loud crash. The airbag deployed, knocking my hands off the steering wheel. Nate slammed into me as the car spun in circles.

This was way worse than a scar.

24

OLD TRAPPINGS

George followed Padma, careful to remain a few paces behind, as they made their way outside. Padma enjoyed being watched. She'd spent hard calculated hours sculpting her curves. Spent hundreds of pounds to dress it. And he remembered losing entire weekends caressing her body.

But something was different now, aside from his lingering mistrust. Something was slightly off.

The way she walked. Instead of confident and brash, it was confident and seductive. There was a heavier swagger. This was the Padma he couldn't reconcile with after the accident. After he had noticed her freshly manicured nails when she had finally come to visit him in the hospital. Before the accident, she had occasionally been aloof, never uncaring and cold, self-reliant never selfish.

She continued past the terrace and walked along a graveled path, heading to a large garden.

"How private does this conversation have to be?" he asked.

She pointed at the sky. "It's a full moon. I think there is a place to sit in the garden. Or we could walk to the river."

As soon as she said the word, a hint of laurel hit his tongue. "It's a bit chilly. And it's never a good idea to leave Nate alone with Vic."

"George, it's not like I'm going to take advantage of you out here in the open. Christ, can't we talk?" Her eyes welled up.

"Of course. I'm sorry. Lead on." He rubbed the tiny hairs at the base of his neck. Why were his hands clammy? Where was this new malice coming from?

She tossed her tiny clutch onto a cement bench and sat. How could he be so daft? The last time they had shared that bench, it had been a warm afternoon in August. And she'd given him the most discreet blowjob. That was a year ago. He remained standing.

"I'm sorry," she said. "For everything. I was stupid and careless." She patted the bench. "I miss you."

"Has Stuart passed you up for the American?" He hated himself for crossing his arms, but he was cold. Down to the bone cold.

"I don't care about him. Not the way I care about you. I made a mistake. I panicked."

"You didn't look very panicked about having his head between your legs."

That was the toughest recollection from the accident. The one he couldn't reconcile. The old Padma would've paled with disgust and left. But this new Padma wasn't going to budge. She wanted to fight. Or she was determined to make him feel bad for her error in judgment?

Tears streamed down her cheeks. She twisted her hands around her clutch. "Do you ever have something, and it's so beautiful and precious, you can't help but wonder how fragile it is?"

There was a new note in her voice. It was distinct and struck a chord of warning. Padma appeared ageless like the statues accentuating the perfectly designed garden. He blinked away the black spots dancing along the edge of his vision.

"All the wedding plans in the midst of my first year at the clinic. It was more than I planned for. Hoped for. Everything was going right. Everything. It was like a train that couldn't be stopped."

When had he taken a seat next to her? Her siren call wasn't subtle. Why couldn't he fight it?

"I hadn't felt that kind of happiness. There was always another obstacle to tackle or plan for, but now the path was clear. I was invincible and scared as hell."

There was a haunting scent to her words as they left her violet lips. She was compelling, but instead of sympathy, he suddenly felt mortal and terrified. Like being trapped in a black widow's web.

Her tears warmed his chilled fingers. He hadn't felt this cold since the accident, when he was sure his life was slipping away. Dread pulsed through his veins.

"I wanted to see if we would break." She sniffed and her eyes dilated.

She leaned in and placed her full lips on his parched ones. His skin iced over, but his heart raced, betraying every cell that was screaming a warning. There was a bitter taste to the kiss. It was earnest and empty, passionate and feeble. It filled him with an odd combination of sickness and health.

She jerked away, but it was too late. Darkness seeped in. "You're not what I was expecting," she said. But he couldn't see or feel her. "You're a different kind of play thing."

25

REALLY BAD

The dull pain radiating from the left side of my face was the least of my worries. My restraints had been cut and I had two escorts, one on each arm, and a hood pulled over my face, making it impossible for me to see. They had asked me to remove my clothing and had handed me a white robe. They'd stuffed my mouth with a rag, that's when I knew this wasn't one of Nate's pranks. I had learned the hard way that screaming wasn't a good idea. It triggered my gag reflex and I had come close to choking to death twice.

The chill from the cracked tile floor bit my bare feet with each stilted step. They forced me to take a right turn, another right, and then a left. We went down a smaller set of stairs, twelve steps, where the hall had grown narrower. The ground had become uneven and coarse, rich with dirt and deterioration. Wherever we were, it was dark.

Cemetery dark.

The tour abruptly stopped, and my hood was tugged off. I blinked quickly, forcing my eyes to accept what little light they could catch. A large wooden door as old as a monastery and as solid as a chastity belt loomed ahead. Two guards flanked the door. Both males of equal height and build, roughly five-foot-ten and one-hundred-seventy pounds. They wore nondescript black uniforms and they looked remarkably alike, not identical but brothers. Where had these people come from?

Although the odds of me successfully running were slim to none, I turned to assess which direction to go. The only source of light burned from oil lamps mounted on the slate walls of the hall. The glow from the lamps illuminated a two-foot arc and the oil lamps were spaced fifteen feet apart. Eventually, the small cones of light disappeared into an obsidian abyss.

I was in an underground tomb, deep in the world of the dead, with an irrevocable invitation.

This was the risk I had not assessed when I agreed to help James. This was the risk of pretending not to be involved in something dangerous. This was the risk of helping a monster. I had failed to calculate what was really at risk.

One of my escorts stepped ahead and pushed against the dense wooden door. It opened to reveal a softly lit chamber.

Wasps of apprehension buzzed beneath my skin. This wasn't like what had happened when James was upset. This was the alarm of clearly realizing I wasn't going to make it out of this room. The same.

Shoved from behind, I stumbled over the threshold, landing on my hands and knees.

My two escorts aligned themselves against the interior doorframe and stared straight ahead. I awaited instructions, but their dark eyes were vacant and empty of life. My unsteady breath clouded from my mouth. I wasn't sure what to say, what to ask, or what to scream. The full moon shone through a circular opening in the ceiling. It gave the impression of a large eye, watching my every move, even the invisible ones.

The room stretched out twenty feet in all directions and the edges of the room faded into darkness. The room had to be round like a rotunda. At the center of the chamber, a large marble table reflected the moon's light. It looked large enough to be an altar, definitely large enough to hold a body. I heard something scuttle along the wall behind me like a rat caught in a bucket trying to claw its way out.

"James?" I whispered into the darkness.

I listened with intent, but only heard my staggered breath. My skin didn't feel the lick of electricity or the hum of discomfort. Maybe I was alone. Maybe it was just a rat. Or maybe James wasn't in the chamber at all, but someone else. Someone worse. I wasn't prepared to meet his maker or mine.

I approached the table in the middle of the room, sensed a shift in the air, and turned. Something brushed my left arm. I spun around in panic, reaching out into the darkness in the hopes of grabbing something or someone.

"What the hell am I doing?" I whispered.

I bolted for the door only to run into Padma. She was no longer in her silk purple gown, but a white gown, much like my own. I staggered back but my panic helped me find my footing.

"Do you think you're going to just run out of here?" she asked. Her backhand came out of nowhere and I fell to the ground.

It took me a few seconds to shake off the shock from the slap and that Padma had delivered it. I stared up at her with rage. She looked different—stronger, less runway model, more menacing. A shadow swam under her skin, lifted from her face, blurring her features. This wasn't the second-year intern. Oh no. This was hell personified.

"Nice to meet you too, Charlotte." I wiped my bleeding lip on my sleeve.

"Astute for an American." Her eyes scanned me from head to toe, calculating something I didn't want to guess.

I blotted my swelling split lip with the robe. Charlotte extended her hand to help me up. I refused and stood on my own.

"Where is James?" I asked.

"You're not bleeding enough." And she slapped me again.

Behind the bright spots flashing on my eyelids, I saw red. I lunged at her. She wrenched my hand back and slammed my face against the marble table. Blood and saliva dribbled onto the slab. I watched it slide down its surface, disappearing into a hole.

The marble table had a slight concave surface with random quarter-sized holes drilled into it. I traced the rim of a hole and pushed a finger through. The holes were strategically placed to collect blood from all major arteries like an autopsy table.

"Oh God." I barely got the words out.

Charlotte whipped me around, pinching my face in her hand. Flecks of excitement and anticipation lit up her eyes. She drew a knife and held it to my neck.

"Enough." A voice pleaded from the darkness. It was hoarse, desperate, and hauntingly familiar.

Charlotte smiled and pulled away the knife, keeping the tip extended at my face. If I ever saw her again, I would land the first punch.

A guard turned a large wooden dial on the wall next to

the door. The chamber rumbled with loud grinding noises. The ceiling rotated and I planted my feet, expecting the ground to open beneath me.

Dust rained down and more moonlight poured into the chamber through smaller openings in the domed ceiling. The grit of decay coated my throat and I rubbed my eyes clear of debris. Charlotte stood motionless and watched like a hungry predator.

"I was hoping we would get to this much sooner, *Abigail*." She blotted dust from my cheeks and I held still, afraid of her touch, afraid of her excited smile. "But I wasn't sure if you were important or just a decoy. We love our games."

The tips of her cold fingers pulled at my bottom lip and she ran them inside my mouth. I pulled away, trying to dredge up any clue to as to what was about to happen. But all I saw was Padma. And her hijacked body.

"What do you want from me?" I asked.

"I want to watch you die."

An electric current whipped up the length of my spine, causing me to stand painfully tall. James had confirmed his presence. Maybe I had a way out?

I shoved passed Charlotte, ran into the dark, reaching out like a blind woman hunting for a wall. With blackness encroaching and the current reaching a violent pulse, I gasped for air.

"Let me see you, James." I wasn't going to die without seeing he was okay.

"I'm sorry." His breath caressed the back of my neck.

I turned but he wasn't there. "Don't be sorry. You haven't done anything." I kept palming the blackness. "Just come out of the dark, where I can see you."

"This isn't going to end well," he whispered into my right ear.

I spun around and was welcomed with more darkness. "You won't hurt me." I said it with conviction, but the knot in my lungs didn't believe a word. A hand snatched my hair and pulled me back toward the light.

"He isn't going to hurt you. He's going to kill you," Charlotte said. "And I'm going to love watching you die. At least this way, he'll finally fuck you."

I spat in her face.

Her hand reared back for another strike, but someone grabbed it. She looked over her right shoulder into the dark. "Do this now." Charlotte released me. "Or I will. We're at the end of your line." She wiped the spit from her cheek. "No more ghosts to chase along the river, my love."

"I will. You always get what you want," James said. His voice caught between a promise and a prayer.

I froze in terror. I didn't even take a breath.

"I've always wanted to play an American," Charlotte said with a wicked smile. "The poison will take affect in ten minutes." She walked out the door. The last guard followed and shut the door to the chamber. The clang of metal sliding into metal sealed my horrible fate. I walked to the light for its warmth.

I wanted to run, bang on the door until my hands bled, but I couldn't move. James's trembling hand emerged from the darkness. His hand was multiple shades of purple, like he'd sustained bruises from a fight. Cuts lacerated most of his knuckles and his nails were torn, jagged or completely missing. Mesmerized, I watched him emerge from the dark. Once his face stepped into the moonlight, my chest constricted with pain.

Never in all my life, could I have imagined his beauty would be reduced to such degradation. If I were religious, what stood in front of me was unholy. Blasphemous.

His body was riddled by violence. Deep blood-caked divots slashed his chest and abdomen. His flawless porcelain skin was translucent like the fine, dry layers of an onion. Streams of old blood pulsated through his veins, thick and dark as molasses. His once icy blue eyes were jet black and sunken into his skull. I had never feared looking into those eyes, until now. Now, there wasn't an ounce of his civility left.

The tips of his fingers landed on my cheek. A tear caught and rolled over his fingertips.

There would be no escape.

There would be nothing after this exchange, only death.

He hadn't fed in a very long time. The control of his most basic instincts was at bare minimum. His eyelids pulsated in rhythm with my heartbeat.

I prayed he was no longer taking the time to listen to my thoughts. I prayed my fear was a resistible aphrodisiac. For the first time since being a frightened, disappointed child, I prayed.

"You don't have to do this," I pleaded.

He reached out to cup my face. Millimeters from my skin, he examined his mangled hand, and dropped it to my shoulder instead. The corners of his eyes twitched at the physical contact. His touch emitted no heat, no secret signal, no friendship. And I made the mistake of gasping.

"Whatever you do, please don't run." James ran his trembling thumb over my injured lip. His eyes pulsed with hunger. Time was expiring, and my options were dead on arrival.

I sprinted for the door. His nails slashed my shoulder, sending a hot burn of pain across my back. His arms wrapped around my chest, trapping my arms. He lifted me from the ground before I reached the door. His movements were primal and swift, mine were clumsy and all too human. My legs kicked in the air, trying to find traction for escape. He wrenched me back toward the slab. All I saw were the pattern of holes and their purpose—to drain my blood.

I planted my feet against the edge of the table but failed to shove him off. The more I struggled, the tighter he squeezed until air became harder to purchase. I stilled but didn't calm. He loosened his grip, and I gulped for air. His scent of sandalwood and spice had ripened into something sour and sinister. He nuzzled the back of my neck.

"Do you know how many days it's been?" he asked.

"Roughly twenty-two days."

He laughed at my precise answer. But it was no longer the sound of warmth, nor a token of his humanity. It was the sound of dark despair. His hands snaked around my wrists and he bent me over the slab. His tongue lapped across my shoulder, searing me with fear. Through the haze of shock, I heard laughter pour into the chamber—a woman's laughter.

James stilled.

The room darkened and dropped from a heated panic to an arctic paralysis. Something deep purple and lethal slithered in and out of the openings of the ceiling. I heard the clap of thunder, the snapping of bones, the chaos of hell.

"I have to place you onto the altar," he said. The statement less a warning, more like a bad omen. "Don't. Struggle." His eyes darted to the apertures in the ceiling. His haunted gaze acknowledged the audience I couldn't see through my fear. He scooped me into his arms.

I grabbed his face. "Please don't do this." He wouldn't look at me. The darkness held him now.

I heard his teeth grind. He wrestled my hands from his face and placed me across the cold table. He stepped away, the ropes of muscle in his neck tightening like bands of steel. His hands encircled my ankles, and he tugged my body a couple of inches down the slab. The walls amplified my scream.

James jumped atop the altar, straddling my hips. My hands struck, slapped, clawed but I still remained pinned. He caught my left wrist.

"This is going to hurt."

He punctured the meat of my palm below the thumb with his fangs. They rubbed painfully against bone, causing me to see white pain. He placed his hand over my mouth, attempting to quell my scream. I snagged his fingers and bit down.

His fangs drilled deeper, causing another blinding burst of pain. I bit down harder and his fingers relaxed. Thick blood coated my tongue and gums like hot syrup. He withdrew his fangs and held my throbbing punctured hand above my chest, watching my blood slither down the length of my forearm and splatter onto the white gown. I thrashed under him and a chorus of hisses poured out of the walls.

He leapt off of me, landing in front of the door. "Stay out! I will do this my way." He punched the door.

I heard a sharp snap and hoped like hell he'd broken his hand. There was no more time to think. I rolled off the slab. My vision constricted and the room morphed into soft edges. Edges that murmured, breathed, caressed.

Sure my hallucinations were the result of his blood, I spat onto the floor but saw no red evidence. I shoved my fingers into my mouth and scraped at the lingering bitterness. What poison had Charlotte rubbed in my mouth? The floor reached out, trying to pull me through. I scrambled to my hands and knees and crawled for the door.

James snatched me into his arms and smiled with the

venom of adoration. "Why do you never listen? You're only feeding my hunger." His bloodstained tongue slipped out of his mouth and he ran it along the side of my face. He shuffled me back to the table.

Through my shifting vision, I noticed the streaks. Streaks of arctic blue cracking the black surface of his irises, clawing their way back from oblivion. His skin was taking on color, his bruising lightened, and the divots along his chest were healing. Awed by his transformation, I didn't notice him leaning in until his lips rested on mine.

"Lay back down," he whispered.

My body reacted to his voice—the anger blew out of my chest, the fear flew out of my mind, and my limbs went lax. I had no control and my body complied. The warmth of the moonlight danced along my face and gown. I stared through the oculus. The hazy moonlight and the effect of James's blood made it look like a halo.

My childhood angel of darkness hovered above me, but there was no longer the weight of fright between us.

James inhaled the scent of my hair and I closed my eyes. His teeth caressed my jawbone, and I remembered the hot pain of his bite and the consequences of his blood. His arousal rubbed against my abdomen, then rocked down lower.

"Grab it," he demanded.

I groaned with desperation and my eyes pleaded no. But something had changed. His eyes held no trace of black. Not a hint of menace. They were icy beacons of blue in a sea of darkness. His eyes dilated and he reiterated the order.

A foreign urge coursed through my blood and my hand slipped between our bodies. I felt the tip of something inanimately hard and jagged poking through the waist of his trousers. My hand slid down the shaft, my fingertips fumbling. No skin, no pulse, grained texture. I was holding a stake of wood.

I held onto the end of the stake and he rocked against me, sliding it onto my belly. James captured my mouth and kissed me hard. I felt the smile of approval across his lips. He stroked his nose tenderly along my neck up to my earlobe.

"When things get really bad, you need to use it. But you need to wait until it gets really bad," he said.

He kissed my forehead, reared back, and extended his fangs completely.

26

ACCIDENT PRONE

George punched at the darkness.

Get up. Get up. Get up, you bloody idiot.

His limbs were made of cement. Paralyzed.

No. No. No!

The copper of blood coated his mouth. He smelled the decay of death. There was a voice off in the distance. Someone was hammering at the door of his mind. But his mind stumbled to remember nothing.

He heard a scream. A piercing, terrified scream. It curdled his blood.

"George!"

Why couldn't he move? He groaned and kicked and spat and cursed.

"Everyone back up and give him some air."

Vic, please help me. I can't move. Get me out of here.

There was another scream and his heart braced for pain. Something cold and bitter spilled into his mouth. Someone was making him drink poison.

He shot up and sucked in air.

George was sitting on the cold ground next to the bench

in the garden. A crowd of a dozen onlookers stared at him with alarm and uncomfortable concern. The moonlight bounced off their shiny dresses, confusing his eyes. Vic and Helen were crouched next to him. Helen was clutching a bottle in her hand. What had she given him?

His breath was frantic. His mind was racing. Every part of him pounded to get the hell out of that horrible lavish party. He had blacked out. For the third time this month.

"You okay, mate?" Vic asked.

"I smell gasoline. Do you smell gasoline?"

"What are you talking about? Do you even know where you are?"

"The fucking gala. Where is Abby?"

He attempted to stand, but a sense of vertigo overtook, and he leaned against the bench. This wasn't what he wanted. Not now.

"Hold up. Let's take a minute to assess you." Vic turned on the crowd. "Alright, everything's tip top here. You all go off and enjoy yourselves." She pulled something from her back pocket and flashed it to the crowd. They dispersed.

George searched the horizon for fire. He smelled burning gasoline and oil. The scent of fresh blood punched him in the gut. He used the bench to help him up.

"Whoa, where you off to, boss?"

He staggered away from Vic down the footpath.

"Abby. Something's wrong. She's in trouble."

"I think you need to take a seat."

His phone rang and he patted his pocket.

"Hold on. You're not going to get that?" Vic asked. There was no mistaking the alarm in her voice. "What happened out here? Your hand is bleeding. Where is Padma?"

George examined his hand. It didn't hurt. The call went to voicemail. He shook his head, less to answer her question and more to clear the cobwebs from his memory. Why were his lips numb? There was no way Vic was going to let the questions go unanswered.

"I dunno." He closed his eyes and shook his head again. "Padma wanted to talk. She wanted to patch things up. It got really cold. And I blacked out." *And I was so afraid.*

"And she just left you?"

"Uh...I guess so." He heard screaming. "Let's go. There's something wrong."

"No shit."

His phone rang again. He inhaled deeply through his nose and exhaled through his mouth. Padma's clutch was still on the bench. What had happened? His phone vibrated against his hip.

"I know this looks strange. But please, answer me. Where is Abby?" George asked.

"She left with Nate." Vic kept her expression matter-of-fact.

Déjà vu taunted him to the edge of a memory. He pulled his phone from his pocket. It was Nate. The call dropped into voicemail. There were six voicemails, all from Nate. All in the last twenty minutes.

"Shit." George huffed.

"What?"

George hit the call back button. Nate's phone rang four times and then dropped into voicemail. He cursed and redialed. George snapped his fingers at Vic, pointing at Padma's clutch. She snatched it from the bench. After two rings, Nate picked up.

"Where have you been?" Nate's voice was in a high panicked register.

"Not really sure."

"What?"

"Never mind. What's going on?"

"There's been an accident." Nate's tone was agitated. "God, not again. Abby. Abby's gone."

"What?"

"She was driving. We were hit. I was out of it, but I can't find her. I think someone took her."

"Where are you?"

George listened to Nate retching.

"Nate! Nate, where are you?"

"Ah, where am I? Right. Country road. East of the estate."

"Are you still in the car?"

"No. I climbed out." Nate's breathing was fast. "Don't bring the fucking cavalry, okay?"

"Who took her?"

"I think I'm going to pass out."

"Nate!" George death gripped his phone, attempting to squeeze a reply from his friend. "Was is it James? Did James Stuart take Abby?"

"...blaming the wrong person for all of this. He's only protecting—" George heard Nate retch again. "Christ. I need a drink."

"Stay put. I'll come get you." George turned to Vic. "We gotta go. Nate's been in an accident."

"Fuckin' hell. I told you we shouldn't have come," she moaned.

The scent of burning oil coated George's tongue once more. It had to be a sense memory of his car accident. Nothing more. He hustled down the path to the parking lot. The cool evening air was a balm to his confusion. He reached for his keys and heard a sharp whistle. Vic pointed to his car, off to their left.

"Are you sure you can drive?" she asked.

"Yeah, I'm good." Despite the blackout, he felt like a straight arrow, searching for a target. He popped open the boot of the car.

"Why not wait until we get there to see what needs fixing?" she said.

George tossed her an emergency aid kit and pulled a latch, lifting a hidden compartment. He unlocked his gun box and slipped his Brown 9MM into the small of his back.

"What kind of accident are we talking about?" she asked.

"I'll explain in the car. Are you armed?"

"Give me sec."

George fired up the engine and impatiently waited for his partner. The scent of blood filled his nostrils, grinding away his sense of normal.

27

SLIPPED AWAY

R ibbons of blood threaded the air. James pummeled another guard, his fists splattering blood against the wall, striping my face. I was crouched next to the first guard's limp body, frozen in shock. The back of the guard's head had been bashed in, a mash of brain and blood pooled around his head. His eyes stared at the moonlight, his pupils fully dilated.

"Abby!"

I closed the dead man's eyes. Afraid of what he had witnessed. Words fell from my mouth, but I no longer understood them. I was lost in a nightmare.

James sauntered toward me, wiping his blood drenched hands on his tattered trousers. "Abby, can you hear me?"

I stared up at him. There were deafening bangs against the door. I curled away from the noise, leaning over the dead body. My robe soaked up blood. It was barely white now. So much red. I tried to get the robe off but James grabbed my shoulders and pulled me to my feet.

"Stop with the Lord's prayer." He shook me. "You need to run."

"Where?"

"Away from me. Away from here. Before I lose control."

"You won't."

"Snap out of it. Come back to me." He shook me again, hard like a ragdoll. "Stop calling me your angel."

I didn't. Did I?

The door burst open. James shoved me backward into the dark. I tripped over something and fell. There, on the ground, was Mathieu Tousain. What was left of him. He was lying on his side and rigor mortis had set in. His skin was the color of storm clouds and he had multiple puncture wounds on his neck and wrists.

James tossed a guard across the room. The man hit the wall with a thud just a few feet to my right.

"Abby! Run!"

"Can you at least put on the bloody heater?" Vic pleaded.

George had opened the windows, following the scent of burning oil. Vic huffed, and started tooling with all the dashboard buttons.

"Listen, I found something buried in those files," she said.

"What? All those boxes only prove he's a master who can't be outdone."

"There are some files in there that weren't like the others. Medical files."

"So? They could've belonged to a project Tousain was working on."

"I don't think so. There are roughly thirty files for thirty children who died in an epidemic of some kind."

"I'm not following."

"The medical files are from America. I think one of them belongs to the American."

"You said they died."

"All but one. And I think it's Abby. The age is right. Her last name has changed. What if she came after those files? What if Tousain wouldn't give them to her? Or what if… what if Stuart lured her here for them?"

"Why would he slip those files in there? He's not careless."

"Right. But I think they're important."

Two miles out, he saw the smoke from Nate's car. He hit the gas.

Vic reached for the dashboard and braced. "What is it? Are you going to answer me?" She spotted the smoke. "How did you see that far out?"

He didn't answer, pulling his Volvo off the road next to Nate's crumpled car. The car had been hit from the left at a decent speed. Someone wanted them incapacitated but not killed.

George jumped out of his car, running toward Nate.

"Please tell me you still smoke," Nate said to Vic. The left side of his face was covered in blood.

Vic pulled out the emergency kit.

"Where is Abby?" George asked.

"Do you have water?"

Vic ran back to the car.

"Did you see where she went?"

"I don't know." Nate leaned against the hissing car. "I have a concussion."

George spun around and looked for any kind of clue. There was no other car or tracks, which meant the other car had stayed on the road. He leaned into the driver's window of Nate's car, finding blood on the steering wheel. He ran his hand across.

The blood was still warm and if he wasn't so wound up, he'd swear it held a heartbeat. He sniffed his hand, he wasn't exactly sure why. When his tongue tasted apple blossoms, he staggered away from the car.

Why could he smell her on his hands? And in the air?

"Where are you going?" Vic called after him.

"There." He pointed to a wooded glen.

"I'm doing just grand by the way." Nate waved his hand.

"You don't even have a torch. How can you see?"

George looked at Vic. Every emotion he was sequestering registered on her face—confusion, surprise, disbelief. What was he going to tell her? He had the very same questions. He pointed up. "Full moon."

"Okay." She said the word slow and steady. He must've looked mad.

He heard a scream. No, not a scream, an order. He heard someone yelling. Yelling at Abby to run. George bolted for the trees.

THE CRISP NIGHT slammed into me as I sprinted through the woods. The downward slope from the crypt helped my momentum. My head jerked from left to right, scanning a world I didn't recognize. A floor of leaves and branches snapped under my bloodied feet. I ran into the darkness, ran away from the orchestra of death inside that pit of hell.

And I didn't look back.

I would run until I saw light. I would run until there was water to wash my skin. I would run until there was no more darkness. Run. Run. Run. Away from bones snapping. Away from children crying. Away from death.

The full moon lit up the woods in a soft blue halo. My vision sharpened. Tree branches lashed my arms and face, but I felt nothing in my new skin. James's ancient blood had intoxicated me with strength and endurance. Adrenaline had nothing on this. My heart was a drum, the beat steady and hypnotic. Air left and entered my lungs in a primal rhythm.

The ground continued to slope downward, but the trees and saplings thinned. I heard the whirr of car engines in the distance. I entered a clearing and slowed my pace. Streaks of white light bounced around the walls of the woods. Footfalls scattered through the clearing, followed by shouts and static.

Two pairs of glowing yellow eyes emerged from the trees —one pair off to my right and another pair to my left. I stilled and tried to assess the new threat. They waved beams of light at my face, barking in some foreign language. I lifted my hands to shield my eyes. My hands and arms were covered in blood. Red blood, not black blood. Human blood. Whose blood?

The yellow eyes closed in.

GEORGE WALKED out of the brush with his hands raised. His torch lit Abby's shocking figure. Her hair was slick and matted. The strange robe she wore was drenched in blood and clung to her figure like a hungry snake. Eyes wide with terror, she looked like a feral animal.

He signaled to Vic to lower her torch. Abby crouched and swung a makeshift weapon toward them with a grunt. It looked like a wooden stake and it too was covered in blood. Nothing was adding up tonight.

"Abby, it's me, George."

She turned her head side to side. Either she was confused or unable to hear. He carefully closed the distance between them. Nothing she did indicated recognition. She was in shock.

"Dr. Whiting? It's me, DI Cooper. I'm not going to hurt you."

She grunted and drew the weapon higher. George watched Vic shuffle in closer, flanking Abby on the left. Feeling threatened, Abby swiped with the stake. George directed Vic to back away.

"Abby, you're safe. No one is going to hurt you. I'm your friend."

He lowered his torch, laying it on the ground. He turned his hands palms up, showing them empty of harm. She lowered her hands. She scanned his face and he was met only with confusion.

Vic snatched the stake out of Abby's hand.

"No," George yelled and rushed to her, but it was too late.

In a heartbeat, Abby had tackled him to the ground, straddled his chest, and punched him repeatedly. He attempted to catch a fist, but they slipped out of his grasp.

Her head jerked back and she arched her back. He heard the clicking noise of Vic's taser, saving George from another blow. Air flew back into his lungs after Abby jumped off and staggered toward Vic. Vic deployed another charge, and Abby collapsed, her hand twitching by his ankle.

"Fuckin' hell." Vic held a quavering Taser gun at Abby's immobile body. "It was the only way to get her under control. Sorry. What the hell is happening?"

George stood and spat blood to the ground. He cursed,

not at Vic but at their circumstance. Nothing was making any sense.

"How did you know she was here?" Vic asked. Her breath clouded in quick huffs.

"I don't know." Because admitting he could smell Abby's blood in the air was complete nonsense. He stripped off his jacket and laid it across Abby's shaking body. He quickly removed the small electrodes from her back and shoulder and leaned over. "Abby. It's me, DI Cooper. We're going to take you to hospital." He eyed Vic and Vic called 999.

Abby's skin was cold. Her chest rose and fell with great effort. The air she exhaled wheezed out and her mouth twitched. Her pupils were fully dilated. Whose blood was covering her?

"James," she managed to squeak out.

"Did he do this? Did he hurt you?" he asked. The level of rage surging through his body was at a breaking point.

"Back...there. Help him," she said faintly.

The tin of blood still flavored the air, but he saw nothing. There were no more screams weaving through the night. The world had quieted, but why did it feel like the storm hadn't even begun? The ground shook, and he reached for Abby. Her body convulsed violently. He only saw the whites of her eyes, and her pulse began to slip away.

28

NIGHT VISITATION

George sat next to the hospital bed, fingering the small bruise in the crook of his arm. He listened to Abby breathing, finally in a normal rhythm. It was token comfort. They had come terrifyingly close to losing her.

When Vic had shoved him out of the way to administer CPR, George had felt an overwhelming emptiness. A feeling he hadn't ever felt, not even after the car accident when he thought he would never see the light of day again. Not even in Afghanistan.

When she had flat-lined, minutes from the clinic, he became hollow. There was no flutter of panic, no fight, no seizing of heart or breath, just a complete gutting out.

The wheezing sound she had made as she sucked air past her blue lips continued to haunt his thoughts. When they had placed the oxygen mask over her mouth, she had chanted one name over and over.

James Stuart didn't deserve that level of affection. Or whatever it was they shared.

Despite all the tubes attached to her, she looked peaceful. He had dimmed the harsh lights an hour ago, to help her sleep, and he no longer wanted to stare at the pallor of her skin. Her face was diminutive, but not delicate, the only sharp angles were along her brows. A faint patch of freckles dotted her nose. How had they escaped his notice?

Her lips looked lovely in their full symmetry. A small drop of dried blood hid in the corner. Pink foam had flowed out of her mouth through her second seizure. He stood, moistened a tissue, and wiped the residue away.

Gross clouds of purple, blue and green mottled her arms. He was going to find the man responsible for this violence. He was going to inflict just as much harm. There was movement shifting under her lids. He gripped his kneecaps and watched as she pulled away from unconsciousness.

The heart monitor picked up its pace and the panicked look of questions in her eyes sharpened.

"You're safe. We found you. You're back at the clinic," he said. He placed his hand on hers. She was cold, but no longer dead cold. He swallowed his anger.

The harsh beeps from the heart monitor settled. She reached out to touch the oxygen tube but her arms only moved a couple of inches and then caught.

"You have restraints on. It's just a precaution. You were a little out of sorts when we found you."

She pulled again and the restraints clinked.

"I'm going to be sick." She lifted and turned her head quickly. Her body folded in on itself.

George stood and caught the fluid with cupped hands.

"I'm sorry," she said.

"No matter. It happens." He walked to the sink and washed his hands. "After the car accident, I was tossing my cookies all the time. Pain medication doesn't agree with me." He picked up a cup with a straw. "Here, have a sip of water."

"Did I do that?" she asked.

He brought his index finger up to the bandage on his nose.

"It isn't broken." But God, did it hurt to fake a smile. He scrutinized her face, examining her readiness for questions. Being a detective didn't come with an off switch.

"Where's James?" she asked.

The name hit like a punch. His brows wrinkled and he pursed his lips. "We haven't found him yet."

A nurse walked into the room with a tray, holding a needle.

"He's in danger. Charlotte is out there with him," she said. "She's very dangerous."

"We have people out looking for him. You don't need to worry. Just get some rest." He stood out of the way for the nurse.

"What are you giving me?" Abby's voice broke.

"Pain medication, with a mild sedative. You need to rest," the nurse replied.

Abby pulled harder on the restraints. "I need to find him. He isn't alone. You don't understand what he is. What she is."

The nurse administered the sedative and gave him the polite look, the one asking him to leave.

"We've got people searching for him."

Abby grimaced at the nurse as she repositioned the heart monitor on her index finger. Her heart rate picked up.

"Can you give us a minute?" George asked the nurse.

The nurse nodded. "But only a minute, she'll be under soon. She shouldn't be agitated."

As soon as the nurse left, Abby's words rushed out. "He's

been blood starved. He's dangerous. Charlotte wants him back."

"What do you mean by blood starved?"

She blinked hard, trying to fight the sedative. The woman was tenacious, he had to give her that.

She tried stretching her mouth. "She's going to kill me." She struggled to keep her eyes open. "He's a vampire."

"You need to rest. We have an officer posted at your door. I'll stay here with you. Wait, what did you say?" Because he heard vampire. Which was pure fiction. But so were grave robberies and men who never aged.

And men who could scent a woman's blood while running in the dark.

Her eyes closed but she managed a few last words.

"Paaaa...ma. Not. Her. Danger. Shar...Lots."

I STARED at flecks of paint peeling along the edge of the ceiling. This room wasn't in one of the approved photo-op areas of Hastings. Was I in the same clinic? Corners of the linoleum were worn thin from use and age. All of the new medical equipment looked out of place, like a new Jaguar parked next to a mobile home. From the absence of windows, I guessed I was underground, in some experimental research area, far from public view.

While attempting to slide my wrists out of the restraints, I had triggered another dose of sedative, and had lost another two hours to the abyss of sleep. This time, I didn't pull on them. I just held the restraint against my thigh and attempted to wriggle my hand free. If they wanted to make me feel safe, it wasn't working. My body was drenched in sweat, not from infection or recovery, but from panic. My mind couldn't differentiate my current state, my painful past, or my haunted dreams. The sedatives were removing physical pain from the equation but not emotional pain.

The paint on the walls began to ripple and shimmer.

I screamed. Why wasn't anyone coming to help? There was no nurse. There was no shuffling of feet. I was trapped. But I wasn't sure if it was a dream, a hallucination, or a textured, layered, tangible version of hell.

Like a death toll, the sound of children's laughter seeped through the walls. My heart pounded, fighting for a way out. The laughter hit a high pitch then morphed into cries. I was going to drown in my past.

My night visitor was coming. The angel was coming. Coming to catch me. A light glowed across the walls. I shut my eyes and held my breath. The hooded angel would come. Come to claim her kiss, the kiss of death, but not before I suffered.

The floor swam with blood. Hot garbled cries brushed against my skin, the cries of frightened children. Their last gazes flashed in my head, the purple flesh circling eyes of brown and blue. So many sets of eyes, looking at me, empty of emotion but full of accusation. Their fingers laced within mine, their cold cheeks against my burning one.

"Oh God, oh God, oh God," I moaned. He would never answer my prayers.

The heart monitor beeped, a chaotic chorus marching me to the buried past. I would not look at that fucking machine. I didn't need anyone's permission to die. After I had held them, had comforted them, the monitors would slow and end in an awful drone.

I struggled against the restraints, my hands turning purple.

The door burst open, but I didn't see anyone. I was

trapped in a world hemorrhaging with death and pain. The death angel was coming. She would finally claim me.

My restraints loosened. I shot out of the bed, falling to the floor, ripping my IV line and oxygen tube. Blood shot from my hand to the white floor, and I scuttled to the corner terrified.

Strong hands touched my shoulders but I curled up tighter afraid to look. I wasn't ready for my trial. I wasn't ready for my sentence. My penitence would not be mild.

"Abby, it's okay. You're okay."

The heart rate monitor rang a flat note.

No, no, no. Not Sam. Don't take Sam. I'll do anything, please don't take Sam. I had begged. The angel had hovered at his hospital room door ready to take his hand. But I had begged and pleaded. And made a terrible promise.

Hands pulled at mine, pried my hands from my face and shame.

"Please, make it stop," I choked out. "I didn't mean to kill them."

"Shhh...it's okay. You're safe."

"She's coming for me. I have to go." I had run from her for so long.

"Shh...shh...no one's coming for you."

My body rocked back and forth until all I heard was my staggered breath and George's whispers.

29

PUSH THEN TWIST

George watched Abby from the hall. She sat on the bed, bundled in a blanket staring at her feet. He wasn't sure if she was silently pulling herself together or still lost to the terror of her panic attack. The trauma room doctor came down the hall, holding Abby's chart and a bottle of paracetamol with codeine. How was it that at twenty meters, George could read the label and see all fifteen pills? What was happening? The world had been tossed upside down.

"How is she?" George asked.

"Settled, I think." The doctor consulted Abby's chart. "She may have had an allergic reaction to the sedative. Instead of blocking the pain, it had enhanced it, sending her into a slight psychotic episode. And you really shouldn't threaten the nursing staff, alright?"

"I'm sorry. She just...she was pretty convinced someone was coming for her." He glanced at her over his shoulder. She was still staring at the floor. He heard the pitter-patter of her heart. The monitor had been switched off a half hour ago. He rubbed his left ear.

"Are you sure you can't convince her to stay a few more hours?" The doctor touched his shoulder. "Detective Inspector Cooper?"

George blinked and shook his head. "I don't know if I can keep her in there for five minutes." He wasn't sure he could keep it together for five more minutes. Between what she had said and what he had sensed, nothing was making any sense.

"Her BP is good, it's low, but good. She's breathing without assistance. But without the IV, she'll be pretty weak. Can you get her to drink some water? Make sure she eats something? Her blood panel is still being processed. I won't have those results for awhile."

George rubbed his forearm. He closed his eyes and shook off the growing nausea. What was he going to do with her? There was his place. Or maybe Vic could take her for the night. Fuck, where was Vic? He checked his phone. No messages. He scraped for all that he had left. "I'll see what I can do, but I'll make sure she's looked after, closely." The doctor nodded and handed him the pills.

He walked into her room and closed the door. She snapped out of her trance and looked an awful lot like an innocent girl with an awful secret. Her gaze immediately moved to the door behind him.

"I need to go find James," she said.

"We have people out looking for him. You're really not strong enough to leave." George pulled a chair and sat in front of her, blocking her access to the door, but giving her his full attention. "Can you tell me what happened last night?"

"I have running clothes in my office."

"Why won't you tell me what happened?"

"I wanted to leave the party and asked Nate for a ride.

Nate had been drinking more than me, or so I thought. I drove. I shouldn't have...the car was hit and I was taken somewhere. I don't know where. James was there. And pah..." She looked at George and he saw a wall go up. She touched her split lip.

"Did he hit you? Do you remember why?"

"No. Someone else hit me. Because James needed..." She stared at the black bruise on her left palm.

"James needed blood?"

She looked at him, her mouth struggling with words she couldn't set lose.

"You said some things. In the ambulance. And before you were sedated. I'm not sure if you meant them, but I think you did." She leaned away from him. "Did he drink your blood, Abby?" Had he really just asked that question? He intentionally looked at the marks on her neck. James Stuart was some sick bastard who had everyone under a spell. "Is he the one who's been attacking dead bodies?"

She slammed her eyes shut. "No. He needs his transfusions. Or else, he's going to do things he doesn't mean."

"Mathieu Tousain's body was found at the crypt. Along with four others. We're well past things that don't mean a thing."

She examined her mangled hands. "How did you find me?"

That was a very good question. He had examined Nate's car. There was a blood trail but it had faded. Then he sensed something in the air and he followed that sense. She moved to the other side of the bed, far from his reach. He was losing ground faster than he was losing his grasp of reality.

"You were running in the dark, covered in blood," he said. "Most of it not your own. If you're mixed up in something you don't understand or want to be, you need to tell me. Let me help you."

Vic had no leads on Stuart's whereabouts and it was nearly four hours from sundown. She had secured the mausoleum at four in the morning, only to watch the evidence incinerate at sunrise, leaving no trace of the depravity they had found. Vic also had a shitload of questions for him. And he still didn't believe the answers.

"He's my patient and he needs help," she pleaded.

"Help? I've seen some terrible things in my life, behavior I don't always understand. Or want to. But I don't believe Mr. Stuart needs your help. Are you involved in the occult? Because if you believe covering an abandoned crypt in blood is a normal activity on a Friday night, we have a strong difference of opinion."

"I'm not involved in the occult. James is my patient. And I'm the only person he will trust. So if you want to find him, you need to let me go."

Seconds ticked off in extended beats as they stared at one another. George had spent his youth playing chicken with boys who had outnumbered, outweighed, and outfought him. He wasn't going to flinch now, despite the extraordinary traits Abby possessed. She had said she was the only person Stuart would trust, but she didn't say he was innocent.

What was so bloody special about this guy?

"After last night, I no longer see a reason to consider Stuart your patient but the prime suspect in the murders of five people. Making you an accessory to murder or something worse," George replied, his tone cold as nitrogen.

Her lips trembled. "Please, it's not what you think. I have to find him. She's going to kill others. Make him do terrible things."

"Who is?" And if George could hasten that outcome, he'd gladly do it.

"Charlotte."

"Who is Charlotte?"

Abby backed away, her body not as rigid, giving him a little ground. "I think she's a former companion." She looked at the floor, then the walls, then his shirt, but she wouldn't make eye contact. "She's a revenant, some kind of evil spirit, who won't rest until she possesses him." Her words were so rushed, he wasn't sure he had followed the freight train. Perhaps she knew she sounded ludicrous. "I think she lives off the dead. The blood of the dead. Something like that. You need to believe me."

Maybe the psychotic episode was still in play.

"I know it sounds crazy." She glanced at him and her desperation tasted painfully sad and bitter. "She'll kill anyone who keeps her from him. That's why she took me to the crypt. To kill me in that tomb. To make him do it, so she could have my body."

"So he was going to kill you?" George hitched his hands on his hips. They were no longer consulting professionals. She was delusional and he was going mental. "Did Charlotte do this?" He grabbed her left hand, showing her the puncture wounds.

She yanked her hand away, and hid it behind her back. He pointed at her neck and she stared at him with contempt.

"No, she wanted James to do it. He hasn't fed in weeks. He's very weak."

"Weak?" He let out an audible sneer. "One of the bodies we found had every one of his ribs shattered and his skull fractured." He closed the gap between them and she backed away. "Fed? Do you hear yourself? Did you let him drink your blood? You said he had been blood starved. That he was a vampire. We found you running from a crypt covered in blood. You didn't recognize me. You had two seizures before we got you here." Her shoulders curled in and her eyes welled up. "And you flat-lined for two minutes and twenty-eight seconds. It took them two hours to get you stabilized." He had backed her into the corner of the room, as far from the door as possible.

She slammed her hands over her ears and shook her head. He listened to her uneven breaths as he towered over her. Her heartbeat was erratic. The bitter notes of her fear wafted off her skin.

And he felt like a monster.

He backed away. "I'm sorry. You've suffered a trauma and aren't one hundred percent. Rest and regain your strength, your sanity at least. I can have an officer here to watch your room."

She drew in a long breath that sounded like surrender. God, maybe he was better at bluffing than he thought. She walked to the bed and leaned against it.

Silence swallowed the room. He wondered when she would say something, anything. After all that had happened, he wanted some assurance she didn't hate him. He just wanted the truth. More than that, he wanted her safe.

"I'm sorry," he said. "I'm trying hard to understand." Understand why he was dizzy but strong. Why he tasted her emotions in the air. Why he hungered for a truth he couldn't accept.

"Do you know when my Dad died?" she asked.

He looked at her in confusion, and she didn't wait for his reply.

"He died April eleventh, 2010, the third day of spring

break my last year in premed. He had pushed through a shitty chemo schedule during Christmas break so that I wouldn't need to worry when classes resumed. He didn't want to distract me with his health." Her nostrils flared. "Because even though I was four years younger than my peers, I was still obsessed with keeping up. Can you believe that?" She walked around the bed. "So he was kind enough to wait until spring break to die. I didn't cry at his funeral. I tried. Tried really hard, but all I could do was get through it without feeling anything." She licked her trembling lips. "You want to know when I finally cried?"

He blinked.

"Seven weeks later. Two days before finals, I found a stuffed horse crammed in a bag from his hospital room. I thought I had lost that little generic brown horse a long time ago, in a place I no longer wanted to remember." She clenched her jaw. "As soon as I touched it, I broke down. Because even though he said he didn't need me, he took a piece of me with him to that fucking hospital to die. Alone.

Because he knew how much I hated hospitals. I didn't eat or sleep. Just cried, alone in my shitty apartment, for thirty-six hours. Which was probably nothing like what he went through." Her stare glassed over. "My first final was in anatomy, it was an oral exam. I don't even remember if I had showered that morning. I don't remember how I had gotten out of my apartment. Don't even remember the walk through campus. I just snapped out of it, in that classroom." He tasted the confidence in her breath. "Do you want to know how many questions I missed?"

He listened to his strained swallow.

"Not one. So don't give me some shit excuse about resting to regain my strength. Because this is *nothing* compared to those two days." She tapped his chest with her index finger. "I don't care that he bit me. I don't care about how much blood I lost. I don't even care if you believe me. I have an obligation to help my patient, and I need to find him. Or there will be more bodies to add to the ones already in the morgue. And unless you have *evidence* that proves I killed someone last night, I believe I'm free to go."

Her indictment became a knot of pain lodged at the base of his neck. George rolled his head, making an ugly snap. Neither of them budged. He shouldn't let her out, because he cared about what happened to her. He shouldn't let her out, because someone was trying to kill her. He shouldn't let her out, because he wasn't sure he could protect her.

The air no longer held notes of sickness or bitter pain. Fear didn't waft from her skin, it was something sweeter —determination.

"And where would you like to go, Dr. Whiting?" he asked.

30

BEHIND CLOSED DOORS

Ten minutes into the drive to Heritage House, I thought my skin would peel off. I kept checking the side-view mirror every twenty seconds, knowing the blue sedan a half-mile behind us was still following. I forced myself to forget the look of complete betrayal on DI Cooper's face when I told him where I wanted to go. I wasn't the bad guy.

"Is your Sergeant following us?"

He didn't answer. I have to admit, he made me a better doctor. The only time I believed I was fighting for James was when I defended him against DI Cooper. So despite what this was costing me personally, I was growing professionally.

Fucking fantastic.

The immaculate hedgerows of Heritage House came into view and I gripped the door handle. Once DI Cooper pulled up the winding drive, the taste of lavender hit my tongue. The calming effect erased by the car following us up the drive.

Did he really think I was capable of giving him the slip? I was flattered. Now, how was I going to pull it off?

With no time to adjust my formulating game plan, I took a half-hearted inhale of the crab apple scent in the parking lot. I sprinted up the stairs, through the entrance, and up the stairs to the Gallery. The detective humored me by not running after me. A uniformed hostess stopped me from entering the gallery.

"I'm a member," I bluffed.

"I'm sorry, there is a strict dress code."

Compared to her soft silk tunic, my faded Stanford t-shirt felt insubstantial, kind of like American credit. "I need to see Helen. It's an emergency." Even to me, the request sounded lame.

The woman lifted her hand and gestured for me to leave. For some reason throwing a fit and appearing like a nut job didn't seem like the next appropriate choice. But I took a last cursory scan of the room. Helen wasn't there. I knew of two secret hallways leading to different parts of the house.

At the bottom stair, I noticed DI Cooper was still outside. There were two uniformed police officers talking with him. He did not look happy, but I was relieved he was occupied. I hooked a right and jogged down the passage James had taken me through after the companion interviews. I raced up the hidden stairwell, knowing I would attract attention, and finally render Helen's appearance.

The second floor held the small interview room and the row of closed doors still begging to be opened. Maybe they were occupied? Maybe other secret interviews were conducted in those rooms? But the floor was silent. I hurried to the interview room, the tip of my index finger touching each antique doorknob. Each one screaming, "Pick me, open me, look inside me." One door shy of the interview room, I turned a knob.

"Hello?" I called through the crack of the door.

No answer.

I nudged the door wider. "Is anyone there?"

I stepped into the room and drowned in splendor. My mind couldn't begin to catalogue all the rich details. The tiffany blue and gold décor as light as honey dripping in the sun was beyond stunning. There were dozens of portraits hanging hip to crown molding in the hall of the gallery, but the portraits in this room held me captive. The level of detail pulled each face from the past into the present. This was James's room. Those faces were his history. His origin.

The furniture was arranged for people to gather, talk, read, listen to someone play piano. Not a twenty-first century entertainment room designed to distract, but a nineteenth-century centerpiece. A room designed to bring a family together. The room evoked a luxurious peace. An emotion I no longer believed to possess.

They had lived in this room.

I touched everything to verify its authenticity. Every bit of it was real, beyond genuine. Every object I lifted carried the weight of its construction—silver, brass, nickel, walnut. There was no such pride of possession in my family. Everything had been scattered to the winds of convenient fabrication.

A set of double doors lay behind the silk upholstered sofa. If I had gone this far off the reservation, why not see the border?

I pushed the double doors open and entered a small formal dining room. The smell of smoke from the small fireplace was recent. It kindled a wariness I couldn't categorize. Across the French oak dining table with oxblood leather chairs were the next set of doors. My desire to discover the other rooms pushed me ahead with no hesitation. This was the terrain I could never cover in an interview with James. It would require intimacy, which implied friendship or love or one of those things I had banished from my statistical outcomes.

The large canopy bed with a carved cornice frame took up half the room. The citrine linens shimmered under the late afternoon sun. It was sumptuous, like a peach begging to be bitten. The giddiness from my hunt dissipated into a heavy sensation of regret.

I sat on the bed, naïve desperation my only companion. Did I really believe I'd find him tucked away? After the night we had survived?

I rubbed the covers with the back of my hands, afraid my palms would soil the million-thread count coverlet. The heavy silk soothed and sang to me. I wanted to lie back and wrap the linens around me, bury myself under the canopy, and lose my war against loneliness. The familiar scent of sandalwood and resin sunk into my skin.

I shot off the bed and looked down the row of open doors. And remembered my patient and who he had been this entire time—an experienced monster posing as a man, a priest, a lover, a patient. I realized we had all been classified by species, genus, family, and usefulness. This wasn't the room I had been placed in. I belonged in a sterile lab, examining deadly things.

Another set of doors sat on the other end of the bedroom. I pulled those two open and walked into another bedroom. Color scheme deep crimson with black trim. With limited interior design knowledge, I guessed French boudoir. His heavy musk wafted from the king-size mattress. Another set of doors waited on the other side of this bedroom.

I yanked those doors open to find another bedroom.

Color scheme hunter green with burgundy accents, very masculine. Colonel Pride in the bedroom with a titanium prosthesis. I wanted to slam my head into the wall for being so stupid. He had respected my clearly drawn boundaries, so why was I so pissed?

"Abby?" Helen's maternal voice cut through four rooms.

I held onto the door for support, and attempted to hide my embarrassment. I looked at Helen and tried to form words, but they didn't come.

Helen closed the doors to the sitting room and walked across the dining room, rubbing her hands as if they were stung by the cold. "James hasn't been here." She closed the doors to the dining room, noticed the wrinkle in the citrine bed, and waited for me to speak. Or answer for myself. I didn't have answers. I needed them.

"These rooms, they're his, it's where he..." Gives them *incomparable pleasure*. But my voice disappeared beneath the weight of my envy.

Helen closed 'the remaining rooms until we stood together in the hunter green bedroom. She placed her hands on my sore arms. The heat from her touch calmed the wind blowing through my barren past. A past well self-constructed, there was nowhere to misplace the blame.

I wore my loneliness like a lab coat.

"Did James do that?" she asked.

I touched my neck. The punctures were no longer sensitive and the scabs had all but disappeared. "I'm not sure. I think so. He was not himself last night. Tousain is dead. And who knows how many others. Charlotte is back." Her eyes pulsed. "Charlotte has...has taken Padma's body."

A nerve rippled across Helen's upper lip. "Are you sure?"

"I'm not sure of a whole lot right now. Just that I need to find James."

"Where did you last see him?"

"An abandoned crypt. It was underground. But it had a domed ceiling with a large circle opening in the center."

I walked to the window, trying to clear the image of the chamber painted in blood. A crowd of poplar and ash trees across the large estate glimmered in the fading sun. In a flash, I was running through the woods. The blue glow of moonlight lit up the ground. The tree limbs whipped my face and arms. I touched the cold glass of the window, freeing myself from the recollection. My reflection revealed the damage I didn't want to remember. I tugged at the collar of my t-shirt. "How does Charlotte choose a body?" I asked.

"She'll look for someone with a weaker spirit. Someone who has crossed over into death. The emptiness will give her room to maneuver. It's always someone he trusts and desires."

That left me in the clear. Almost.

"Do her victims know?"

Helen walked up behind me, her glowing face lighting up our shared portrait in the window. "No, she's a subtle kind of cancer."

"And if you kill the host?"

"You force her back to square one."

I rubbed my throat, trying to force air in and out. Was I ready to sacrifice everything?

"I need to get out of here, but I have—"

"George with you? I don't think that's going to be a problem."

Guilt twisted my stomach. I didn't want to let him down or hurt him. I didn't know what I wanted when it came to the nice detective. I guess I wanted him to be left out of my equations.

"Does he know?" I asked Helen.

"I told him James is a vampire. I told him Charlotte was coming for him. That she's dangerous. But I didn't tell him about Padma. Because he doesn't believe any of it."

There was a knock at the door. Two women entered the room. They looked remarkably similar. Straight black hair that fell just past their shoulders, five foot three, petite builds. They looked a lot like me.

"Abby, this is Margot and Rachel."

Dumbfounded by the resemblances, especially Margot's, I forgot how to shake hands.

"You're going to need to swap clothes with Margot."

Margot removed tight designer jeans and a red linen tunic with elegant efficiency and handed them to me. She stood in her French lace underwear, leaving me stranded in fully-clothed awkwardness. Helen gave me a visual shove and I got on with undressing. I handed Margot my lame running clothes. Her level of mortification registered on my shame Richter scale. "Sorry," I said to Margot.

I turned to Helen. "What happens here exactly?" I asked.

"Do you really want to know?"

I looked at Margot then Rachel. They were stunning, young, college-aged girls who were probably available for company for limited amounts of time. "No, I don't want to know."

Margot giggled and slipped on my clothes. "May I have your hair tie?" she asked.

I pulled it from my hair and handed the rubber band over. Margot's jeans fit latex gloves tight, and the tunic revealed breasts I had always tried to hide. Something about my mother crept up the back on my throat. I shoved it well below my self-esteem.

Margot pulled her hair into a neat ponytail and Rachel followed suit. Although Rachel's running suit looked way better than my flimsy one, the resemblances were uncanny. Helen had a damn good eye.

"Wait," Helen said and pointed to my feet. "Shoes."

"What?"

"You need to swap shoes."

I eyed Margot's three-inch wedge heels. "I don't know how to walk in those."

"Learn." Helen tipped her head to Margot.

Margot gently pulled me to the bed and removed her shoes. "I'm a thirty seven. What about you?"

I compared my slashed up feet to Margot's cherry red pedicured toes. "Six," I said.

Margot slid her black shoes next to me. "They're not that bad."

"Why do I get the feeling you've done this before?" I asked Helen as I wrestled on Margot's shoes.

"Things got a little grim during the Thatcher years," Helen said. Margot and Rachel left the room. Helen opened a small dresser drawer and handed me something cold and heavy.

God, what the hell was Helen? I told myself I didn't have time. I didn't have the capacity. I certainly didn't have any disappointment left. "I can't take this." I attempted to give the gun back, but she wouldn't take it. "I'm not a murderer."

"But she's already dead. They both are."

I shook my head and carefully placed the weapon on the bed. "Not to me."

"You said yourself he wasn't himself last night. Nothing is simple any longer. You need to protect yourself."

"That isn't going to protect me." I pointed at the gun.

"Neither is your degree in medicine or your lack of faith."

We were at a standoff. Arms crossed, staring at a five-foot Persian rug divide that would not be bridged with a Glock 9.

"Fine," Helen said. "I'll have a car waiting for you on the other side."

"Other side? Where am I going?"

31

HIDDEN TREASURES

The initial quarter-mile of the three-mile hike was no different than walking into a large movie theater. It was dark, but not completely dark, the air smelled slightly used, the floor sloped, and the air conditioning was set way too low. Helen had lent me a flashlight, the first clue that where I was going, wasn't going to be in broad daylight. The antique charm of my new life had finally worn thin.

The low ceiling hovered five inches above my head. If I spread my arms, I could touch each wall, and the rough plaster occasionally snagged my borrowed sweater. I didn't even want to think about my feet. Stupid heels. I flashed the light down the tunnel and squinted, swallowing the heart pounding in my throat.

After the second half-mile, the walls dampened, indicating a change of terrain. The floor was no longer worn smooth from use but rough with loose dirt and gravel like a dry creek bed. I flashed the light ahead, keeping my courage focused. My breath shook a bit, but I chalked it up to physical exertion not fright. Yep, leaving the gun behind was a moment of sheer brilliance.

The light beam caught a series of cup-sized iron rings along the sides of each wall. They sat slightly higher than my head. Each ring was evenly spaced at twenty paces. I grabbed a ring, the rust-encrusted surface cut into the cold of my fingers. I ran my hand across, picking up oily soot. My fingertips held the scent of kerosene. They had to be old torch posts.

I continued forward until the wall on the right took on a different canvas. The rough plaster gave way to chiseled granite and an archway. I flashed the light behind me and gauged the distance traveled to a little over one mile. I was still under the estate. But not within screaming distance.

The archway held a solid metal door forged of iron. The oxidized metal was caked with a layer of burnt sienna paint. My light beam swung like a pendulum from where I had walked to how much farther I needed to go. There was a faint glow of light at the end of the tunnel. Natural light, my final destination. The sun would be setting soon.

Move forward. Walk past the door. Walk towards the light. Don't be curious. I repeated to myself.

It took four good shoves to get the door open.

Three stone steps lowered me into a sunken room. My flashlight only cut a few feet ahead. The darkness resided in the room with unyielding resistance. The air smelled of earth, rusted metal, sweet rotting wood, and misery. I didn't get the sense that I'd been here before. This wasn't the crypt. But something close to it.

A tower of melted wax stood in the corner of the small room. Boxes of large kitchen matches littered the floor, inviting me to reveal the hidden room. I lit the tower and found two candelabras. Similar iron rings lined the ceiling and a few scattered around one wall at waist height. The metal rings were caked with rust and black soot, perhaps blood. They had to have been used as restraints. Maybe I'd found an old dungeon? Whatever I had found, it was old. Perhaps older than James.

I circled the room, studying it for more clues. One corner never caught any light. I lifted the flashlight above my shoulder like a club and walked to the dark corner. There was a small door no wider than a pantry cabinet made of the same forged metal. I didn't even give myself the benefit of a logical debate. It took one good shove and I passed over the threshold to another smaller room.

The floor crunched under each footstep. The room smelled of dried plants. There were notes of anise and chamomile, the soothing aroma of lavender. Bundles of wrapped twigs and flowers covered the floor. Untouched tokens of affection left for the dead inhabiting the room. Taking up the room were four coffins, one adorned for a woman and three smaller ones, each smaller than the next like a set of Russian dolls.

"Did you have a family?"

"A wife and three children, but that was a lifetime ago."

A sharp pain rose up my throat, and my lungs pinched.

"Oh James." My words were swallowed by the emptiness of the room.

I lifted the flashlight and scanned the sacred secret room. The walls were covered with a repeating pattern. It wasn't wallpaper, but tally marks. I ran my shaking hands over the wall, felt the slick of wax, and smelled hints of decay. The markings were made from blood mixed with wax used for ink. But to tally what? One wall held twenty five thousand marks. They went from ceiling to floor, repeated and repeated. Going on forever. He had marked days lived like time served in a prison.

My shoulders curled to my ears, attempting to hush my growing unease. I had trespassed well beyond the scope of my employment.

A tall apothecary cabinet peeling with black paint rested against the far wall. In some areas the paint had stripped away completely. In this hidden room filled with anguish, I wanted to learn about the man instead of the disease.

"I'm sorry," I said quiet as a prayer.

I pulled a drawer open and found ornate hair combs. A pair made out of mother-of-pearl, another made of silk with strands so brittle they flaked into my hand. Another drawer held pressed flowers. Hand-carved toys. A rattle. It became difficult to see or breathe.

"Why do you have this tucked away?"

I moved around the cabinet and found more items. Newspaper clippings. Hermes cufflinks. A drawer filled with business cards. A tie pin with a rusted out blue insignia. I found a box wrapped in a Chanel silk scarf similar to one Helen had worn. I unraveled the fern green scarf from the box. With each turn, something rattled and I followed the drumbeat of my conscience.

Inside the box was a burned, mangled piece of metal. I rubbed the charred object. It was a Volvo decal. Judging by where I had found the item, it was the most recent treasure to be hidden.

I heard metal clang against metal and froze. Stood firm without breath or movement, and listened to the room. Listened for a shift in temperature, a shift in chemistry, waited for my sixth sense to shift into gear.

The room inhaled all its secrets and waited for me to move. There was no electric hum, no seismic lash, nothing snagged by my intuition's web. And in that long eon of silence, I recovered my courage and tripled it. I wrapped the box, replaced it in the drawer, and pocketed the car ornament.

I turned back to face the room, my light casting soft white ribbons against the walls, the coffins, and the floor. I remained alone with his secrets. There was a part of me that finally understood the depth of his despair. Another part of me wanted to pull him free of it.

I shut the door to his shrine and crossed the antechamber. The room continued to eat all noise as if starved for sustenance. The door clanged. I threw my light back to the door and watched the door ebb open and close. A natural phenomena.

From the inside the room, the forged iron door had a different patina. It was pock marked with fist-sized craters.

"I had tried not feeding once before, but the hunger overrides everything."

With an enlightened pair of eyes, I examined the room again. The iron rings were at waist height. James had shackled himself in that room. Four of the iron rings were twisted, three more twisted open like shattered cartilage.

"I knew locking myself away wouldn't be enough, I always found a way out."

I placed my fist into one of the craters in the door.

"The hunger overrides everything." The metal door amplified my voice.

I crossed the room and extinguished the candelabras. The hot wax had added another ridge to the tower in the corner. I cupped my hand, whispered another heartfelt apology, and blew out the last candle. When I walked back to the door, the tiny hairs along the nape of my neck rose. The room had become as cold as hell.

The air gathered energy and polarized. There was nothing to my left, right, in front of me, or behind. But my skin pulled tight with alarm. I took one step back to the door, and another until my foot hit the first step. Wisps of my hair floated to the ceiling. I had forgotten to look up.

I reached behind me and touched the metal door. One more step and I'd be out.

A cloud of darkness slithered along the ceiling and the walls closed in.

32

TUNNEL VISION

"What seems to be the problem?" George asked Constables Tuner and Hsu.

The two uniformed policemen were beat cops, good for following up on minor details, squaring off a crime scene, and, occasionally, for picking up suspects. They were all on favorable terms, not warm and fuzzy but proficient and professional. Neither of them seemed very comfortable at the moment.

"DCI Helderman has a few questions," Sergeant Turner said. He kept his gaze above George's shoulder on the scenery.

"I'm a little busy right now following up on a lead. How about I give him a call in an hour?"

"That's not going to work. He needs you back at the station." Constable Turner put his thumbs in his belt and widened his stance. And Constable Hsu rocked back on his heels.

George rubbed his nose. "Okay, I will follow you to the station."

"We have instructions to bring you back personally."

"Ryan, what the hell is going on?"

Constable Ryan Hsu looked at the ground and winced. "You need to come in, sir." He finally looked George in the eye. "It's your ex. She's been roughed—"

"You're going to get us suspended," Turner warned Hsu.

"What's happened to Padma?"

Constable Turner placed his hand on George's arm. "Let's go over it at the station."

George flung his hand off. "Is she okay?"

Hsu glared at Turner. Turner nodded and shook his head. "She's pressing charges. For assault."

"Against me?" George pulled his phone from his pocket. There were a dozen messages from Vic. Fucking fuck.

"Sorry, sir," said Constable Hsu. "We have to take you in."

George looked back at the estate and growled. "Can one of you stay back and go after Dr. Abby Whiting? She's looking for someone dangerous and she shouldn't be without protection."

Hsu looked at the ground again. "Sorry, sir. We've been instructed to stay clear of the estate."

"DCI Helderman doesn't want you going into Heritage House?"

"No, sir. Ms. Robson doesn't want us making guests uncomfortable."

Brilliant. His day was coming up roses. He faced the large mansion and scanned the windows. Helen was on the second floor, observing the situation from her beautifully constructed false pretense. She smiled and waved. She was waiting for him to ask for help. He hadn't asked her for anything since he was twelve years old.

"Can I make a quick call?" George asked. Turner nodded. Vic picked up on the first ring.

"This has gone to shit," Vic said.

"Where are you?"

"Home. Suspended."

"What? But you didn't. I didn't—" She didn't let him finish.

"You need to call Nate. We kicked a hornet's nest."

George looked back at Helen. "Is she okay?"

"The American? I don't know. I've been warned off the clinic."

"Abby's fine. She's at Heritage House."

"She's up and walking? Are you having a fuckin' laugh?"

"It's a long story. Is Padma okay?"

He listened to Vic take a long drag from a cigarette. "I don't know what she's on about. Call Nate. Have him get you a decent barrister. And don't, I repeat, do not go after James Stuart."

"Right." He put his phone back in his pocket. "Right." He hitched his hands on his hips and looked at the two uniforms, looked back up at Helen, and swore. He cleared his throat, rubbed under his nose and turned his back to Helen. She was going to eat this up like cake. He slipped his hand behind his back and flashed two fingers. Those two fingers were going to cost him every roadblock he had ever placed in front of Helen.

"Fucking grand."

"Pardon, sir?"

George shook his head and followed the two constables to their marked car. Hsu opened the passenger door to the back of the car. George slid in and looked back at the house. Helen was gone.

THERE WASN'T a word for what I felt as my feet lingered on

two steps, my hand touching the cold door, and my mind bracing for death.

Courage? No.

An eerie calm settled across my body and my mind became a barren desert.

Brave? Definitely not.

Time slowed, my heart slowed, everything moved in slow motion.

Stubborn? Probably.

My eyes followed the beam of light. It moved up the far wall and crawled along the ceiling. I caught sight of his feet first, covered in dirt and dried blood.

"I killed six people feeding in twenty-four hours."

The light beam continued across his tattered pants and mottled torso. His arms crossed his chest and his face was ashen with slumber. A cloud-like gas swirled around him, mimicking a hurricane. It had the hazy quality of natural gas. The noxious cloud shimmered against the light. I watched the cloud descend.

A woman's figure took shape. She had ashen gray skin and dark eyes outlined with white lashes. Her brown hair was severely pulled back into a knot at the base of her head. Three small children peeked from around her waist.

Like Russian dolls.

I reached out to touch her and she vanished. A thick black cloud backed across the room, gathering momentum.

Shit.

"James wake up!" I screamed.

He was unresponsive. There was an awful howl in the room. Air drained from my lungs and my skin itched with panic. I threw my flashlight at James. It stopped inches from impact, hovered in the air as if time had stopped, and shot across the room making a loud pop like a bullet. Shards of metal littered the floor.

I was lifted off the ground and my throat tightened. I attempted to wrap my hand around the apparition's hold, but my fingers found nothing to grip. My feet flailed and fluttered in fright. I tried screaming, but it came out in stutters and gasps. I was hurled out of the room.

My back and head knocked into a wall, and I slumped to the ground. Warmth from blood trickled down the nape of my neck. A high-pitched ringing filled my ears.

Someone crouched over me. They lifted my chin and leaned in, close enough to kiss.

"Help me," I said.

"Your curiosity will get you killed, Abby. Don't ever go in there, again."

I inhaled the ice from James's warning. My vision clouded, my throat screamed with pain, and my chest burned.

A thud reverberated down the tunnel, interrupting the intimacy of my pain. James ran, drawn to the disturbance. I pushed myself up and staggered toward the light. And fell knees-chest-face to the cold ground.

Dirt caked my tongue. The light at the end of the tunnel had faded like a cloud had crossed the sun.

AFTER AN UNINTERRUPTED DRIVE across the estate, all the while keeping his attention locked on the rearview mirror, George finally gave up hope Helen was going to help. The sky had a soft clamshell pink glow but it didn't fill his cockles with any warmth. Instead, he ground his teeth on impatience and anxiety. What had happened to Padma? And why did he suspect it had something to do with his blackout? He rubbed his scraped knuckles. He wouldn't hurt her. He didn't have it in him.

The car followed a sharp curve, cresting a hill and came to an abrupt stop. A flock of sheep had congregated on the road, blocking their way back into town.

"Lucky I was going the speed limit," Turner said. The constable tapped on his horn but the animals didn't move. "They came out of nowhere."

George's phone chimed. The text was from Helen.

LOOK FAMILIAR?

What the hell? George looked out the window. The road was just a quiet, windy country one. It was the only road in and out of the estate. It was also the road where he had the car accident six months ago. There was a pair of old oak trees fifty meters ahead. Not unusual this far out in the country, but George had remembered peering up at those trees from his overturned car. He remembered thinking they looked like lovers' hands reaching out for each other across the road. George pulled at his collar.

"Are you okay, sir?" Hsu asked.

"I need some air."

George got out of the car. He wiped the beading sweat from his upper lip and stared at the pair of trees. He heard the hiss of oil splattering against the engine. He heard the tires spin round and round, searching for road to grip. He remembered gurgling and choking on his own blood as he aspirated. He unbuttoned another button. A cold sweat had flushed his skin.

He overheard Hsu explaining the accident to Turner. Turner gave George a you're-one-lucky-bastard cursory glance.

He called Helen. "Where's Abby?" he asked.

"No longer here."

"I don't have time for games. Is she okay?" he gritted.

"Keep an eye out for her. Bottom of the hill, to your left."

"What the hell—" but she cut the call. He swore under his breath.

The two constables had left the car unattended. They were attempting to move the flock by waving their hands. At the bottom of the hill, the two oak trees loomed. He eyed the unattended car. Taking the squad car off-terrain in the same area where his car had flipped and overturned three times would be the fastest route. It would make a handy getaway. The two fellow officers were distracted enough.

A strange sense of alarm crept up the back of his neck. It wasn't that he was back at the accident site. It was that he didn't have a sense of what was happening to him. Physically, mentally, and now, emotionally.

"Where are you going?" Turner called after him.

"I'm going to walk. Once you guys get the road unblocked, you can pick me up. Sound alright?"

The constables were now completely surrounded by the flock of sheep. George didn't wait for them to reply. It's not like he could disappear. At the bottom of the hill, to the left over another knoll was an old cemetery, replete with moss-ridden headstones, broken fencing, and crosses jutting from the ground like arthritic limbs.

Why would Abby be hiding in a cemetery? How could he rationalize any of this?

A soft wind blew up the road, and he swore he heard a whisper.

George glanced across the macabre landscape. Three mausoleums stood perched on the hill. A peculiar revulsion hit him square in the chest. Someone had come to the car when it had flipped. He remembered seeing her feet. He remembered being terrified.

Help me.

The plea was clear. But there was no one around. He wasn't even in the line of sight of the two constables now. But it was Abby's voice. Abby's voice in the wind. Just like last night.

Help me.

The sky devoured all residual heat and the temperature dropped a good ten degrees as he ran across the cemetery.

He eyed the three mausoleums. One appeared on the verge of collapse, another looked well maintained, and the last chilled him to the carotid artery. A hard gust of wind pushed at his backside, egging him on. He noticed the last mausoleum's door was cracked open.

The door opened into a tight space as big as a garden shed. He peered in and searched for an obvious passage. He ducked to enter the small hut for decayed bones. A rattle from the cement tiles on the floor caught his attention.

He hammered the tiles with his foot until they shattered and fell down a hole the size of a sewer grate. He ran his hands around the inside of the hole until he found an iron bar, reached in deeper and touched another.

When he pulled his hand back, it was covered in blood.

"Abby," he yelled, but there was no answer.

George dropped down the hole and crawled into darkness. He waited for the rush of apprehension, adrenaline, but he felt oddly comfortable. The darkness possessed texture and it touched him in a way that was second nature. It bothered him a little to realize he could see perfectly in a part of the earth holding no light. He peered down a tunnel a foot too short to stand comfortably.

A cold wickedness brushed his flesh. And he smelled pain.

Help. Help me. Please help.

George continued through the tunnel with the conviction of a predator. "Abby," he called out.

Thirty yards ahead, her body lay prone, her fingers scraping the ground. She was trying to crawl away. He saw a man lurch into the tunnel and leap a top her frail body.

"Stuart. Stop."

Panic focused his senses. He watched Stuart cradle Abby in his arms and lean into her neck. He sprinted for him.

He ran up behind Stuart and dove at his rib cage, ripping him off Abby. They tumbled into the darkness. They rolled and twisted, arms and legs entangled. A regiment of steps busted them free of one another.

Stuart recovered first and yanked George up by his collar.

George watched blood trickle from Stuart's mouth. The hint of satisfaction hung on his lips, driving George into a rage. He shoved Stuart away and waited for him to swing. Stuart didn't, he dusted dirt from his hair and chest, like he was bored.

"I like you, George. Granted things are not going the way I had ever planned. Welcome to the afterlife."

George cross-hooked Stuart in the mouth. His head cocked back, returning with a smile as wide and deep as the English Channel.

George was tackled to the ground. Stuart sat on his chest, swatting punches away like they were tedious flies. A gleam of anticipation sparked in his eyes. George watched thick curved canines descend from Stuart's insidious smile, screaming to be fed. George held him off with his hands, shoving Stuart's distorted face away.

"Are you ready for this dark new world?" Stuart snarled.

"What are you?"

"My doctor didn't tell you?"

"Keep away from Abby." Oh God, he had to get to Abby.

Stuart wrapped his hands around George's neck and squeezed. "Let's see just how strong you are now."

Every last cell in George's body fought to hold off the darkness speeding in from the periphery. His fingers gripped over the tendons of Stuart's clutch. He didn't want his last memory to be of the prick's hauntingly calm face.

"Where's that hungry boy from Bristol? I've watched you take on six boys at a time."

How did he know where he was from? George kicked and thrashed until panic stampeded through him. He palmed for any weapon. He wrapped his hand around mangled metal.

George shoved the piece of metal into the side of Stuart's neck. His jugular artery spurted blood in small arcs but Stuart's grip didn't loosen. It was like Stuart wanted to test which of them would blink first.

A smirk slithered across his face and he finally let George go. "Interesting. You exhibit self-control. That's hopeful."

The rush of air hit George like another round of punches. He rolled and pulled his legs into his burning torso. The high pitch whistle of his gasps polluted the dark's quiet. He heard the shuffle of Stuart's feet, and prayed the bastard had stumbled from blood loss.

The scent of James's blood cuffed George in the stomach. Hard.

George sprang to his feet. Stuart rubbed at his neck. The injury plugged, but the residual blood still streamed down his neck. And it smelled of life, and irresistible power.

"Are you still here, George? Or are you about to blackout? You can't afford to be afraid now."

How did the monster know about the blackouts?

"Do you lose pockets of time?" Stuart taunted. "Do you sense things more deeply?"

George took a running leap at him, toppling the monster to the ground in the tunnel. It happened so quickly, too quickly, and before he knew it, he had bit Stuart in the neck. Stuart's blood tasted like comfort, and pain, and the will to survive both.

The realization that he was aware of his need, his desire and his hunger collapsed George with disgust. He shuffled off Stuart, ran out of the strange dark room, and tripped over Abby's lifeless body.

Her cheek was pressed against the cold dirt. Her back didn't lift to breathe. Her fingers were curled but he couldn't taste her pain. Suddenly, his confusion and agony no longer mattered.

"Abby."

She didn't respond.

Emptiness consumed him. Back at the hospital, she had been terrified to die, to meet her maker. She had run from an invisible enemy, an angel of death, ready to dole out punishment for a crime he couldn't understand. He had promised to protect her from the darkness. He had failed, twice.

A sharp pain radiated from George's lower back and he collapsed, his hand curled over hers. She was cold, deathly cold.

"Now be a good boy and leave us alone," Stuart whispered in his ear.

"I'm going to kill you." Blackness coated George's vision.

"Not today, son."

33

COMING CLEAN

The sound of water hitting water pulled me to the surface. My body felt warm, buoyant, and free. My head throbbed but the warmth eased through the beats of pain. James's dead family had knocked me down, crushing me into the dirt. But I had seen light. I'd caught its last beams with my hands. Maybe I had crawled my way to the light? Out of the cold earth to the warmth of what felt like a womb.

The synapses in my brain battled for connection. Was this heaven? Cocooned and protected, I didn't want to leave. There is no heaven, I argued. The haze of white poured through the slats of my eyes. Other colors seeped through, blacks and blues first, next yellows, pinks and oranges. I saw James with a halo of light behind him, soft and aglow with life. No more black oozed through his veins. No more bloodied hands. No more angel of death.

It took massive effort and coordination to get my hand to lift from the water. I reached out and touched his face. His cheek gave under my touch. He had form and mass. He was alive. James was alive. But I was weightless and empty. My hand slipped and he caught it. He returned my hand to his face.

"Come back to me," he said.

He kissed the inside of my palm. The firmness of his lips flooded my body with a strange desire. James smiled and his eyes stared past the frightened girl holding the locked gate to my childhood. I settled back into a comfortable unease. There was the safety of his normal appearance—clean-shaven, clean-cut, but his deceptive cleanliness had led me into some very dark places in the last thirty-six hours.

Feeling exposed and naked, I covered my chest and crossed my legs, and water sloshed over the side of the tub. My hands felt around my partially clothed body. I was immersed in a large bathtub wearing wet underwear and a dampened sense of awareness.

James shook his head and clicked his tongue. "Now, what kind of monster do you think I am?"

My nervous laugh reverberated against the water, tickling my bottom lip.

"You had dirt and blood in your hair. And you got sick all over yourself."

I reached for my head, patted down my skull, looking for proof of injury. There was a bump at the base of my head the size of a walnut. But I wasn't bleeding. Thank God. The water in the tub ran clear as an alibi. My throat tightened with speculation. And I stared at him, raging with accusation.

"You had a nasty gash on the back of your head. I couldn't let you bleed to death."

"You could've taken me to the clinic. Called Nate. Or a paramedic..."

"It's not really safe to call anyone. Things have gotten a little complicated."

I tried to sit up but the room swam and my stomach ebbed with waves of nausea.

James placed a hand behind my neck and his other on my chest, steadying the disruption in the water and my body. "You shouldn't try moving so fast."

The steamed air tasted of lavender and eucalyptus, reminding me of runs through the rolling hills of Stanford. It smelled of a lost home, one I might never see again. My eyes stung with confusion. I swallowed my desire to cry.

"How many blood exchanges are we up to?" I didn't adjust the cold revulsion from my voice.

His hold on me eased and his gaze grew heavy. "You have nothing to worry about." He released me and reached for a towel. I instantly hated myself for missing his touch.

I watched him unfold the towel, his hands smoothing the surface like he was ironing his excuses. He draped the towel over his shoulder and leaned over the tub.

"I've taken your blood twice. I have given you my blood twice. But we have not made the *required* exchange." He leaned in closer, and I sunk into the tub deeper. "You have not *consented* your blood to me with love or affection and you have not *taken* from me what is rightfully yours. Although I would kill to know what that feels like." He rolled his eyes to the ceiling in feigned prayer.

Bath water filled my mouth. It tasted sweet, seductive, and slippery. His gaze swept over the water. "Why do you hide your body? It's tan, fit. Not painful to stare at for an hour. It is a walking billboard to move to California."

"We don't all drive convertibles, wearing bikini tops."

"That's a damn shame."

I almost laughed but I caught the hidden truth in his empty smile. "You've never been to California."

"I've never been anywhere. But here."

It was one thing to live and die in the same town, but after 184 years it would be hard not to want to set the place ablaze. He was trapped in permanent exile within his home. I almost wanted to forgive him for the last forty-eight hours.

"Why haven't you left?" I asked.

"What I need is here." He looked down at the floor, seemed to looked through it, to the hidden room below. He held out his hand. "Ready to come out?"

I stared at his long manicured fingers, and examined my own dirt-caked nails. The tunnel grime taunted me to ask the million-dollar question. But that meant admitting to things I should not have seen. His hand stayed outstretched and steady, unwilling to break our last moment of peace. I had trusted him under worse circumstances.

I slid up slowly and allowed him to help me stand. His firm grip was like a steel buttress holding every arch of my weak body. My legs gave out and in one quick swoop I was out of the bath and in his arms. The cold swept over my body, and my teeth rattled, and I pushed my head against his chest for warmth. He held me tighter.

The heady scent of sandalwood and temptation seeped through my pores, through my steadfast belief there could be nothing harvested in my growing attachment. He carried me into the citrine bedroom. Every muscle in my body stiffened.

"Put me down."

"But you're—"

"Put me down. Please."

Before he made it to the grand centerpiece of the bedroom, I jumped from his arms.

"What the hell is the matter with you?" he asked.

Unable to reel in my discomfort, I gripped the towel harder to stop shaking. I'd taken an oath to protect his condition. To protect his secrets. I certainly didn't want to become one of them. The room glimmered and I half-expected murmurs and moans to come through the walls. I fought toppling over, and stumbled to the edge of the bed.

"You're shaking," he said. "Badly."

"It's normal." I gripped the towel tighter, thinking I could squeeze the tremors away. I glanced at him. He was worried. Worried for me.

"It's normal to have tremors after a traumatic experience," I chattered.

"What can I do? Because watching you shake like this isn't helping."

I needed to get warm but crawling into the beautiful bed, his bed, wasn't an option. "Whiskey. Whiskey will help." At least I hoped it would.

He left and my eyes darted all over the room, assessing how I could get warmer, where would I find clothes, and how soon would I have the strength to leave? Because a part of me desperately wanted to stay. It was fear, exhaustion, and need, the need for answers, not his affection.

It had nothing to do with affection.

With all the talking, and his confessions, all I had discovered, even when he'd hovered over me in darkness and threatened harm, I enjoyed the intimacy. Enjoyed his touch, his kiss, his danger and pain. It was like walking on the edge of a cliff made of sand.

I wrung water from my hair and watched it bead on the rug. How many pairs of feet had crossed this room? Images of the companions flashed in my mind and I understood their purpose. They were temporary measures, rotated medications to treat symptoms. What could I dispense that would be any different?

When had my constant companion become so painful? Loneliness was the only assurance against loss.

The door opened and James glided in with a new look of calm and confidence. I hated that nothing got under his skin and now he lived under mine.

He handed me a highball glass of amber liquid, brushed a loose limp strand of hair from my forehead. I slinked away from him and sat on the bed. The heat from the whiskey hit my nose and I held my breath. The glass clinked against my teeth. I counted to five and swallowed a mouthful. Fire whooshed down my throat and tumbled into my stomach. I cupped my hand over my mouth, fought the need to expel the whiskey from my system, and sucked air through my nostrils.

"How does anyone drink this stuff?" I asked.

James arched his brows, almost offended by the comment. The alcohol was working on multiple levels.

"Who is Charlotte?" I asked.

I watched the name slice through him like a scalpel. His weight shifted to his heels and he widened his stance. "Why did you come back for me?" he asked.

Always a question answered with a question. We were back on the dance floor, back to our routine. The question surprised me because it implied my answer mattered. But my actions mattered more.

"You're my patient. I couldn't just leave you. And you saved my life."

"I came awfully close to ending your life."

"But you didn't." I took another sip of whiskey. "Why?"

"Do you know how difficult it is to find a good doctor within NHS?"

I choked on my laugh, which he interpreted as a white flag. He took two steps forward but I held him at arm's length, the length of my reach, and the length of my wavering patience.

He took my injured hand into his and traced small circles around the puncture wounds. "I'm sorry. Sorry for hurting you."

He wanted me to forget my pain. Perhaps all of it, even the pain he knew nothing about. He wanted me to forgive and forget. But we were well past that. I no longer wanted to dance.

"Who is Charlotte?"

The circles stopped and he squeezed my fingers and let go. He walked across the room and stood at the window. Someone wanted me dead and it wasn't James. It was someone stronger and crueler. And when James didn't answer, I scanned the room.

"Where are my clothes?"

He shrugged and grinned with boyish menace. I walked to the door.

"You're going to walk through Cambridge in a towel?"

"I'll walk through Cambridge stripped of everything. And I'll get my ass on the first plane for the States because I'm tired of being lied to. I don't want to play. You either answer my questions or we're done." Funny, I no longer chattered or shook.

The skin around his eyes grew tight. I reached for the door.

"We were lovers. And she has cost me everyone. Almost everything."

I felt his aggravation across the room, the prickle of static in the air between us. But it didn't stop me from crossing the room. The moonlight should have cast his reflection against the glass but it remained empty. Which made our time together more surreal.

"How old are you?" he asked.

I cleared my throat. "Twenty-eight."

"I didn't notice Charlotte until she was twenty-four. She was on her second husband by then. Married a Duke, acquired a title and a reputation. Quite an accomplished woman at twenty-four, much like you." He glanced over his shoulder at me. "But there was a price she had to pay for her rise in station. She came to me for help, because we had grown up together. She was clever that way. And as her priest, I wanted to help. I thought I was capable. But I had sorely underestimated how far she would fall."

"And she took you with her?"

"All the way to hell and we haven't made it back yet."

"Are you going to kill me?"

He snatched me around the waist. "Do you have any idea how many incredible women I've had to kill because of her? Do you think it will be easy to kill Padma?" His disappointment tasted crystal clear. "It hardly seemed fair to take your life, Abby. You've yet to live it."

I fumbled for words, his mouth too close, but I pressed. "Can I have my clothes?"

He let me go and pointed to the French settee by the closet. A red wraparound dress hung over the back.

"I don't think so," I said.

"Humor me."

I grabbed the dress and walked into his walk-in closet to change. The closet was as large as a guest bedroom. Neat rows of suits hung across one wall in every shade of black, grey, blue and brown. Another two rows of pressed tailored shirts. A shelf of sweaters, a wall of shoes, drawers of ties, handkerchiefs, pocket squares. The volume of good taste and disposable income swallowed me like a virus.

"Did you get lost?" he called out.

"No." *That happened a long time ago.* I peeled off my wet underwear. It took me a few seconds to figure out the configuration of the dress. I eyed a black sweater, yanked it off a shelf, and pulled it over the dress. And after pulling each drawer open looking for boxers, I found women's underwear.

"Of course. What did you expect?" I mumbled.

James lounged on the settee and swung his legs to the floor when I reentered the room. He pulled my running shoes from underneath and laid them in his lap. It was like he had offered me a get-out-of-hell free card.

"Let's go for a walk. Go see the river." His face held a haunted longing.

"I don't want to go anywhere except home. Not with your girlfriend hell-bent on putting me in a grave."

"She can't hurt you. Not here. It's sacred ground."

"Can't hurt me? What about down…" My voice caught. I remembered being tossed from his secret room. Remembered the taste of dirt in my mouth. The drawers filled with all of his remembrances. My guilt had snatched my tongue. I couldn't admit to seeing his precious family.

"Have you ever met someone, and understood in that moment, they were what was missing? That they were the key to everything?" he asked.

I was afraid to answer the question. More afraid I couldn't live up to the commitment.

He stood and leaned his forehead onto mine. "You see… I'm lost. I'm stuck between two needs." His hands were on my hips and he nudged me backwards. "I want to give you the answers you seek. But that only puts you in more danger." I felt the wall behind me. "Or we can stay in this room and we can forget everything we already know." His mouth trembled over my hungry lips. "Give me your *consent*. Take me where you want to go."

The weight of his soft words coursed through my blood. I remembered the power he held over me in the crypt. How powerless and safe I felt. I wanted to give in to his words. I wanted to feel his hands unwrap the dress. I wanted to feel the marble skin. I stared into the cold abyss of his blue eyes.

It took every miserable ounce of my restraint to answer.

THE FOG HOVERED over the river like a satin sheet. The cool mist made tiny droplets across my face. I tilted my head back, welcoming the fresh air, hoping to cool my overheated cheeks, hoping to eradicate my polluted thoughts. After two sips of whiskey, the sweater I had borrowed clung too close and made my skin itch. It pricked at the craving I was trying to suffocate.

I swatted branches with the back of my hand and dug a trench in the back of his blue cashmere sweater. I followed him into the darkness. Again.

"I've never met anyone like you," he said.

I made no comment. He snuck a glance. I had never met anyone like me either—stubborn, stupid, and determined to remain alone. The moon was veiled in ribbons of cotton.

"I haven't met anyone who hasn't wanted my blood." He ducked under a large oak branch. "Don't you want to live forever?"

His condition was an incurable curse, but I couldn't say that to him. Not after what I had found in his secret room. I scratched my head, rummaging for a polite answer. "I appreciate deadlines."

James buckled with laughter. His laugh cut through the fog, tumbled over the arms and legs of trees, and rippled over my skin. It was a rich and rare treat, and I was sure it would haunt me for a lifetime. The way his kiss had haunted my dreams.

He ran the last few meters to the bank of the river. I didn't pick up my pace, just cautiously watched. He untied a flat canoe from a small walkway then reached out for me. This must have been the punt Detective Cooper had mentioned. A strange exhilaration flushed from my chest, like ditching school or hopping on a motorcycle or dating the wrong guy. I had picked a terrible time for a bucket list.

I climbed onto the punt and sat down on the bench facing the stern. He lifted the pole and pushed us from the shore until we drifted with the slow steady current of the water. The evening was strangely silent.

"Why the river?" I asked.

"It's peaceful out here. Helps me with my memory. I want to give you the truth."

Even in the moonlight, his eyes glimmered blue mocking the river's black. I dropped my hand into the cool water, fanning out my fingers and the water curled under my nails.

"You killed those men last night," I said.

"Yes. I needed blood. And I didn't want to take all of yours." He didn't even turn to look at me. It was a simple answer for an awful question.

"And Tousain?"

He gave a cursory glance, lifted the pole, and the water rippled. "Yes."

I drew in the cold air. Where did anyone go from here?

"When?"

"A few days after you arrived."

I waited for the shock of surprise. It didn't arrive. "Why?"

"The world is full of enough monsters. He wanted more.

More money. More secrets. More time. And he was going to risk the only one I have left to protect."

He had murdered Tousain to protect me? I was almost flattered. The scent of moss and deciduous leaves tempered my thoughts of the beautiful murderer at the stern.

"Do you still love her?" I asked.

The look James gave stripped me of ease, and in a heartbeat he replaced it with torrential kindness. "Charlotte promises you everything. And then she delivers. You don't even question the price." He closed his eyes like he was savoring a morsel of a memory. "It's excruciating and irresistible." The night smelled ripe with haunted happiness. "Tell me something, at work, do you work hardest to easiest, or easiest to hardest?" he asked.

The moist wood frame of the punt gave under my grip. I didn't like his questions tonight. "You identify the givens and then eliminate possibilities. So easiest to hardest."

"The curse of my condition isn't the killing or the guilt. It's the isolation. Knowing you are other, different. Forgetting your past. We can never go back to the comforts of human identity. You have to give up everyone in order to have everything."

"But you have companions. You're around people all the time."

"Not family. Not ever. Something we have in common."

"I have a brother."

He gave me a harsh look of pity. I spent my days and nights isolated at work, nowhere near family or friends. All by choice.

"I had a brother," he said. His eyes locked on the water. "And two sisters. A feat we all made it to adulthood. Proof money can purchase assurance."

The fog thickened and I lifted my gaze to the shore.

Three figures stood along the river's edge in eerie silence. They were thin as paper but as clear as his sadness. It didn't occur to me to panic, I was too engrossed in his story.

"I guess we all felt entitled to our comforts. Pride is a shameful possession. I imagine I didn't care about my siblings at first. Honestly, I didn't. But if I hadn't forgotten my own family."

I blinked, trying to clear the ghostly vision along the river. The figures along the bank didn't look like the present. They didn't look like the future, but they bore a strange distant resemblance to James. More apparitions walked out of the fog and my throat was full of coarse sand.

"After fifteen years of not changing but being totally changed, I checked in on my brother. I wanted to see how he was doing. If he had had any children, squandered the family estate…"

I wanted to look at James, to acknowledge his pain, but the growing crowd had me captivated. Women and men of all ages, shoulder to shoulder dressed for a strange stage play. And the children. Huddled next to knees and hips and waists. All of their eyes locked on one person.

"James."

I said his name, heard it in my head, but it hadn't made it past my tight throat. It was trapped between not wanting to believe, and not wanting to remember the ghosts of my own past. More individuals came out into the night to stand at the shore. I cupped the icy river water and drank. It didn't matter how the water tasted or what organisms resided in it, I needed my voice to grow.

"It's funny the things you miss, the people you need, the memories you lose after you realize you have all the time in the world."

"James." His name shook past my lips, enough to jar my eyes away from the shore. "Who are they?"

He tilted his body away from them, his gaze transfixed on the water, no longer in concentration, but in dedication to denial. The long oar lifted and fell into the water with less grace. A horrible twitch tugged at his left eye.

Had he murdered all of those people? All of those witnesses at the river's edge.

"Charlotte would find out. Find them. And reward me with their executions."

Ridges of goose bumps shot across my arms. Over eighty apparitions hovered along the shore, along the edge of my ability to comprehend. I couldn't remember how to breathe. The ghosts continued their stranglehold.

"Why?" I murmured.

James heaved the pole from the water and dropped it into the punt. He yanked me to the stern and wrapped his arms around mine, locking our view. His ragged breath at my ear shoved me well past fear and deep into dread.

"What do you see?" His voice sounded thick with agony.

My nerves were coiled around my heart, but they burst like a flock of black birds after a loud clap of thunder. "Your dead."

"Charlotte interpreted my interest as regret. And she was right."

There were dozens of faces. And I catalogued all of them. How they were grouped. How they stood not in militant hatred, but in casual unity. Bound by time, bound by a bloodline, bound by death.

His grip loosened, and he rubbed his jaw along my temple. "I should've stopped loving her after she killed my children. I tried. Again and again, I've tried. But with every cull she made, I would forget."

"Forget?"

"Forget the man I once was. Forget where I came from. Forget the family I had adored and worshipped. Forget the identity I had lost. I was left with no memory of them. Nothing but drawers and drawers full of mementos. And I don't know who they belong to."

My legs bowed, nearly tipping the boat and throwing us into the black water. He counterbalanced and set me back on the bench. I watched the figures evaporate into the fog. Desperate, I fought harder to see each of them. Fought to recognize features and match them to his. For the first time since I childhood, I wanted to see the dead.

"Charlotte works hardest to easiest. Eliminates the biggest threat first, enjoys the challenge, savors my pain. The easiest victims don't even know. It's almost natural. She went for my brother's children three months after I had watched him lose a card game. Waited thirty years to kill him."

My eyes burned. "What do you want from me?"

The sound of my voice was no longer familiar. It sounded steely, sharp, and held the edge of a knife. The punt had glided back to the bank and everything stopped. The river didn't churn. The night was a sleeping giant heavy with silence.

Everything leaned in.

James sat across from me, took both of my hands and wove them into his. "Everything changed last night. I'm going to kill Padma to send Charlotte back for the last time." His fingers fastened like cuffs. "And then, I want you to kill me."

I shot out of my own skin. Strange to look at something so beautiful, and want to shred it, only to stitch it together again. Endings were awful nuisances I had avoided by not having beginnings or middles with anyone. And I surely wasn't going to change now.

"No," I blurted.

"Do you really think you have a choice?"

"Yes." I jumped free of the boat and the ground sank beneath my feet. It took me a few heartbeats to adjust, but there would be no rest for the damned, no matter how hopelessly distraught.

"She has systematically eradicated my family," he called out.

I stumbled and clawed my way up the bank, mud seeping into my running shoes.

"My bloodline has all but disappeared. Been wiped from existence. She always returns for me." His anger scraped at my dignity.

"I took an oath. I can't take a life." I shook my head, hoping it would erase the last half hour. Hell, the last forty-eight. He snagged my elbow.

"You must help me end this."

"Go to hell."

"You forget that I'm already there. If she takes my last descendant, I am hers forever. I will never make it back. I will never remember. And they will never be at rest. How can you not help me?"

I stared at my feet and bit my tongue. Tears spilled free, dropping onto the ground like fat raindrops. If I believed the man I saw in the crypt the night before was beyond repair, the man standing in front of me was beyond saving. I walked toward the lights of Heritage House.

"Your blood is different," he said.

I staggered and slowed.

"You shouldn't be able to sense me before I sense you. No one has ever slipped free of her grasp. No one has ever slipped free of mine. You should be dead. My blood should've killed you."

Death sounded like a good option.

"What happened in Sturgis? That tiny hospital. That tiny town. All those poor children dying. I saw your memory. How did you ever survive it all?"

His words looped around my neck. The more he spoke, the harder it became to escape, I was caught in his sticky web of deceit and despair.

The soft lights of Heritage House danced across the expanse of lawn and perfect hedgerows. I tried to imagine their warmth traveling across the newly devastated evening. The luxury of the citrine bedroom wrapped its arms around me, toying with my hopelessness.

I marched to the lights. There would be a safety hatch. There would be a place to run. I knew how to hide. I had managed it for years.

Just feet from the house, he dropped his last argument. "No one has seen what lies across that river. No one but me. How can you see the dead?"

I rounded on him. "You knew. You knew I'd choose the walk over staying in that bedroom. You've known every choice before I ever make it. Because you've created the experiment, the lab, the samples. You know every given. I will not kill anyone. Never." Never again. I managed to find the door and yanked it open. It didn't matter whether I recognized the hall. I followed it. Despite the silence, I knew he followed. "Why didn't you just kill yourself, you selfish bastard?"

"You don't think I've tried? It doesn't work, and they're left trapped here, never at rest. Never at peace."

I ran down the hall, ducking around the corner, anger fueling my speed.

"You were amazing last night," he said, hounding me. "Fearless and determined to save them. To save them all from being trapped here."

I stopped cold. Blood thickened in my veins, ran slow as sludge. It churned through my head and I remembered the bloodstained robe, the stickiness of death on my skin.

"What are you talking about?" I asked, not wanting to know.

"You performed the Last Rites. Sang to them. Blessed them with a kiss."

I stood locked inside my hidden childhood. Remembered the beds holding small bodies. I heard their ragged last breaths. Saw the bloodstained sheets. Remembered how the only light came at dusk, when their souls and smiles were carried away. Sorrow had ruled the universe of my childhood, which is why I chose never to return to it.

"Leave me alone," I screamed, at him, at my memories.

"You said you'd help me." His eyes glimmered with desperation.

I spun around the room. How did we get back into the citrine bedroom? "I'm losing my mind." I rubbed my eyes. "I can't. I won't."

"Then at least forgive me."

My confusion and fear fell off my skin like yesterday's clothes. There was his offer, an offer rich with comfort, and a distraction from our mutual heartache.

"Help me feel like the man I once was."

His timeless kiss quashed my argument to run.

34

JUST A FEW QUESTIONS

George sat in the interview room surprised by his level of discomfort. He was on the wrong side of the table, staring at two coworkers who were trying their damnedest to stay objective.

"You can't account for a fifty-minute window?" DCI Helderman asked.

George ground his molars and shook his head.

"But you remember sitting with Ms. Venkat out in the garden, talking to her and kissing her, is that right?"

"Yes. I did not hit her."

"And how did your hands get bruised, DI Cooper?"

"Like I said before, I got into a scuffle with James Stuart."

"Under a cemetery?"

George took a deep calming breath. "Yes." The breath had not worked.

"Did you follow Mr. Stuart under the cemetery?"

"No."

"How did you know he was there?"

"I was walking. I heard Dr. Whiting scream and followed

the noise. I was worried Stuart would attack her again. And I was right. I found him crouched over her..." It hurt to say the words, like a good kick to the gut.

"You found him..."

"Over her prone body."

"He was attacking her?"

"Yes." George didn't like how shaky his voice sounded. "Like he had attacked her the night before in the mausoleum."

DCI Helderman slid aside his tea and pulled an open case file. "Right. We've sent a couple of officers to the mausoleum. And aside from a few broken tiles, they have found no trace of the attack you're alluding to. No trace of any blood, of any kind. The only person who can corroborate your story is your sergeant. Even she is unclear as to what the two of you found aside from Dr. Whiting running away from the place in an incoherent state."

He licked his finger and flipped through some papers and continued. "The bodies that were supposed to be sitting in the morgue, including Dr. Mathieu Tousain's, are missing. And the coroner has no record of them." He slammed the case file closed. "But I have Ms. Venkat claiming you assaulted her." He fanned out four photos of Padma's bruised face. "And you say you injured your hand in a scuffle with Mr. Stuart. The same man who had an affair with your former fiancée. Do you understand how this is stacking up?"

George understood how it all looked. He also understood that if he explained everything they would lock him up. In a sanitarium. He ran his tongue along his teeth. Had he really bit Stuart?

"If you could speak with Dr. Whiting, I'm sure this can

be cleared up." What if they had tried? It was mid-morning. They would have followed up with her by now. What if she couldn't be reached? The other what if was too hard to consider. "She was checked into the clinic. She was in critical condition when she arrived."

"But she walked out of there roughly twelve hours later?"

The interview room became more confining. "You need to find her. She's in danger." He needed to get out of that room. The same way Abby had wanted out of hers. Why had he let her go? Dammit, he would never forgive himself.

"Do you need some water, Cooper?" DCI Helderman asked.

George stared at the two men across the table, lost in all of the actions he needed to take but couldn't.

"We have a call into the clinic," DCI Helderman said. "And a call into Mr. Stuart's office. We have spoken to Dr. Nate Rothschild. He confirms Dr. Whiting and he were in a car accident. That they were both attended to at the Hastings Clinic. And that they both sustained minor injuries."

"Minor injuries?" George attempted to steady his voice. What the hell was Nate doing? George was going to strangle him. What had they done to him in that bloody clinic? All of those treatments. The dialysis. The prescriptions. Was he some sick experiment?

There was a knock, and Constable Turner walked in with a slip of paper. Turner didn't extend George so much as a passing glance. Shit. DCI Helderman scanned the paper and leaned back in his chair, furiously rubbing his bottom lip. He placed the paper into the case file.

"The samples we took when we swabbed your hands and scraped under your nails." George folded his arms, tucking his hands under his arms. "Most of it doesn't match

Ms. Venkat's blood type. But there were trace particles that match her under your nails."

"I didn't hit her. I wouldn't." George closed his eyes, rummaging his mind for any memory after that bitter kiss. "This all has to do with James Stuart." But he couldn't explain how. It was too unbelievable.

DCI Helderman turned to his sergeant and motioned for him to turn off the recorder. He leaned across the table. "Listen, you're a good copper. But you have me in a tough spot, George. I want to believe you, but sometimes the most obvious answer is the right answer. I think you went to that event and something in you snapped."

George pinned his fists harder.

"When you say this all has to do with James Stuart, I have to agree." He leaned away and and tapped his fat sausage fingers on the table. "Six months ago, you found your fiancée entangled with her boss at Heritage House. That very same night, you had a horrible car accident, and the two of you split up shortly thereafter. While you were recovering from said accident, am I right?" Helderman didn't wait for George to answer. "You've put your head down, back into work, everything is fine. You've moved on. Or so you think.

Mr. Stuart invites you to their fancy event. You man up and show, and then you realize everything's changed. You ask Ms. Venkat to have a chat, things don't go the way you want, and then you lose it. I get it."

"No." George slammed this fists onto the table, sending tea and files into the air. "I went snooping around a rich, entitled prick and now he's going out of his way to destroy my life." He regretted the words immediately. They were emotional and complete conjecture.

DCI Helderman stared at George, his nostrils flaring. He

gingerly picked up his overturned tea. "Sergeant, can you escort the detective back to his holding cell?"

George stood and waved off the sergeant. "I apologize for the outburst. You have to find Dr. Whiting. Just tell me if she's okay. Please." Because if she wasn't, George was going commit murder.

35

CELL DIVISION

My phone woke me up. This was alarming on two fronts: one, I had managed to fall asleep—amazing the level of exhaustion a few traumatic experiences will cause—and two, I was alone in the citrine bedroom.

I didn't recognize the phone number, but this was their third attempt to reach me. I had slept like the dead. I shook my head and answered the phone.

"This is Dr. Whiting."

"Dr. Whiting, this is Constable Turner of the Cambridge Constabulary. I was wondering if you could come by the station today and answer a few questions?"

My heart raced past my brain.

I checked the time. It was a little after ten o'clock. "Huh, yeah. Sure."

"And what time can we expect you?"

I attempted to put things into a mental checklist. Avoid running into James. Call James. Call Nate. Where was I with Detective Cooper? Since he was having me brought in for questioning, probably high on his never-talk-to list. James needed a transfusion. I needed to shower, eat, and consume three cups of coffee. Damn. Did I need to create an alibi? Shit. I needed to recreate my entire universe. I stumbled out of the bed.

"How about after lunch?" I was an idiot.

"Shall we say one o'clock? Just mention DCI Helderman at the front desk."

"DCI Helderman?" Was that George's boss? I snatched my running clothes from the foot of the bed. When did those get there?

The officer spelled the name for me. "Yeah, I got it. I'll be there at one." I tossed my phone on the bed. I got the rest of my clothes on and brushed my teeth. James hadn't left a note, but he had made sure I could walk out of there with clean clothes and fresh breath. How considerate.

I carefully opened the door, peeked down the hall, and kept my eyes locked on my feet as I made my way downstairs. The very public foyer was lit with mid-morning sun. The doors hadn't been open for guests, the staff was busy shining the floor and polishing the brass. There had to be a back door. I didn't make eye contact and followed my nose to the kitchen.

Every staff person I passed gave me a nod and showed no reaction. Clearly, I hadn't been the only random civilian to walk down these halls in search of another exit. One of the kitchen staff offered me coffee and a scone. I pocketed the scone and kept up my brisk pace. This was quite the walk of shame. There was a small door leading up a few steps to the back of the property. I raced up them and found Helen having her morning coffee and paper in a small garden.

With a uniformed police officer.

How was I born this lucky?

Helen looked at me over her coffee cup, her stare warm but cautious. I attempted to back down the steps, but the officer turned around.

"Dr. Whiting?"

I don't think I'd ever regretted the title until then.

"Yes."

"We're following up on a complaint regarding an incident that took place at the Hastings Clinic gala. We're hoping you can answer some questions?" He didn't seem as interested in my response as much as he was interested in the way I looked. He scrutinized my face, clothing, and hands.

I pocketed my hands, palming the warm scone. "I just spoke with Constable Turner. I told him I'd come in after lunch today."

The officer looked at his watch. "You don't have a few minutes now?"

I looked at my phone, pretending to check the time. "Actually, I have business to attend to at the clinic. It's a little time sensitive. Life and death."

The policeman moved aside and I said goodbye to Helen. I walked to the parking lot at a brisk pace, scarfing the scone, and then remembered I didn't have a car.

Screw me.

There was a lone car in the lot, a blue Volvo sedan. I squinted at the car. This was the car DI Cooper had driven when he had brought me to Heritage House yesterday. Why was it still in the parking lot?

Frantically, I looked back at Heritage House. Had he come back looking for me? Wait, the policeman had wanted to ask a few questions. About the gala. Not about vampires or crypts or James? Murder wasn't a complaint.

I stared at the sedan. My eyes fixated on the Volvo logo.

Coincidence is statistically possible, I just didn't know how often James allowed for them. My phone chimed.

KEYS ARE IN THE SUN VISOR.

The text was from Helen.

"What is going on?" Talking to myself wasn't abnormal. I had left abnormal behind hours ago.

I was surprised to find the car unlocked. Who did that? Was that standard for cops? I pulled down the visor and caught the keys.

JAMES WALKED into the Cambridge Constabulary. He asked for DCI Helderman and made an effort to take in the lack of décor of the police station. There wasn't much to note, it was very bureaucratic and charmless. Nothing like the original Constabulary. At least that one had given you sense of guilty until proven innocent fear factor.

A uniformed woman peered up from her work. He smiled at her, which thanks to the split lip hurt slightly. She returned the gesture. Plans had changed, but his charms had not. He heard the shuffling of feet from the other side of the office. It sounded like DCI Helderman needed an entourage. Interesting. George would've come unaccompanied.

Two junior detectives came through the door first, followed by DCI Helderman. The DCI had a more than passing resemblance to a classic British bulldog, but with much better teeth. James knew the man wasn't a native of Cambridge, had transferred from Liverpool three years ago and it still showed. Helderman paused and assessed James. The DCI was taken aback by James's obvious bruised lip. Had he believed George to be a liar?

"Mr. Stuart, thank you for coming in."

James shook the man's big hand. "Not a problem. I think there has been a misunderstanding. So I'm happy to clear the air." James eyed the two inferior detectives. "Is DI Cooper here?"

"Why don't we go back to an interview room?" Helderman said.

"Alright." James followed the trio of officers through the doorway down a small hall to a set of rooms. One of the junior detectives opened the first door on the left.

Despite the soundproof rooms and the lack of windows, James knew George was in the second room on the right. James noticed there were only four chairs available in the interview room. He paused before entering and turned to the big detective. "I would appreciate if you could round up DI Cooper. He's been very helpful on the Tousain case, and I believe he's been charged with a crime he didn't commit. And I want to assure him I feel no ill will." James smiled and locked eyes with the DCI. "And I don't think we need the extra help."

Helderman blinked. "I'll see what I can do. In the meantime, can we get you anything to drink?"

"No, thank you."

James walked into the interview room and took his seat. The three officers whispered game plans to each other, noticed James was paying attention and closed the door, leaving James alone.

A series of small windows filtered sunlight into the room. Across the room was a mirrored observation window, which at present was empty. James ran his fingers across the recording device. There was a knock and DCI Helderman entered with a cup of cold tea and a very thin case file.

James crossed his legs and ironed the crease of his trousers between his fingers. He heard the door to the observation room open and two figures entered—a man and a woman. James stared directly at the woman and kept his face neutral.

"Again, thank you for coming in." DCI Helderman took a seat.

"Not a problem, I assure you."

"Would you mind if I record our discussion? My note-taking ability isn't the best."

James eyed the case file and nodded. DCI Helderman went through the usual legal requirements for the recording.

"We're following up with various attendees regarding an account of an incident that took place at Heritage House the evening of your gala. Can you confirm Ms. Padma Venkat and DI Cooper were at the event?"

"They were both on the guest list. I don't believe they came together. I'm sure you can confirm that with the staff of Heritage House."

"You were not at the event?"

"I had arrived early and fell ill. Stomach bug. Ms. Robson was kind enough to lend me a room, while my staff and I reworked the announcement and event schedule. There was no point in risking everyone's good health."

"And how long did you remain at Heritage House?"

"Throughout the event. I'm a bit of a control freak. And didn't want to leave until the festivities had concluded."

"Did you see DI Cooper at anytime during the evening?"

"I had seen him later in the evening, after most of the guests had left."

"Because you were feeling better?"

"I think it had been something I ate." James looked at the observation window.

"And what did you two discuss?"

"DI Cooper had some questions regarding Mathieu's disappearance."

"And is that what the two of you discussed?"

"At first yes, but then the discussion became personal in nature and escalated."

"Did DI Cooper hit you?" Helderman touched his upper lip.

"We both got a few good punches in." James smiled.

"I'm sorry. We should have removed DI Cooper from the case sooner. Given that you two share a past."

"I don't think we share a past as much as we share an interest in the same woman. Don't apologize for the good detective. If anyone owes an apology, it would be me."

Helderman scraped his cheek with his thumb "And where did this scuffle take place?"

"Outside, in the parking lot."

"Not in a cemetery?"

James knitted his brows together. "Pardon?"

"Never mind. And did you ever see Ms. Venkat?"

"I saw her earlier in the evening."

"And had she seemed injured or upset?"

"No. She was in mint condition." James looked at the observation window.

"And what did you two discuss?"

"Not much."

"I don't understand."

"Let's see, how do I put this delicately." James licked his lips. "She was looking for some company for the evening."

There was a quick knock on the door. One of the junior detectives escorted George into the room. George stopped in his tracks. "Where is she?"

Helderman pulled the chair next to him for George to sit. George didn't move.

"Hello, DI Cooper." James offered his hand. George did not accept. *Don't piss your career away. Take a seat.*

Helderman pointed at the chair. "Detective Inspector George Cooper has entered the room. The time is eleven twenty-two. James Stuart has confirmed there was a physical encounter between himself and DI Cooper. Do you wish to file a complaint?" Helderman asked James.

"No. Our scuffle had nothing to do with the detective's case. It was personal and was long overdue." James smiled at George.

George licked his front teeth and reluctantly sat.

"And what time would you say you saw Ms. Venkat?"

James looked back at the observation window.

"A little before nine thirty."

"And she appeared fine?"

"Yes. Never more beautiful." James continued to stare past George at the observation window.

George opened his mouth. James uncrossed his legs, knocking the table and spilling Helderman's cold tea.

"Gah, these tables are crap."

If you want to come after to me with the freedom of your reputation and profession intact, you will not question why I'm here, George. Or what I say.

George shook his head as if he was attempting to clear his ears. But James knew he had heard every word.

George leaned across the table. "Did I just hear you right?"

James's heart fluttered to life. George was such a good man. "I said she never looked more beautiful."

Helderman stopped wiping his spilled tea and gave George a quick warning glance.

I believe your inferior superior wants you to mind your

manners. *So don't make a scene, George, and just play along. Please, humor me. It'll be the last time, promise.*

"Where is she?" George asked.

Helderman turned his head slightly toward the observation mirror.

"I'm not sure who you're talking about, DI Cooper," James said. *Where o where could your little lamb be?*

"Did you hurt her?" George asked.

DCI Helderman leaned into the recording device. "I'm pausing this interview. I will remove DI Cooper from the room and restart after a short break. It is eleven twenty four." He turned off the device and stood, motioning for George to stand up.

"If I hurt Ms. Venkat," James said. "It was by consent. I think Ms. Venkat is a little confused as to which man she really wants. She has trouble with her attention. But she has interesting predilections, wouldn't you say, DI Cooper? A bit on the darker side, no?"

George lunged at James. But DCI Helderman yanked him back, pulling George by his elbows.

Why do you have to be so sensitive about Abby? She's all yours, after I'm done.

"If I find out you placed a finger on her or she has so much as a scratch, I'm coming after you. Do you hear me? I'm coming for you."

It took every pound of Helderman's two hundred and forty to get George out of the interview room.

James inhaled the heated air. George was such a passionate man. With such a long fuse. Hatred didn't come to George easily, which made everything harder. James stared at Charlotte through the observation window and wondered if he had been unforgivable enough.

DCI Helderman entered the room, this time, with a hot

cup of coffee. The man had recently stopped smoking. A smart decision, considering how poor his health was. The black tumors were spreading.

"I'm terribly sorry about that. I'm not sure why you wanted DI Cooper in the room if you knew he'd react with such hostility."

Helderman wasn't a terrible detective. "I like DI Cooper. He's a good cop and a better man than me. I just can't keep my hands off his lady. Regrettable, but true. Whatever charges Ms. Venkat has filed, I assure you, he's innocent. He cares for her. Deeply."

James heard the door to the observation room open and close.

Helderman rubbed his burning forearms. "Were you aware he had blacked out shortly after speaking with Ms. Venkat?"

"No. That's not good."

"It isn't. And it's rather inconvenient."

James sat up straight, took a slow deep breath, and placed his hands on the table. "I believe DI Cooper still comes to the clinic for dialysis. Perhaps that is why he blacked out?"

Helderman glanced at his thin case file and rubbed his ear lobe.

"Wouldn't you agree, Detective Chief Inspector Helderman?" James asked. He kept his voice flat and his stare intense.

Despite the look of confusion, Helderman nodded. "It's possible."

"It would make sense. If he had missed treatment, or was under duress, he could be prone to passing out. Wouldn't you agree, DCI Helderman?"

Helderman nodded. "Yeah, that sounds right."

"He would never hit Padma." James shook his head.

Helderman shook his head. "No. He's a good copper."

"That's right. And you're going to let him go. But not until Dr. Whiting shows up."

Helderman nodded. "Who is Dr. Whiting?"

"She's the American. And when she gets here, you will leave her in the waiting room. And let DI Cooper go."

"When the American gets here. Let George go."

"But make sure he sees that she's alright. He's so very worried."

Helderman nodded.

James stood. "Thank you, Detective. I hope I've cleared everything up for you."

Helderman looked at the recorder. "I forgot to turn that back on."

"Imagine that." James shook Helderman's hand. "Doesn't matter. It doesn't catch my voice anyway."

36

PAST THE LIMIT

I drove DI Cooper's car back into town, minding the speed limit and checking the mirrors every two minutes. The country drive gave me plenty of time to get used to navigating the wrong side of the road. The weirdest part was looking over my left shoulder. As soon as I got to the police station, I was going to stretch my neck and shoulders.

DI Cooper kept a fairly neat car. No empty drink containers or food wrappers. Not even receipts for fast food or gas or whatever convenient goods a cop would purchase. There were two water bottles in the backseat, one half empty. I know I had a strong misconception about police work from television, but it was just so orderly. There was the lingering scent of chlorine, which made me suspect he swam as often as I ran. He was a fit man, and it probably kept his mind clear.

I wasn't looking forward to handing him his keys. Or seeing accusation written all over his face. Or hearing another reason I should stay away from James. He was right, but I wasn't wrong either. Although what I had done last night was wrong.

I would just leave the keys at the front desk and catch a cab back to the hotel. And get my act together for the questions coming after lunch.

The parking lot of the Cambridge Constabulary wasn't packed. There wasn't a lot of crime being committed in the college town. Aside from whatever James and Charlotte did. I scanned to see if there was an employee parking area, and decided the spot near the front of the building would do. I put the car into park, killed the ignition, made sure nothing was out of place, and saw James walk out of the police station.

I ducked and covered.

Wasn't sure why I was holding my breath, but I didn't have the instincts required for any of this vampire subterfuge. Why was James at the police station? I had to believe a man who had lived across three centuries knew how to keep clear of the cops.

I peered over the dashboard. There was a car with a driver waiting for James. Did he have a car with a driver? He probably had many cars and many drivers. James got into the passenger seat. The car drove off. I spent a good five minutes attempting to get my heart rate back to normal.

I rubbed the panic and exhaustion from my face. I made sure the car was locked. Twice. There was no sign of an accident with this car. No uneven paint. Even the front axel of the car was original. This car had not been in an accident. I shook the idea from my head. It had been a long, crazy couple of days. And I wasn't a detective.

Swallowing as much of the lingering shame about last night as I could, I entered the police station. The front desk was a mere ten feet away when I heard my name.

"Abby?"

The day couldn't get any worse. I attempted a smile and tried to figure out why Nate was standing with one of James's companions in the police station.

I was not equipped for any of this. The scone I had eaten tumble-dried in my stomach.

"What are you doing here?" Nate asked me.

My mouth opened but there were no words. I glanced at the companion who seemed rigidly set on not acknowledging me. Okay...

The keys to the Volvo dug into my palm. I had spent hours upon hours with a pathological liar. I'm sure there were a few tricks I had picked up.

"You're good friends with DI Cooper, right?" I asked. Always follow a question with a question.

Nate's eyes bloomed open. "Yes, it's why I'm here. For George. Both of us, actually. This is Devon Cerin. We all went to school together. He's a barrister."

I knew exactly who Devon was, but how had the world become so small?

"Detective Cooper left his car at Heritage House." I handed the keys to Nate. "Wait, why does he need a barrister?"

Nate scrunched his mouth. "Uh, well. I'm not sure."

"Abby?"

DI Cooper stood on the other side of the front desk, wearing the same tuxedo shirt from Friday night, except it was muddled with dirt and bloodstains.

"Hi, are you okay?" I asked.

The question knocked him off balance and he took a step back to steady. "Am I okay? Are you okay?"

"Yeah, I'm fine."

The scorch of Nate's scrutiny was far from subtle, but his

wasn't anywhere near as intense as DI Cooper's. He examined my face and clothes, the way a devout mother would check her daughter after a broken curfew.

Heat flushed my neck and cheeks. His nostrils flared and there was a slight quiver at the corners of his mouth. He was upset. Very upset. There was no way on earth for him to know what had transpired between James and me. Was there? And this couldn't be explained away by saying it meant nothing. It was something, I just wasn't sure what.

A large man dressed in a gray suit that seemed to keep him from falling out of it came through the corridor.

"I've called Vic, she can come back in tomorrow," the man said to George. "Why don't you take the rest of the week off?"

George didn't answer. He just continued to silently cross-examine me.

I had made a terrible mistake.

"Dr. Whiting, I'm DCI Helderman." He shook my hand. Actually, his hand swallowed mine. "I was expecting you later but I think we've gotten all the answers we need. Sorry if we've caused an inconvenience. Thank you for coming down."

I looked at George for some sort of explanation. He closed his eyes and shook his head. When he opened them, it was as if he were a different man. A cold man. He was shutting me out. "Devon, what are you doing here?" George asked but looked at Nate.

"Dr. Whiting?" DCI Helderman asked.

"That's alright. I'll just be on my way." My stomach cramped and I leaned forward, grabbing the counter. "I'm sorry, is there a restroom?"

George halted his discussion with Nate, and Helderman pointed down the left hall. Sweat beaded my upper lip. I gave them all a curt nod goodbye and quickly walked down the hall.

I shoved the ladies room door open and ran to a stall and threw up the scone.

"Here." Nate held out a set of keys to George.

"How do you have these?" George asked.

"Abby brought them." Nate hitched his thumb over his shoulder.

At this point, there really wasn't a good fucking reason to ask any follow-up questions, everyone was too busy lying. So why bother? He turned away from Nate. "Sorry you were dragged all the way out here for nothing, Devon. But it's good to see you." He shook Devon's hand, gave Nate a glance and headed out of the office.

"That's it?" Nate called after him.

"Not now, Nate."

George exited the building and scanned the parking lot for his car. It was right in front. Brilliant. He clicked the unlock button. He heard Nate's attempt at a jog.

"What the fuck?" Nate called after him.

George rounded him. "What the fuck? Really? What the fuck have you done to me? What happens in that clinic?"

"Do you really want to know?"

Nate's eyes were dead serious. If George wanted the truth, now was the time. George noticed Devon walking toward them. "I can't do this right now. It's been a long fucking night."

"You think I've clocked in a nap?"

"The one thing that was refreshing about you being so posh is you couldn't be bought. So what has Stuart given you to shut you up?" George opened the door to his car.

Nate slammed it shut. "What happened with Padma?"

George shoved Nate back. "Nothing." Devon picked up his pace towards them. "Why don't you be the affable host and take Devon out for a good time."

"I'm going to let that one go. If you want answers, and you want to stay upright, you need to come into the clinic. Sooner rather than later."

George backed away. "Oh, I won't be going back there for treatment, mate." Devon was a few feet away.

"Everything alright?" Devon asked.

Nate put his arm around Devon. "Let me take you to The Crimson Head. They have a fantastic meat pie." He nodded at George. "Get thee to the clinic. It's where life-changing miracles happen."

George watched Nate walk with Devon out of the parking lot, heading east to the pub. What the hell did Nate mean? And how long had Nate betrayed him?

He yanked open his car door and fired up the engine. He peeled out of the parking lot and drove to the Fen Causeway just ten kilometers away. He parked the car, walked to the river, and once he was sure he was alone, he screamed a series of expletives.

There was no good explanation as to why he could smell James Stuart all over Abby's skin.

37

RUNNING ON EMPTY

It was Tuesday. I hadn't seen or spoken to James since Saturday night. In fact, work and life had been quiet and uneventful. All thanks to the security detail following me around at every hour of the day. They weren't police. Too well dressed and too many to escape, the Cambridge police didn't have the budget nor the capacity. Did it bother me that James had steered clear of me for the last few days? A little. He was probably working up another argument, one he would never win.

At least Nate was still speaking to me. He had confirmed James's transfusions were back on track, thanked me for the killer scar along his temple, and assured me his lovely car had been donated to a movie set. It had been fully insured and he had wanted to give the Tesla a go anyway. Of course I argued that was a step down and wouldn't turn a head in my old neck of the woods. At which he huffed an interesting turn of phrase. I still didn't think I had it completely figured out, anatomically speaking.

I increased the speed on the treadmill and enjoyed the view out the window. The treadmill facing the wall was good for clearing my cluttered mind to needle out theories. But now, clutter was good. I had to keep my mind occupied. My role had not changed. And my mind hadn't either. I couldn't kill James, but I could save him. To have him stay a little longer. There were too many unanswered questions.

How would I stop Charlotte? And why did any of this involve DI Cooper? Perhaps he'd been at the wrong place at the wrong time, had witnessed or seen something he shouldn't have. How would I ever convince him to arrest his former fiancée? I kept seeing the look of betrayal on his face. The one he gave me when I asked to go back to Heritage House. The one he gave me at the police station. I had deserved the latter, I think.

My vision blurred for a second. I wiped sweat from my eyes and slowed my pace. The bruises and scrapes along my arms and legs had faded, but my stomach wasn't one hundred percent. I began to worry my appetite had changed, was leaning toward liquid sustenance. But I pushed against that theory. It was stress.

This morning's breakfast hadn't been substantial enough to pull off thirteen miles, but I could manage ten at a slower pace. I took a swig of water and noticed DI Cooper walking across the minty lawn, carrying a box, a small moving box for files or papers.

I continued to watch him, knowing I had a protected vantage point. The slight hitch in his left leg had returned. This hadn't been a stellar five days for the nice detective, but he still held his head high and his shoulders back. The man had great posture. Must have been from all that swimming. As he walked passed the gym, he turned his head and looked straight at me.

He stopped walking as if he had recognized me, which I didn't think was possible through the mirrored windows. He lifted the box as if to say hello. I checked behind me and grabbed the bar of the treadmill, almost losing my footing. I shook my head. But he still remained in my line of sight. I slowly raised my hand. How could he see me?

So much for privacy.

I flashed him a five-minute sign and stopped the treadmill. There was no way I could be dry in five minutes. Dammit. I really needed to learn how to give better estimates. I flashed him another five.

It took me seven minutes to get showered and changed. I walked out and the warmth of the summer afternoon hit me. My hoodie had not been the correct post-run choice. I wiped sweat from my face with the back of my hand.

DI Cooper waited on a bench, the box seated next to him. He stood when he saw me. "Sorry, I didn't mean to put an end to your workout."

His voice was still congenial but his gaze was distant. "I was wrapping up anyway. What brings you here?" We were back to being professionals. Totally great.

"I've decided to use another clinic for treatment. I came for my medical file. I thought it fair to bring back yours."

"Excuse me?"

He lifted the lid. Inside the box were two, maybe three, dozen medical files. The Sturgis General Hospital logo emblazoned across the fronts of the files. I wiped the sweat from my upper lip, rubbing my hands on my jeans.

"How did you get these?" I asked, afraid to touch the box.

"They were delivered along with dozens of other boxes. Stuart likes to be thorough when he's trying to prove his innocence."

"I don't understand."

"Neither do I. But I wanted to make sure they went back to the right person."

Funny, I thought I'd feel more vulnerable when they arrived. At least anxious, or excited. There was just detachment.

I didn't know what to say to DI Cooper. Part of me didn't want to see him leave. Another part of me understood this was protocol—no more entanglements with me or the clinic. Why was he suddenly more important? I placed the lid back on the box.

"That must've been hard. To survive that," he said.

"It was." I couldn't lie to him anymore. Well, not about me.

"Is that why you became a doctor?"

"It's why I became a pathologist. To understand disease and prevent it. So that maybe it doesn't happen again."

"I never realized how deadly influenza could be."

"Is that what the files say?" I glanced at the box. Of course, he had read the files. It was his job. "That wasn't my guess."

"Your guess?"

"I've never seen them. It's why I came to Cambridge. What brought me to Hastings."

"I see." He stared at the windows of the gym. "Did you know Tousain had them?"

I nodded. "I thought he would let me see them the first week I arrived." That was a lifetime ago. "Then things changed." I stood and lifted the box. It was as big as I had expected, but the weight of it forced me to readjust my footing. DI Cooper reached for the box.

"How about I take those up? I've got to see Nate anyway."

I stared at his offer. He had strong hands, safe ones. It's not like he was going to take the files hostage. Because he was a good person. Despite knowing that, I hesitated. My life's ambition was the box. All the answers I had ever sought or hid from were in it.

"Abby?"

"Right." I handed him the box. He'd had them longer than I ever had. Why had James given them to him? When wasn't James playing me for a fool?

I threw my workout bag around my shoulder and we walked without conversation to the research building. Even as we entered the elevator, there was a quiet, a new barrier between us. Since the night in the hospital, every conversation, every look we had exchanged, and now with the files, DI Cooper was pulling away. And I wasn't ready to let him go.

"I know you probably don't want to talk to me about this, but how much of your accident do you remember?" I asked.

He rolled his eyes.

"Please. You've seen my medical file."

"I remember that day at work." He squinted. "I was upset about having to be home so early and changing into clothes I hated." He blew out a breath. "I had to meet Padma for a work thing. And then I have fragments of the car accident. The sounds, the smells, how everything seemed to be coming to an end."

"Did the accident happen after the work thing?"

"Yes. It was at Heritage House. I found Padma with..." He closed his eyes, struggling to remember, perhaps. "I found Padma with James."

He didn't sound convinced as much as he sounded resigned.

"Are you sure about that?"

"She never denied it."

"I don't think you can take Padma at her word. And I don't believe James would do that."

"What?" His tone had a little bit of confusion mixed with a whole lot of anger. "Stuart will do whatever he pleases, including kidnapping, hitting women, creating shell companies, hundreds probably, blatantly lying to people, consuming blood. Oh, and getting away with murder."

I watched the elevator count off floors. DI Cooper didn't want to believe in the make believe. He wanted facts. And I certainly didn't have them all. "What's the statute of limitations on murder in this country?" I asked.

"Why? Are you hoping I'll wait until you leave to build my case?"

"Why would I leave?"

"Why would you stay now that you have these?" He lifted the box. "Or can you not walk out of here a free woman?"

He had made a very good point. The elevator opened and we exited, relieved to have a time out. I pulled my badge from my bag. We passed Nate's office and turned the corner. A dreadful cold slithered up my spine. The collar of my hoodie was soaked with sweat. Great.

I swiped my badge and pushed open the door to my lab.

"You keep a tidy office space. Where would you like the box?"

It wasn't tidy as much as it was underused. "Counter is fine."

I watched him place the box on the counter. Even noted how muscular his arms were. He examined the room and wrinkled his nose.

"Do you keep blood in here?" he asked.

I pointed to the refrigerator to his left. "I have some

cultures growing." I glanced at the other units. "But no, no blood."

He sniffed. "I thought I smelled blood."

I guess he would have a nose for it. "Thank you."

"Not a problem." He turned to the door.

"No, I mean, thank you for letting me go the other night. And looking after me. And listening. I know that wasn't easy for you. None of this has been easy for me."

He folded his arms. He appeared to be making a serious effort to come up with a reply. Maybe this was the moment to thank him for the curry too.

"It would..." He uncrossed his arms. "It would make me very happy to see you take that box and leave here. I don't believe Stuart has your interests at heart. Go back to Stanford. Before it's too late."

It was a slap to the face. I dropped my gaze to the floor. My eyes burned with pain. I pulled open the door of my office, and held my tongue. He walked through without another word. What would be the point of telling him to stay away from his possessed ex fiancée? He wouldn't believe any of the reasons.

Screw that.

I yanked open my door and called after him. "DI Cooper, the car you drove the night of your accident, was it the same model you drive now?"

He didn't turn to look at me, just stopped in the hall and looked up at the ceiling. If he thought it was fine to push me away, well, he had figured wrong. I was getting used to it.

"Yes. It is."

"Why would you get the same car?"

I heard his sigh. He turned to answer me.

"Because I didn't want to run away from my fears."

Everything he said had become a barb. I wasn't running away. Not anymore.

There was a shimmer along the ceiling, not unlike the way water catches sunlight. I watched it undulate on to the wall in waves. My throat tightened. I walked out into the hall and approached him.

George sniffed again and grimaced. Something about his eyes, they had changed, no longer warm with concern. They were policeman's eyes, on full alarm.

I watched a shadow creep around the elevator, near Nate's office.

"Take care, Dr. Whiting."

I sprinted down the hall and snatched his arm before he could knock on Nate's door.

"I don't think he's in." My voice sounded unnaturally high.

George knocked with his other hand. There was no answer. There was no one in Nate's office. He shot silent questions at me. Ones I couldn't answer.

"I smell blood," he said. His eyes glistened.

"Don't go in there." I gently pulled on his arm.

He tried the door, but it was locked. I gasped with relief.

"Abby." He placed his hands on my shoulders. "Please step away."

I silently pleaded with him to not follow his instinct, but I had already asked for more extensions than I deserved.

It took him one kick to bust open the door.

"Oh God," I whispered.

A small river of blood ran across the middle of Nate's office floor, almost making it to the door. Nate was in his office chair—his lips were purple, his eyes clouded, his head slightly tilted as if he were confused. There was a hypodermic needle in his arm with a missing Vacutainer collection kit. His blood had drained onto the floor. There was a note on his desk.

George called out Nate's name. His voice wasn't loud or alarmed. It was lost behind brotherly love and loss. I reached out for him but the barrier was already up and it was impenetrable.

I heard the elevator ping. Two employees came out. One screamed. It was Padma.

The next few minutes played out in a sick slow motion —Padma screaming and collapsing as George kept her from Nate's office, security officers rushing to the floor and pushing me aside, sirens out in the parking lot, red alarm light flashing in the hallways.

I stared at the shimmer hovering above the door to Nate's office, watched it dissipate, and take a ghostly shape.

There stood Nate, waving at me behind his own dead body, behind the veil of the living. I slumped to the floor and listened to the rush of blood, pulsing in my head.

38

PERMANENT DAMAGE

I didn't go home. I couldn't. There were three interviews, all filled with the same questions. First with DCI Helderman, then Hastings security, and finally, the legal department. DI Cooper had left hours ago. Vic had come to get him. She had given me a polite stop-screwing-with-my-partner glare. The police had cleared me to leave, but I couldn't. I stared out the window and waited for the clinic to approach sleep. I had spent enough hours here to know that it, too, slept.

There was no sleep for the feint of suspicion.

I had called down to the emergency room and requisitioned the record of my emergency room visit. They had run a full blood panel after my panic attack. I also noticed Nate had viewed the results of that panel last night at two in the morning.

He was still alive at that hour. There was a security clearance required for the details of the report. The hospital couldn't deny a patient a physical copy of the report, but I suspected Nate had run his own tests.

Had Nate discovered what I already understood? Or had my blood finally fallen susceptible to disease?

After Gayle, my lab partner, had passed away at Stanford, I had spent days testing my blood. Aggressive strains of lung cancer, H1N1, and Ebola—not a cell had been damaged. I had risked every threadbare professional connection to get access to those pathogens, using equipment that logged every trial. All the while being under investigation. It was a wonder I had pulled off any of it. Only to destroy the miraculous results.

I had universal immunity.

Every single time, through every trial, my blood survived. But now, I was vulnerable. Disease was plaguing my every waking moment. I could barely keep water down.

I needed Nate's clearance, or James's permission, to access whatever trial Nate had run.

The night DI Cooper had found me, Nate had moved and adjusted the blood inventory, ensuring James would have blood for "transfusion" when he returned. The form also indicated James would donate blood, which had to be a mistake. I leaned into my screen, studied the form closer, and realized it had an extra set of details in the corner.

On instinct, I picked up my phone to call Nate, and quickly realized I would never speak to him. Ever.

The phone fell out of my hand and bounced on the counter. Part of me refused to believe I would never see his playful smirk or hear another poorly timed come-on, that none of this was happening, that I could wake up free and clear of this nightmare. My computer pinged again, and I wanted to throw it against the wall.

I yanked James's medical file from my desk and compared the forms in the file to the ones on my screen. The forms were almost identical except for the new column of information. Why hadn't I seen this column before? I entered the new parameters in the clinic's search engine.

One command flashed across the screen.

Please enter security clearance.

Frustrated, I rubbed my face and held my head between my hands. I cracked open a window and watched more cars leave the employee parking lot. There were only a dozen left now. Nothing like a murder to get people home earlier than usual. My stomach gurgled. After James had left with the Cambridge police two hours ago, food had been sent to my office. He had casually waved from the path as he passed my office window like it was any other day at the office. In that moment, I imagined him dead. I imagined him suffering as much as DI Cooper was now.

But death was his normal. And Charlotte was the source of infection.

The food tray sat on top of the box of files DI Cooper had brought. I had ignored my box of secret past. They were no longer relevant or meaningful. I removed the tray to take it to the break room to reheat or toss, I hadn't really made my mind up. On the corner of the box was an archive sticker for the clinic. It had Tousain's name on the label, an archive location code, and another eleven-digit code.

Eleven digits. Just like the security clearance.

My gaze ping-ponged from the box to the computer screen. I entered the number.

Six windows bubbled open across my screen, giving me a panoramic view of James's blood transfusion history. Some of it I had reviewed before, but there were two new windows. Windows I couldn't have accessed before, because I never had the right clearance. But now, I had Tousain's number.

Even though the records listed Tousain as the primary

physician, Nate had managed the blood inventory for the last ten months. Every time James had come in for blood, he'd left blood, at a two-to-one ratio. If he received four units, he donated two. The two processes were not independent of each other either. Which made no sense. The log also displayed a fluctuating inventory. I had only requisitioned ten units since taking on James's case. So who else was using the blood?

If James were a prudent philanthropist, he'd have multiple researchers working on his problem. But that would require an immense amount of trust, which I knew to be of limited supply.

I scanned through the report until I noticed another anomaly. Almost six months ago, the inventory had peaked with twenty units of blood collected over a two-week period. Too much blood to take from a normal person, but he had the power to heal and regenerate.

Nate had approved moving the units of blood not to Tousain's department code, but another. I keyed in the number in the archive directory. I received an error message. The number was too short for the report directory. But it was short enough to be a department or patient record. I stretched and paced the length of my office. I keyed in the number into the patient record directory. And got another error message.

Crap.

It had to be a patient record. Everything about James was a well-crafted secret. All allies were blind, with trapdoors. But the man went out of his way to document his history. The room I had discovered under Heritage House was a testament to his inability to let history go. I printed out the inventory report and raced to the elevator. The doors closed and I felt the intrusive eyes of the security camera. I folded the report and slid it into my pocket.

The archive and research library of the Hastings Clinic took up the entire second floor. The size of the place instantly swallowed my renewed confidence. I gripped the paper and walked up to the reference desk. Unsure I could trust anyone, I carefully folded down the report until only the code showed.

"I'm new here," I said to the reference librarian. "I'm trying to track down a patient file that's gone missing."

The heavy-set woman pulled up her reading glasses and smiled.

I stood a little taller. "Can you tell me which department this code designates?"

"That would be the acute trauma clinic," the librarian said.

I took a step back, dumbfounded. James could sustain a traumatic injury, so why would they risk bringing him there? His body could heal in a matter of hours, maybe a couple of days at worst. He could regenerate muscle tissue, organs, and bones, no medical supervision required.

I pulled a chair up to a computer terminal, swiped my badge, and ran another query. I entered dates, department codes, and physician names. The computer listed twenty matches, all tied back to Nate's employee number. I scanned the file types and noticed an archive code for radiology. I jotted the number down and walked down the rows of shelves, scanning the labels.

After twenty minutes, my nerves had coiled at the base of my neck. I wasn't even close to a match. "Dammit."

All seven employees in the library looked at me. I zeroed in on the nearest fellow employee, a man hogging an entire table with papers strewn about like a file had exploded.

Out of ideas, I walked up to him and asked, "Where do I find archived X-rays?"

The man glanced at me and looked at his papers with longing. They weren't small children about to be abandoned. Jesus.

"You can just point," I said, giving him a soft shove.

He stood reluctantly, circled a number on his work, and marked his place with a ruler for extra assurance. The man was unnervingly tall, almost seven feet, and extremely lanky. His thick glasses eroded any sense of threat. He headed to the south side of the building.

"Where in America are you from?" he asked.

"What?"

"You're an American, right?"

"Oh. Yeah, California. The Bay Area."

"Bay Area? Like San Francisco?"

"Silicon Valley."

"I have a cousin in San Ramon. Is that part of Silicon Valley?"   •

"No. But it's part of the Bay Area. It's the East Bay."

"Are you an intern?"

"No." I kept my tone curt and impolite.

He got the hint and stopped asking questions. We had crossed a quarter of the floor. He pointed to a row of archive shelves with oversized bins. "They only keep film for five years, but everything gets scanned before disposal."

With my current luck, the film had been destroyed. I quickly covered the distance of one row and stared at a lower bin. It had the correct number range, and the excitement vibrated my chest. I snatched the bin and flipped through the records. I found the record labeled 3445-os.

I pulled the envelope and searched for a patient name. The envelope only had a patient number. The patient number didn't match James's patient ID. It was a thousand digits off. I slid the X-ray from the envelope and held it to the light. The X-ray was of a spinal cord, with a clean hairline break four vertebra above the pelvic bone.

"That's a shame. No recovery from that," the man said.

I nearly jumped out of my skin, and shot the man a severe glare.

"Sorry, someone you know?" he asked.

"I'm not sure." I scanned the black transparency once more and found nothing but the patient number. No patient name. But there were two sets of initials in the corner. "Are these physician initials?"

"Yes, but this looks like an outside specialist was brought in, otherwise it would've been coded properly."

"Is there a way I can find the consulting physician?"

"You'd probably need to track down someone in the billing department."

I had no time to hunt down a fucking accounting clerk.

"That kind of injury would've required multiple surgeries," he said. "If he were brought here first, he wouldn't have been moved to a consulting hospital until after he was stabilized. We have a good trauma unit, but not the best. He would've been moved to Christchurch."

I jogged to another computer terminal and keyed in the patient ID. The screen returned no name, just the same numerical code. "Okay, you little shit." My fingers keyed in another query, pulling all files associated with the number. Forty-three results. But each time I clicked a file, only the confidential patient number appeared. I slammed my fist on the table.

My seven-foot coworker walked over and peered down at the screen. "That just means the files have been moved into storage. You have to go through formal approval to pull those kind of files."

"Why?"

"Because the patient is dead. And family has to be notified to have those records requisitioned."

I cradled my pounding head in my hands, fighting my desire to scream. I heard tapping on the keyboard and the mouse clicking.

"Although you can still pull up pharmacy records," he said.

I looked down at the screen and watched the man key in a foreign language.

"I've been to San Francisco twice, it's a charming city," he said. "The food is fantastic. I had squid ink pasta at one place. Better than Venice."

I tried to soften the stress lines fracturing my forehead, but it was too much to ask. He pulled up the basic search form, planted the dates of the X-ray file, and entered the pharmacy code. The computer spit out a screen full of lines by date.

"That's odd. Looks like the patient has continued to have prescriptions refilled. The last physician to prescribe was Nathan Rothschild. As recently as last month. That doesn't make sense, unless someone is, well... scamming."

He keyed in another field and the screen revealed the medications. As I read through the list of medications, my limbs loosened, felt heavy and distended.

"You alright?" he asked.

I leaned over the screen, hoping to shield it from further review. "Thank you for your help. I thought there was an anomaly. This is a very serious violation and I want to maintain the privacy of the doctor."

"Right."

"Can I have your name? So that when I write up my report, you'll be credited for your help."

"Geary. Arthur Geary."

I shook his hand, and watched him walk back to his table. My lungs were straining for air and I prayed I didn't look as red as Author's blushing cheeks.

Of the five medications listed, I recognized three of them. I snapped the X-ray to the light and scrutinized the spinal injury. He should be in a wheelchair. The human spine could never recover, could never repair, and could never walk after that kind of damage. Ever.

39

BROKEN

"Boss, it's time to go," Vic said.

George didn't move. There was a heavy, sharp pain radiating through his entire body. It kept him anchored next to his dead friend. Martin, the coroner, watched him from across the room afraid to approach Nate's body while George remained.

"Let Martin do his job." Vic placed her hand on his shoulder.

George covered his mouth, words swimming to be free only to drown seconds later.

"Why?" he asked Nate. Because the note wasn't enough.

Sorry, mate. Sorry about the accident, about Padma, for everything.

George heard Vic strain to keep from crying. Strange, he knew she never cared much for Nate. Her heart rate was erratic, straining for the calm of nicotine.

There was a knock. DCI Helderman entered the room. He glanced up at Vic and nodded at George.

"The family's here. Do you want to speak to them?" Helderman asked.

George shook his head, didn't look at his superior.

"How about we give you a few minutes alone? And then Vic can take you home."

The thickness of cancer thickened Helderman's already phlegmy baritone.

"Rebus, you should probably schedule a checkup," George said.

"Pardon?" Helderman asked.

"The breathlessness you feel. You should have that looked at."

Confused, they all glanced at one another. But George held them all off with a harsh glare of his own. *Leave me alone.* One by one, they scuttled around his wake and left.

"This isn't happening." George shook his head. "You posh bastard. This is not how you go out. It's too melodramatic. And you promised to call."

He hovered over Nate's lifeless body.

"Why?"

He asked over and over until he couldn't breathe or see.

40

SACRED WORDS

B lack and navy suits continued to climb from cars, meandering down the crowded sidewalk, filing into the chapel. I tried to focus on all the hats, instead of my growing anxiety. There were many hats, but time continued to roll out a sand pebble at a time. Another ten minutes until Nate's memorial service started. I stood off to the side by the parking lot, pretending to scan email on my cell phone. I needed to sit close to the back, close to the door. Just in case.

The chapel was no larger than an old farmhouse, sitting on a grassy hillside. It was made of white sandstone peppered with red and brown bricks that must've been added through restoration. To any other foreigner, it was a stunning remnant of an older time, perhaps a simpler time. For me, it loomed larger than an iceberg ready to tear into the hull of my childhood, revealing its contents to all the mourners.

There had been so many funerals in Sturgis, enough to fill a lifetime. Everything had changed after that autumn, as it should have, but I had refused to let that horrible memory dictate my life. Refused to believe it continued to cast shadows on my life's work—saving others from disease.

My lunch of saltine crackers and water bubbled and squirmed. A cold sweat plastered my skin thicker than Cambridge's constant damp air. I wanted to feel the sun, but the sky was a thick plane of gray. It was uncomfortably dark for three o'clock in the afternoon. The decision to relocate to this old town was crossing from the opportunity of a life-time column into the biggest mistake of my life column.

Someone rubbed my arm, startling me.

"Sorry. Are you alright?"

It was DI Cooper. I marveled at his civility. I shut my eyes and took a deep ragged breath. "No, not really. You?" I tried to look him in the eye, but once the traces of sadness became apparent, I looked over his shoulder at the passing cars.

"You're shaking. It's warmer inside," he said.

"I've never been to a Church of England service. Is it long?" His mouth hung open like I had asked him for a cigarette. "I'm sorry. Nerves. I have a tough time with funer-als." My heel dug into the moist lawn, numbing my cowardice.

"Depends on how long the speeches last, probably an hour, hour and a half."

A woman with a large black hat cast across her face walked up to George and waited for his company. I recog-nized the coral lipstick. My blood ran cold.

Padma lifted her gaze and I was starstruck. Despite the lack of sun and shading from the hat, her skin glowed. She offered a congenial smile, but her borrowed eyes conveyed a deep threat. She looked secure standing next to him, no longer overtly touchy-feely.

"George, we need to get inside." Padma looked like she

didn't like to weather the weather. How could a revenant walk into a church? How could I ever explain to DI Cooper his former fiancée wasn't human?

"Yes, you're running out of time." My tone was far south of polite.

"I'll see you inside," George said to me, and escorted who he believed was Padma into the chapel.

I watched them with a deadly sense for detail. Charlotte's stiletto heels didn't clatter while walking, the grace of her hips swayed with ethereal elegance, and her regal profile didn't flinch a smile for anyone. This was a woman possessed of the poise I lacked. DI Cooper kept his hand at the small of her back. Surely, he suspected she wasn't Padma?

The somber bellows of a church organ announced the beginning of Nate's funeral. I checked my watch, not volunteering any unnecessary minutes of torture. The hymn I recognized—I had two minutes to wait at the back, and pray my childhood phobia wouldn't catch anyone's notice.

One minute and thirty seconds.

The ushers, flocked in white, eyed me with warm impatience. I didn't budge. I watched the crows gather on the rolling lawn. I noticed Colonel Pride sitting in a parked car. He lifted his hand to say hello. Nate had said he'd been a medic in the army. Afghanistan. Of course.

Fifty seconds.

I entered the church. The skin on my face tightened.

The small chapel was swelling to hold its contents. I reminded myself this wasn't a child's funeral or a playmate's funeral or a neighbor's funeral. Just a colleague's funeral, who may have been murdered by my only patient or my only patient's psycho lover.

The organ's wail slowed and quieted. I strategically

examined the layout, counting steps to exits, finding the last three remaining seats, found the one closest to a wall and the door. And sat, ignoring everyone's dismay.

I removed a tissue from my pocket, struggling with tremors in my hand. This symptom was misdiagnosed as sorrow by my pew neighbors and they each gave me a soft smile. I laced my hands together and they quickly wrestled apart. The service had barely begun, and my body was giving out. I shut my eyes, sat on one hand and placed the other on the cold wall, to steady, to feel something tangible, because the untenable damage under my skin was anchoring its claws.

I heard bodies shuffle and move around me.

Please, please, please. Don't seat anyone near me. Please.

Warm fingers wrapped around my wrist.

Shit.

"I've got you," James said.

Relief flooded my nervous system at the sound of his familiar timbre. It didn't matter what had transpired, I needed a life preserver. No matter how damaged. I bowed my head, kept my eyes shut, laced my fingers with his, and gripped.

"I didn't think you could come into a church," I said.

"Where else are the damned supposed to go?"

Unable to contain my wonder, I looked at him. It had been a couple weeks since we had shared a room, let alone a conversation. He wore a fitted slate grey wool suit, with a bright white shirt, and a dark purple tie. Elegant and composed, a sharp contrast to me.

The ceremony started with a welcome from the chapel's vicar. After two hymns, my skin no longer pulsed and the walls didn't shimmer, my anxiety was under a modicum of control. The chapel was beautiful in its simplicity. No garish paintings or portraits of the crucifixion. Clean white brick walls whose only character came from age and endurance. There were a series of stained glass windows depicting the Madonna and child, reminding me of Nate's boyish dimples.

There came the benediction, and my mouth moved, remembering the words that had erased my childhood. Muscle memory was a cold friend.

Nate's father spoke. I listened to find any similarity between father and son, but Nate's father was stoic and formal, no hint of mischief or playfulness. My father was quiet and had a dry wit, but he didn't hide from friendship and life the way I had. Sometimes the fruit falls and tumbles so far from the tree.

DI Cooper stood. His tall frame climbed the three steps to the podium with quiet resignation. My sick curiosity wondered how he would fare. I prayed his voice didn't crack under pressure, the way mine surely would. He pulled a single note card from his inside pocket.

"I don't want to talk about Nate."

A hush overtook the church. His casual, friendly voice had strengthened over a course of seven words to become a full-bodied tenor.

"Because he was a complicatedly bad but good man. Nor do I wish to list the many achievements of a man who had far too many ahead of him."

A lesser man would've choked on emotion, but it was as if DI Cooper's sorrow had doubled his strength. There was no tremor in his voice. His shoulders buttressed the oppression of loss and his hands rested on the podium with the lightness afforded only by courage.

And I was awestruck.

"I met Nate when I was twelve. I had been sent away to St. James Academy for boys. I assure you, it wasn't for my education. I have never known my father, and my mother was a dead junky. Being sent away was my last shot at survival. My last shot at a normal life. I had convinced myself that it would be wise to blend in with the best. To stand apart, by standing above the outsiders and the outcast, and to be rather outspoken about it.

This charmed my new chums to no end, and in three months' time I found myself standing atop a classmate's face. At the time, I believed I had truly distinguished myself."

George's expression softened like an angel had caressed the pain from his heart.

"When I pulled my foot from the boy's mouth to listen to his garbled words, I was struck by his fierce determination to set me straight. After years of eluding classification, he had nailed me with one phrase.

He called me a textbook cliché. A bully not worth footnoting in the school paper. A boy so afraid to stand on his own that I spent all my time showcasing my expected weaknesses instead of serving up my unique strengths."

George's smile beamed from the dais, cutting through my misery, my regret, and my fear.

"Nate never feared telling me the truth." George's gaze roamed the church, and then fell on me. "Never feared pointing out my careless insecurities, my short-sighted triumphs, and my false ambitions. Because he was more dedicated to what I could never acknowledge. My potential."

The air became safe to breathe again. My clothes were no longer ropes twisting and burning my skin. I listened to each of his words, consumed them, and used them to plaster my guts.

"He was always the first to celebrate my success. And I

fear..." George's eyes fell on me again. "And I fear without him I shall always walk with a permanent flaw." His mouth hesitated and hot tears fell onto my hands, rolling through my fingers. "Nothing will be normal, but I will keep his faith. I owe him so much more than that."

James retook my hand into his, which surprised me. I hadn't noticed letting go.

"I'm okay." I folded my hands together in my lap. My attention riveted to the man I had grossly underestimated.

George lifted his note card and slid it back into its resting place, the inner left breast pocket. His bottom lip threatened to make a painful frown, but he quickly recovered when Nate's mother shook his hand.

I had never cried in public, not in my adult life. After hearing the chorus of sniffles throughout the chapel, I didn't feel embarrassed or ashamed. There was a communal unity to the act, and for once I didn't question belonging.

The vicar took the stage and walked the congregation through prayer. James handed me a prayer book. Worried I would offend, I held the book for comfort. There wasn't a standard funeral prayer I hadn't memorized. It was a language I spoke fluently. Funny, I didn't think the wall I had built around my childhood could be climbed.

I mouthed John 6:35 and studied the high-pitched roof. A black shadow undulated in the corner of the ceiling behind the vicar. It looked like a dirty cobweb rippling under a draft but it hadn't been there earlier.

The shadow crept from the ceiling and slithered down the wall like a swath of black silk tapestry. I glanced out the window. The sun still lay buried beneath the overcast gray sky, making it incapable of casting a shadow. I shook off the optical illusion, chalking it up to panic-induced exhaustion.

Like Lazarus, I arose from my dead childhood memories, and distracted my anxiety by listening to James's voice. Watched him recite the words, and wondered when they had lost their value, lost their meaning for me.

"'The Lord is my shepherd.'" The words fell from my lips with ease. Like picking up a conversation with an old friend. A black spot flickered in my peripheral vision. I bit the inside of my bottom lip and began the mental argument.

This isn't happening. I'm tired. I'm beyond tired. Your mind is playing tricks.

The shadow took shape and a boy perched himself on the rail to the side of the vicar. The boy stared right at me. I gripped the pew, my body shaking with dreadful familiarity.

I'm losing my mind.

The boy was no more than seven years old, wore a tight-fitting black suit with a white shirt. The standard outfit any parent would strap onto a child for church, except it clung to his thin frame like he had been baptized in it.

"'He makes me lie down in green pastures and leads me beside still waters…'"

His black suit and the white walls surrounding him accentuated his gray pallor and dead eyes. The boy seemed familiar, like the boys who had lived in my nightmares.

"'He shall refresh my soul and guide me….'"

I slammed my eyes shut and pieced together the mechanics of inhaling air. It didn't help that my body had been deprived of sustenance for almost a week. Sickened by my own cowardice, I opened my eyes and the boy vanished. A moan of relief escaped my lips.

He reappeared in the front row, squatting on the shoulders of mourners.

"'Though I walk through the valley of the shadow of death…'"

Why does death follow me? The boy crept across rows of

attendants with the shiftiness of a fox hunting for his small prey. His eyes crucified me. I couldn't move.

"'I shall fear no evil; for you are with me...'"

Dying boys and girls were with me. Would always be with me because I hadn't released them. I thought I had left them in Sturgis. I had attended every one of their funerals, but I hadn't acknowledged their weight. The boy was just two rows to my right. My panic began to catch the attention of the mourners surrounding me.

A shroud of water covered the boy like a wall between him and reality, the wall between him and me. The water glimmered on his skin, but I saw no trace of water beading on the floor, or on the mourners he rested on. Heads began to turn as he hopped toward me.

"'You spread a table before me in the presence...'"

Tables...tables. In a flash, I was back in quarantine. Medicine tables and medicine trays. Beds, beds. Beds of children crying, praying, dying. Beds, beds, beds. White beds, red beds. My vision blurred, and I no longer knew where I was. I just knew it was hell.

The boy crawled onto James's lap and my bones evaporated.

"'You have anointed my head with oil...'"

The boy reached out and touched my cheek. The cold caress burned and I jerked away, bumping my head against the wall. I wiped my cheek and found water on my fingertips. James wrapped his arm around my shoulder and his eyes said everything I didn't want to hear.

They acknowledged my singularity, and my madness, because he wore the look of concerned confusion. He didn't see the boy perched on his lap. He didn't feel the child's presence.

I was alone with the dead. Again.

"'...and mercy shall follow me all the days of my life,'"

Death will follow me for the rest of my life. The boy smiled, and instead of teeth, water poured from his mouth down his chin onto his suit.

But I saw blood. Blood running from tear ducts, blood staining sheets, and blood splattering my cheeks as my playmates coughed in quarantine. Instead of offering this child a helping hand, I bolted out of the chapel, knocking and shoving chairs and people from my manic escape.

I would never dwell in the house of the Lord. Because I was cursed with immunity. And disillusion.

I yanked my keys from my coat pocket, ripping the lining. The gray sky opened and let loose rain, not an onslaught, but enough to impair my already blurred vision. Shoving the car key into the door with blind force, I pinched my index finger, tearing the skin. I sucked on my bleeding finger, pulling the door open with my other hand.

The door thumped shut and the rain pelted the roof of the car, reminding me there would be no quiet. No peace. I reached for the steering wheel and realized I was sitting in the passenger seat of a British rental car.

"God dammit." I punched a dent into the roof. "I hate this place," I wailed and laid my forehead on the dashboard. The dashboard smelled of cigarette smoke and car cleaner, cuffing my stomach with nausea.

Knock, knock.

I didn't lift my head. "Go away." There weren't enough nerve cells left to handle James or his concern or lack thereof.

Knock, knock.

"Leave me alone."

The driver's door popped open and the car gave under the weight of James taking a seat.

"I told you. To leave me. The fuck. Alone." I whipped my head up to launch a sneer.

At Detective Inspector Cooper.

I leaned my head back and mouthed another expletive.

"What's going on?" His tone was soft like a pat on the hand from a really good friend, or a really worried one.

I didn't have it in me to explain. "I want to go home."

He looked out the window. "Me too."

"No, back to Stanford. I don't belong here." I didn't have the courage to stand apart and above it all.

His eyes darted back and forth like he was examining my vision or gauging my sincerity. He rubbed rain from his chin. The rain continued assaulting the car.

"I'll see what I can do. Maybe not this week, but I'll get you back to where you belong." He gripped my hand, not like a friend, but as if he were making a promise. It rattled me because it was genuine. How would he ever make it back?

"I'm going to be sick."

I ran from the car, holding my stomach. I fought for every step and made it behind a row of rose bushes to retch with some privacy. Between eruptions I listened to the rain pound and sizzle. It was warm, but not enough to make rain sizzle. I stared down and watched the contents of my stomach etch and burn the ground.

Oh God, what now? What was happening to me?

The clip of Detective Cooper's rushed walk rang like an alarm bell, and I kicked dirt over the strange evidence bubbling on the ground.

I tried to lift my head to spot him but my stomach contracted with the force of a pressure cooker. I heard him shuffle to a stop and I waved, signaling him to keep his distance. He disappeared from view. Relieved to be alone, I bent down closer to watch the dark red acid from my stomach bubble. Stomach acid could react with other elements but I was fairly certain the ground didn't have a huge sodium component.

I dangled my head between my knees, my stomach settling, and liquid poured onto the ground off to my right. I spotted DI Cooper's wingtip shoes. Before I could protest, he placed a cool cloth on the back of my neck. My eyes rolled back in relief.

"Better?" he asked.

I nodded, coughed, and blocked his view of the black, bubbling puddle. He tilted a water bottle under my nose. I took the water and rinsed out my mouth, making sure to dilute God-knew-what was on the ground. I pulled damp-ened tissues from my pocket, wiping my eyes and nose clear.

Dark crevices of worry wove across his forehead and he was careful not to stare. He occupied his hands by refolding his handkerchief into a series of neat rectangles. The church organ vibrated, a chorus of voices floated from the chapel across the lawn.

"I need to get back," he said.

I stared at his soaked head of hair and his rain-stained suit, and shame gripped me once more. "I'm sorry. Sorry for everything." *Sorry I'm not strong enough to stay and help you with the truth.*

He squeezed water from his handkerchief and nodded. "Me too." He walked back to the church, and I was adrift. Someone had cut my safety net.

41

EXCHANGING OF VOWS

James stood over Nate's grave, keeping his hands occupied by turning a coin in his pocket. He smelled the sweet aroma of wet grass and the rich dug-up earth. He no longer smelled the perfume of death. It almost brought tears to his eyes.

The cars continued to pour out of the cemetery, heading home or heading to the Rothschild estate in Grantchester. Colonel Pride had called ten minutes ago. Abby had safely made it to the reception. She was finally showing signs of evolution.

There was a comfortable breeze, holding notes of rose water.

Charlotte in Padma's dead body stood next to him.

"You made a promise."

James nodded. "I did. Do you know how much the world has changed these last twenty years?" She always looked stunning in black.

"Smart phones, the Internet, artificial intelligence. Terrorism, pornography, slavery. People are not all that different than I remember."

He bit the inside of his cheek and tasted blood.

She lightly kicked a clod of dirt. "Such a shame. I almost regretted it."

"Why Nate?"

"Why not?" She shrugged and smiled.

"Surprised you waited so long."

"I wanted to see what it would feel like to watch him suffer. He was a little frightened but I think he was relieved to go. The guilt was killing him."

"You still want the American? Or would you prefer a more dazzling person? Someone with a title perhaps? Or at least a legacy." He touched Padma's face.

She pulled away. "Why did you fuck her?"

James pouted. "Felt sorry for her. She's so lonely. And why not test drive next year's model? You'll be pleasantly surprised."

"That whole scene in the church." She sneered and shook her head. "Cleary, she's a little off."

"I've always adored crazy."

Charlotte stood taller. "How many funerals have we attended here now?" She scanned the tombstones.

James clenched his fists. "I can't recall."

"Fifteen, sixteen?" She tapped Nate's headstone with the tip of her stiletto. "How can you stand there and look at all that you've laid to waste?" She threaded her arm into his. "You believe I'm full of malice. But look at all the pain you've caused. Such terrible viciousness. It's almost criminal, wouldn't you say?"

"I'll bring the doctor to the church this evening."

Charlotte beamed. "That's almost cruel." She held her hands behind her back. "And no tricks, my love. Or there will be more funerals for the Detective to attend. I wonder how many it would take to break him? You know how much

I enjoy watching a good man break."

James wrapped his hand around her arm. "Tonight. It will be over." He leaned in to kiss her.

She stopped him short and stared into his soul. "Tonight, it begins. We begin."

He kissed her on the cheek. "You should try a breath mint. You smell of death."

42

A PINT

"I appreciate you ditching the reception with me." I clinked Sergeant Turner's pint glass. "I didn't realize Nate was from such a privileged family. I mean, I knew he was well off, but that was like—"

"Yeah, old money. Really, old and cruel money. I didn't even want to disturb the air in that house. You sure you don't want a drink, drink?"

My tonic water was staying nicely put in my stomach. "I'm good."

"You hungry?"

"No, not really."

She pursed her lips.

"But if you are, please get something. You don't have to worry about me." I was getting better about picking up on other people's needs. "Have you been DI Cooper's partner for a long time?"

Vic rubbed her swollen nose. She had wept pretty hard at Nate's funeral, which was weird. I didn't think she really liked him. "I joined the department a few years after him.

Wasn't really working with him until two years ago, after I had busted my ass on a kidnapping case."

"So you knew him when he had his accident?"

"Yeah, why?"

I shook my head. "Just making conversation."

Vic waved down a waitress and placed an order for chips and samosas. "I think you're being nosy." She lifted her pint.

There was no way to hide the flush of embarrassment crawling up my neck. "Caught me, Sergeant." I raised my hands.

"Do you like George?"

I strained to keep my eyes in their sockets. I shrugged and nodded. I wasn't good under cross-examination. "He's a good person."

She took a generous gulp of her pint. "Yeah, he's fucking swell."

I rubbed my cheek. Her warning had registered.

The waitress delivered Vic's mountain of fried food. My eyes watered. She tossed a couple of fries into her mouth and pointed at her plate.

"Uh, no thanks. Do they have Newcastle on tap here?" I needed to try harder.

Vic smiled, tips of French fries shooting between her teeth. She ordered us two pints.

"What do you want to know about George?" she asked.

"Has he seemed different to you, since the accident?"

"How do you mean?"

"I've noticed the sporadic discomfort in his left hip. Are there any other physical ailments or behavior changes?" I was more interested in the latter.

The waitress delivered the pints. The brown ale was smooth and comforting. I may have closed my eyes and moaned.

"He's been more introverted."

"Introverted?"

"Quiet."

I stole a fry from her plate. She pushed the plate closer.

"He wasn't always this quiet?"

"Jabbering George?" She laughed. "No. He used to talk everyone's ear off. Like he didn't have a shut-off valve. Except when he was working a case."

"And now, he doesn't chat?"

"Didn't even talk to anyone his first month back. Literally, just yes and no, guv."

"He didn't talk about the accident?"

She shook her head. "We all went in to the clinic to check on him. He wouldn't acknowledge we were there, he just kind of checked out. And when he checked back in," she said, letting out a huff, "he was pissed."

We had eaten half of the fries and I hadn't even panicked about where the restroom was located. It was in the back left corner of the bar. Thirty paces away.

"Probably had a lot on his mind," I said. "Almost losing his life and all that."

"He has lost his life." She stared at me, lines creasing her brow and mouth. "His car, his fiancée, his promotion, his confidence, and now his best friend." She wadded up a paper napkin and threw it onto the plate of fries.

I bit my bottom lip and glanced at the television. There was nothing to say.

"Sorry," she said.

"It's alright." I drank half of my pint. We both avoided eye contact for the next few to five minutes. I had never been a fan of soccer, so my eyes wandered back to the cork-board of pictures behind the bar. The happy couple picture was off to the right just below the corner, nested between five other happy couples.

"No fucking way. I forgot about that photo," Vic said. "What an ass. I can't believe he brought you here."

"It wasn't a—" Before I could finish, she had stood and walked to the bar.

She leaned over, talking to the bartender. He brushed her off and she flashed him her badge. He followed her pointing finger and removed the picture of George and Padma. Vic sat down, drank more of her ale, and held the picture in her hand. A third of the picture had been folded over and faced me. I stared at Nate's darling dimples. My eyes stung.

I reached for the picture. "May I?"

I ironed the crease out and examined the three friends. The picture was taken a world ago, the world before the car accident, when the three were light-hearted and happy and hamming it up for a group selfie.

There was a striking symmetry to the photo with Padma as the midpoint.

Vic reached for the picture. She had to pull it from my hand. "I never understood why she liked George."

"Over Nate?"

Her brows crinkled. "Hmmm...I never considered that."

"And he still hasn't talked about the accident?"

"No. It's off limits. I think he believes it makes him look weak."

"Weak?"

"As a detective. That he can't remember all of it. And it bothers him to have to still go in for dialysis. Like he's some cripple or something."

I cleared my throat. "Besides the quiet, has anything else

changed? Does he keep later hours? Eat differently? Display any sun sensitivity? Stronger sixth sense?"

"He always keeps late hours. He always forgets to eat and take his meds. Always been a keen detective. Although his night vision has improved." She leaned across the table. "You know something bad about his health, doc?"

"No. No. He's in great health, and damn lucky. It could've been much worse." I kept my gaze direct and steady. Pretty proud I had pulled it off. She snatched a samosa and dipped it in chutney. "Does the Jantoven make him tired?" I asked.

"Is that the yellow one?"

"No, that's probably lisinopril." Which just confirmed two of the five prescriptions. Maybe I had chosen the wrong profession.

"He gets a little run down before it's time for him to go back for dialysis."

"But nothing else peculiar?"

"Besides the Stuart case? No."

I stared at the samosas. My stomach clenched.

"What happened that night?" she asked. "Off the record."

I interlaced my fingers and held them to my mouth. "Off the record?"

She nodded. Despite the friendly conversation, she was protecting her partner from further harm and I was trying to do the same by protecting my patient's shame. As much as I wanted to give her the truth, I couldn't give her the whole truth.

"My life irrevocably changed that night. I didn't ask for it. I may have deserved it. But you don't need to worry about me. If you want to protect George, you need to keep him away from Padma. She's very dangerous."

"Padma? Dangerous? Maybe when she chips a nail or

screws her boss." She leaned back and examined my face for audacity and perhaps a drop of insanity. "Did he drink your blood?" she asked. How could she not?

"James Stuart lives off the blood of others, but he would never hurt George. Far from it. I think Padma killed Nate." I pointed at the photo.

Vic stared at the picture, her mouth hanging open, her body not rigid with authority but limp with bewilderment. "Why?"

I glanced at my backpack. The X-ray showing George's damaged spine was inside. But there was no name, no record of the procedures, just coded archives. And I couldn't betray George. Not until I had my facts straight. And telling Vic Padma was Charlotte was even more ridiculous. "To have George back in her life." Under her lethal watch.

She continued to examine my face and I held her gaze, whispering in my mind, I'm not crazy, please, believe me. Her lips pursed and she looked at the photo. "She didn't even come to see him. Just left him hanging in hospital that first week."

She didn't believe me. I hadn't earned my way into Vic's circle of trust. She was a damn, fine friend to have. I finished my beer. "So now that DI Cooper is not as chatty, he probably doesn't mince words, huh?"

Vic had nice green eyes when they were fully open and not suspiciously squinting. "Nah, he's always been pretty honest."

I pulled out my credit card.

"No, no." Vic slammed down her glass and reached for her back pocket.

"I asked you for the drink, remember?" I handed my card to the waitress. Vic didn't even attempt to argue. She was growing on me.

"Ta." She lifted her glass. "What are you looking at?"

"Airfares."

"You're leaving? Why?"

"George asked me to." And I needed to go home and face my own demons.

"He probably didn't mean it."

I lifted my brows at her.

"That's not fair. You walked me into that one."

I shrugged. "It wasn't a date." She wasn't buying the fake smile. I pointed at the picture. "Any chance I could have that?"

She pulled out her phone, took a picture, and handed me the photo. "Is Stuart really going to let you fly out of here?"

I stood. "I'm not being held against my will, detective. And once he realizes I'm not that special, he will."

After we had said our goodbyes, I went for a run, a long one. And not at the Hastings employee gym. The rain had stopped and the air smelled of a world scrubbed clean. The footpaths around the university were well thought out, better than Stanford's. I had allowed my fear of the unknown cost me the best running days of my stay. The paths out of the university to the Fen were spectacular and I almost hated the idea of leaving it all behind.

I thought about everything DI Cooper had said. That James didn't have my interests at heart. He was correct. James wasn't interested in protecting me. George would want justice and maybe he would be the only person who could serve it to Charlotte. I wondered if he'd ever be open to the truth.

There was no guarantee that what I understood was painting a complete picture. But I had to hand it to James, he was a master of the art of deception. At the fifteen-mile mark, the sun had set and clarity pumped through my veins.

I hadn't felt this unafraid in a very long time. The ghostly figures had emerged from the river's fog. They tracked my pace, watched me turn and run back to town. I just hoped I could give James a run for his legacy.

43

IN POOR SPIRITS

George rubbed his temples, trying to block out all the chatter. He heard every single word, mumble, and half-ass conciliatory comment. The scent of coffee burning in the pot two rooms away reminded him of an ashtray. This would be the point in the evening when Nate would make a crass comment or lay odds on which special anyone he would take home.

Fuck.

The noise and the static polluted his ability to not think about everything. Why could he hear conversations held in other rooms? Why could he smell the sentiment of pity cast in his direction? Why could he taste the disappointment in the room? It was overwhelming.

Padma crossed the room, a glass in each hand.

Why did she walk that way? That wasn't her walk.

She sat across from him and handed him a whiskey. He thanked her and placed the glass on the table next to him. There was no reason to suffer a blackout again. She placed her hand on his thigh, a little too high. An awful ribbon of regret slithered along his skin. He took her hand.

"Listen. About the other night. That was a mistake. I shouldn't have kissed you. And if I misled you, I'm sorry." He looked at her. She was a wall of serenity. "Things aren't back to the way they were. I still need to sort things out and I can't be with you. Not that way. I'm sorry."

She took a breath. It was forced. "Do you miss him?" she asked. "Does it hurt?"

What kind of fucking question was that? Why was she smiling?

"What's happened to you?" he asked.

There was a spark of light behind her eyes. "You're an interesting beasty." She had purred the words.

He jumped to his feet and ran for the water closet. The noise and chatter followed him into the tight space. But at least he couldn't pick up on everyone's cologne. He cupped cold water and splashed his face. He was losing his shit.

There was a delicate knock.

"Just a minute."

His hands shook and he fisted them into tight balls. The door opened. Padma slid inside.

"I need a minute," he said to her. She ran her fingers along his jaw. He carefully stepped away from her.

His phone chimed. Thank god, Vic. She had texted him a photo. A photo of himself with Padma and Nate with a caption that read: *Stay away from Padma. Why'd you send the American away? Dumb dick.*

She snatched his phone and giggled at the photo. "You need answers."

There was a new note to her perfume. It wasn't rose or cardamom. It was something stronger, more overt. It was carnal.

"Who are you?" he asked.

"Who do you want me to be?" She stepped into his

personal space. "You're going to be powerful. I can taste it." She licked his neck. "So powerful."

She ran her hands along his arms. A tight panic seized his chest. She took his left forearm and bit him, tearing his skin.

He pushed her against the wall. She laughed.

"You taste like the dead. He's never made anything for me before."

"What the bloody hell is wrong with you?"

He snatched a towel from the wall and blotted his arm. The blood coming from the bite mark was black. He turned on the water and ran his arm under it. There was no red. He was bleeding death.

"What is happening to me?"

"I think it's already happened, beasty. Don't you remember anything? I don't know how he did it, but he's pulled off something spectacular. I'm looking forward to finding out what kind of monster you are."

George smelled burned rubber. He heard the spit of oil splashing on the engine. He remembered the accident. The crunch of metal. The snapping of bones. The red, hot rage he felt that night for...No, that can't be right. Nate. He wanted to kill Nate. He stared at Padma.

"You were in the car."

"I wasn't in the car, love. Padma was in the car."

His vision tunneled. The room constricted. He remembered looking into Padma's eyes in the car. Her dead eyes. There was something outside of the car. Something hungry for death.

"Stay away from me." He warned whatever was occupying Padma's body.

Padma cradled his face. "I think we have many years ahead of us to figure this out, beasty." She kissed him.

He yanked her away. "Did you kill Nate?"

She laughed. "Did I kill the man who fucked your fiancée?" She covered her mouth as if she he had uttered scandal. But George felt his stomach bottom out. "No, I like to take the people who hurt the most. They always taste the sweetest after they're gone. Like a crisp meringue. Melts on the tongue. I wonder what Nate will taste like? Betrayal? An Aston Martin? Or rosewater? Do you know he took her from behind at your birthday party? He was a naughty fuck."

Black rage pumped through his veins. "Shut up." He wrapped his hands around her throat. And squeezed, choking her laughter.

She gave him a wicked smile full of pleasure, curdling his blood. "Give me my new body, beasty." He smelled her arousal.

George yanked his hands off her throat and fled.

44

LAST CONFESSION

The chapel was quiet, quiet as my resolve. Somehow I knew James would be late to his own meeting. He enjoyed grand entrances. I hoped while I waited the small boy I had seen during Nate's service would appear. I wanted to wish him well, to help him heal, to confront my past—a little dress rehearsal for the man who filled my life with strange darkness and confidence.

I rubbed the puncture marks on my hand, and wondered how long I'd feel the scar tissue. Perhaps they would be my only memento from Cambridge. The scent of the air shifted from burning candles to sandalwood. I was no longer alone.

James sat next to me, in the front pew.

"Thanks for coming. After the service, I didn't think you'd come back here," he said.

"I wanted to face my fear."

"Make any progress?"

I smiled. "I just started."

Funny, I had hoped to feel nothing when I looked at him, but there was that timeless tether. If he pulled, I would follow. If I pushed, he would tempt. He smiled and cast his gaze at the raised podium. "What happened to you today? You gave the nice detective a good scare."

"I saw a little boy. Or he saw me. I think he was drowned here or somewhere nearby."

"Is he with us now?"

I checked around us and shook my head. "We're alone. But I can't make any promises. It's a chapel with a cemetery outside."

James laughed and his eyes glassed over. "My cousin was married here. It was a cold spring wedding. Rained all morning but it cleared up for the reception. Weddings were so simple then, a community affair."

There was a sharp pain twisting through my ribcage. I breathed through it. "You were married when you met Charlotte?"

James closed his eyes, taking his time to answer. "I never said I was a good husband."

"I never assumed you were."

But he regretted it enough to keep his wife's and children's remains close, a constant reminder of his infidelity. The moon pierced the stained glass windows, filling me with the strength only James believed I possessed.

"How long have you seen the dead?" he asked.

"I guess the logical answer would be after Sturgis, but it had been much sooner." I scratched the side of my cheek. All the slaps resurfacing. "I remember waking up with my mother one time. I think I was five or six. I'm not sure why she was in my bed. Probably had an argument with my dad. Anyway, I woke up and pointed to a child sitting in my closet." James's smile was warm, paternal, making me feel safe. "She told me I was just imagining it. The only person who ever believed me was Sam."

"Your brother."

I pressed my thumb into the scar tissue, trading physical pain for something else.

"What happened in Sturgis?" he asked.

"I got very sick. But so did a lot of other children at my school. We were all quarantined, thirty-one of us." I kept my gaze steady, stared straight through the candlelight. "The younger kids died within forty-eight hours. We didn't understand what was happening or why. None of the doctors had any answers. We all...we just understood fear. After three days, they wouldn't allow our parents to see us because it made everything worse. It's not comforting to be visited by a parent in a hazmat suit. We couldn't touch them and we couldn't go home." I covered the tremble in my voice by clearing my throat. "I had stabilized after the sixth day, but they kept me under observation. They couldn't figure out why I was getting better."

James took my hand. He rubbed small circles in my palm. If I wanted the truth from him, I needed to confess mine. I didn't have as much to lose.

"After a week, nineteen had died and four were close to dying, including my brother. I was terrified. So I did what most children do, I prayed." I stared at the dancing flames of the white candles on the altar. "I prayed every minute of every day in that hospital. And every night, someone came and took those children. She came quietly and she was so gentle. Who would've guessed she was an Angel of Death?"

"I'm sorry." He squeezed my hand.

"Me too." I took a deep breath. I still wasn't sure I'd ever get out all the words. "Because I had stabilized, and my brother was failing, they decided to do a transfusion. To see if my blood could boost his immunity. I even begged that thing. That evil thing to help save Sam. I made her promise.

Swore to her." The intensity of James's stare was layered with hope and salvation. "I don't understand how you found out. How you knew about those records. Or me. But I know that I'm not your miracle. My blood can't cure you. Can't fix your past. You made a mistake. I'm sorry I can't help you."

I stood and walked down the aisle. The weight I'd been carrying since Surges lifted and floated free. It shattered against the rafters. My only regret was I would probably perish to prove my point.

"Abby." I turned, but James kept his body to the altar, his gaze level to the cross. "I've spent most of my everlasting life watching people. Watching behavior and predicting outcomes." He crossed his chest in genuflection and stood. "I might be wrong about circumstance, but I'm never wrong about people." He faced me. "And I'm not wrong about you."

"He died. My brother died. My blood didn't save him."

There was an ugly crack in his confidence. "There is no record of him in that hospital."

"Because my father stole it. And he refused to sign the death certificate."

"But you sent him a package."

"Because I needed him," I screamed, wiping my eyes. "I needed to believe he was still with me. I wanted to believe someone was looking out for me. Because I'm all alone." The air burned between us and I let it consume what was left of my fear and his disappointment.

"You don't have to be alone. Not now."

"I can't save George," I said. "And you already have."

He walked up the aisle and I stood my ground.

"Clever girl." He kissed my forehead. "George is all I have left. My only family."

"Why didn't you just tell him?"

"I ruined his life because I didn't protect him enough. I

couldn't. Not without repercussions. And after Tousain figured out George and I were related, I suddenly felt..." He traced my cheek with his fingers.

"Powerless."

He stared deep into my eyes. "Human."

"Your companions. They're all friends of his?"

"Associates, teachers, classmates, enemies." His gaze was hypnotizing and blatantly honest. "It was the only way to know him without getting him killed."

"What do you get out of feeding?"

"A little peace and quiet. But sometimes I get a memory." His eyes had glassed over. *"A lovely recollection, pure and unedited. And it's beautiful."*

"And the accident?" I asked.

"Was an accident." James closed his eyes and shook his head. "I had been careful not to be anywhere near him. But you can't predict the human heart. One night, Nate called. He was in a complete panic. He'd seen George's car run off the road. I couldn't lose him."

"Nate was a companion? What were you thinking?"

"I'm alone in this world," he yelled, anguish peeling away all pleasantries.

"By choice."

"You made the same choice."

I stepped back. "Did you know she would kill Nate?"

He didn't answer. I backed away and swallowed my disgust. He had my truth. And I understood his. "I'm sorry, but I can't be a part of this. I can't help George. Only the truth can." I walked toward the door.

"What did you promise the angel that night?" James asked.

The edges of my vision dimmed, and I staggered. How did he know?

"Only the truth can save us now, Abby. What did you give up for Sam?"

I fell to my knees, the shameful truth too heavy to bear. The cold concrete cut into my knees, but only the agony in my chest registered. Acid flushed up my throat, the black bile threatening to make another appearance.

"Breathe, Abby," he whispered and wrapped his arm around my shoulders and lifted my chin. "Shhh...it's alright. There's nothing you wouldn't do for family. You and I understand that." He kissed my brow. "After all this time, don't you want to confess?"

I dug my nails into the floor, the uneven surface tearing them to shreds. I fought for air. "I promised..."

He took my hands and we kneeled in the aisle. "You promised..." he prompted, and his eyes grew shiny, lacquered with expectation.

"I promised to shepherd them, to help them go, if she let Sam stay. Their lives for his, the rest of them for him." A dark hush took over the chapel. I had become transparent and hollow. "They all died, she took all of them, except me," I choked. "I'm a monster, no different than you. I bartered the lives of eleven children to save my brother." And I would spend the rest of my life alone with my shame.

"You were a child. A frightened child."

I pulled away.

"And what happened when she came for Sam?" he asked.

I stared into the abyss of his clear blue eyes. "I kissed her. I kissed her until I bled. Until all I saw and felt was death. Until she was nothing."

Tears streamed down his cheeks, and they fell against mine, his mouth trembling over my lips. "Shepherd me from this place, Abby. Set me free." His kiss was as light as an angel's.

Light flashed through the stained glass windows. A car engine stopped. James pulled me to my feet. He brushed hair from my damp face.

"You were a child. What you did was brave and out of love." He wiped away my tears. "Please understand I cared for you very much."

Cared? Why was he speaking in the past tense? James walked to the altar. He lit more candles, casting a tall black shadow against the wall and up the ceiling.

I heard footfalls near the door.

"Do you know what I did this morning?" James asked. He came down from the altar.

I shook my head, my heart pounding in my chest, throat, and head.

"For the first time in over a century, I watched the sun rise. It was beautiful."

James pulled something from his inner pocket. And my mind reeled from his words.

"Are you left-handed?" he asked.

"No. I'm right-handed." I blinked my confusion away.

"You will be for now."

James drove a knife into my shoulder, below my collarbone. The pain was swift, but not as excruciating as the realization of who had entered the chapel.

"Good evening, Detective," James said.

George stood in the doorway.

His eyes were obsidian and fixed with hate.

He had a gun. A gun pointed at James.

GEORGE SMELLED ABBY'S PANIC. It etched his skin and fed

him with an eerie sense of calm. He walked deeper into the chapel. "Let her go, Stuart."

James turned Abby around, using her as a shield.

"You don't want to do that George." Abby pointed at his gun, her hand dripping blood.

God, she would follow that monster to hell and back. He would give anything for her care. He was lost in a world he couldn't navigate.

"Don't listen to her." James removed the knife and Abby muffled a scream. He licked blood from the blade, then held it below her chin.

"Why didn't you just let me die?" George asked James.

"You mean too much to me."

"I don't even know you. You ruined my life."

"Yes. And I saved your life."

George fired, hitting James in the left shoulder. He reached out to counterbalance and Abby ran from his grasp.

"You're a better shot than that," James said.

"No!" Abby ran toward him, putting herself in front of his lethal aim. "You don't want to do this. You'll regret it."

"Regret? What am I?" George yanked up his sleeve and revealed his forearm. The gash from Padma's bite oozed black blood. "What have you done to me? All those transfusions. All that time in your fucking clinic."

"Let me help you," she said.

He stared into her eyes. They were earnest and pure. He needed pure more than ever. Because his world was diseased now.

James dashed to the altar. George repositioned his aim. Abby jumped in front of it. "We can figure this out. No one has to die." But her voice no longer quelled his anger. Her eyes were fully dilated and her lips shook. "Please, put down the gun."

"Come on, boy," Stuart said. "How much more damage do I have to inflict before you shoot me?"

"Don't listen to him," Abby pleaded. "I need you to listen to me. Believe in me."

George listened to her heart race and she took quick sharp breaths. Blood soaked the right side of her shirt. But she didn't even touch the wound. She was too afraid, afraid of him. He lowered his gun.

"You're hurt," he said. She touched her chest and nodded. "He hurt you." George fired another shot, missing James's head by inches.

"Please! You need him. You need his blood." Abby reached out for his gun with her bloody hand. She was so brave.

"I don't want his blood. I don't want to be a monster, Abby."

"You're not. You're a good man. You always will be."

"How long is always?" he asked. Because if it was well over a century, he wasn't sure he could live with that. He hadn't asked for any of this. This wasn't the life he had imagined. This wasn't life.

"You have choices. There doesn't have to be any more death to follow you. I will help you. He will help you." Abby pointed at James.

"You have such a very long fuse, George. We have that in common. I commend you, for patience is a virtue." James tipped a candle, toppling it into the next until a wall of flames erupted along the altar, dropping to the floor, and running around the edge of the chapel. "I ruined your life. I slept with the woman you love. And I'll kill her, just like I killed Nate."

"Shut up!" Abby screamed. "Don't listen to him. He wants you to kill him."

The sacramental cloths framing the podium caught, fueling the flames higher until a drape of fire engulfed the altar. The chapel filled with a layer of black, toxic smoke. George's mind was ablaze with hate. Why wouldn't Abby get out of his way?

"What did you do to Padma?" George asked.

James sauntered down the aisle, the flames following. He was the devil incarnate. "Padma didn't survive the car accident. Surely, you know that now." He turned the knife in his hand. Abby's blood glistened on the blade.

George remembered the night he had found Abby covered in blood. How she had collapsed and had a seizure, and that awful drone of the heart monitor, when she had flat-lined.

Abby shook her head, her eyes fixated on something behind him.

"She's a monster," James said. His malevolent eyes locked on Abby. "She must be killed."

James was the sinner. Abby was the only saint in the church. The only person worth dying for.

James hurled the knife, piercing the air. George pushed Abby aside, shoving her to the ground. He fired two shots into James's chest. James smiled, mouthing "Thank you" as he fell backwards. The knife landed with a thunk instead of a clatter.

Padma stood at the end of the aisle with a knife in her chest. She stumbled into the chapel, and flames leapt onto her body.

WET GURGLING NOISES joined the ugly chorus of hisses from the fire. James writhed on the floor, spurting blood from his mouth as he tried to breathe. I crawled down the searing aisle until I was next to him. I tore open his collar and he coughed blood. His crisp white shirt turned crimson red. I placed my hands over the bullet holes in his chest and pressed. The warm blood seeped through my fingers.

"Stubborn asshole," I panted.

His body could sustain injury, but it wasn't immune from pain. He winced at the pressure. It was fine. In a matter of seconds, he would begin to heal. I counted to five. His blood remained red. I continued to count and swatted the obvious questions out of my stream of logic. I had made it to ten. His blood remained red, no black.

"No, this can't be." My hands were stained red. "Come on." I wadded up my jacket and pressed against his wounds. Tears burned my cheeks. The flames closed in around us.

A ball of orange and red staggered down the aisle. Charlotte in Padma's body with outstretched arms and hands drew closer, clamoring with want. I shoved a pew, blocking her from getting any closer. George pushed another pew behind, trapping her for death.

George called for me to come. A window shattered behind him.

I sat next to James. He grabbed my wrists, coughed blood, and groaned.

"Wasn't wrong," he gurgled. "Wasn't wrong about you."

"No," I sobbed. "Stay with me."

He smiled, his white teeth cutting through the blood. "Overstayed my welcome." He arched his chest and his legs kicked. He was drowning in his own blood.

I fisted his shirt, my face over his until we shared the same breath. "He needs you." *I need you.* His body stilled—he'd seen the truth in my plea.

"He has *you* now. You can save him." He wove his fingers into mine. "If I go, Charlotte can't come back."

The chapel roared with fire, the night air hastening its desire. My skin grew hot, my heart blistered with pain.

"You're his angel now." He wiped tears from my mouth. "Give me your consent. Shepherd me from this place."

I shook at his words, and blood seeped onto the floor warm and red.

Life began to dim in his eyes, and I laid my lips over his, blood coating my mouth. "I consent," I whispered over and over, until all that looked up at me were lifeless blue eyes.

The ceiling screeched under the pressure of heat. A high-pitched scream cut through the roar of the flames. Two arms shot out from the wall of fire, reaching for me, desperate for James. Charlotte's fiery figure thrashed and clawed.

"Go to hell," I screamed.

The remaining windows of the chapel shattered, raining glass to the ground.

An arm snaked around my waist and pulled me from the inferno.

45

LIFE IN RUINS

The last fire engine pulled away from Lazarus Chapel. I had no idea an old church could burn that long and irrevocably. The air smelled thick with singed wood, charred flesh, and seared intentions. I didn't really sense any of the noise or lights. They were like ghosts floating along the periphery of my attention. I sat still, perched on the edge of the ambulance, staring at the remnants of that sacred place, waiting for James to walk out of it, unblemished.

"Doctor Whiting, we really need to get you to hospital. The staples aren't enough."

I gave the medic a look, a look armed with my medical degree's veneer of superiority. "If you want me to sign a fucking waiver, I'd be happy to absolve you of any liability."

"You were stabbed with a four-inch blade."

"Below the collarbone, above my lungs and in the middle of my pectoral muscle. He didn't even knick my shoulder blade. It's a very well-crafted flesh wound. And the bleeding stopped hours ago." Because James's aim was always on target.

"No one is coming out of that church."

I shivered and pulled the wool blanket tighter. My attention didn't waiver.

"Fine. I'll let the police know you're up for questions."

Questions? I had a few of my own, but it was too late. I had answers to some of the questions George had asked in the church. When he was engulfed in anger. I had partial truths for myself. And I had listened to a few too many beautifully executed lies. Would I ever have enough time to sift through it all?

Two plainclothed police officers walked toward me. I recognized the larger one from the police station when I had driven George's Volvo back. George? Where was George? I scanned the parking lot. He was talking to two uniformed officers. He was intentionally not looking at me. I didn't blame him.

"Dr. Whiting, do you remember me from the other day? I'm Detective—"

But I cut him off, "Detective Chief Inspector Helderman." I closed my eyes, wincing in pain for effect. Yes, there were a few tricks I had learned from James. Misdirection being one of them.

"I'll make it quick, so they can get you to the hospital." I nodded, filling my eyes with fake tears. "Why were you in the church this evening?"

"I was paying my last respects."

"To Dr. Rothschild?" Helderman didn't mask his confusion.

"Yeah, I had a little trouble at his funeral. So I wanted a do-over." I eyed George. Could I do it all over again?

"And when did Mr. Stuart join you?"

"I'm not sure. He's always so quiet. Maybe after an hour."

"You sat in an empty church for an hour to pay respects to a coworker?"

"I lost track of time." Because I had assumed I had all the time in the world.

"And at what point did your conversation escalate?" Helderman asked.

I stared at DCI Helderman. His eyes were bloodshot and his complexion was sallow. He looked like a man that had once withstood the hours of the evening with little more than a pack of cigarettes and coffee, but had forgotten those years were well behind him.

"Dr. Whiting? Did you hear my question?"

"You asked me when our conversation escalated." When did James hit the detonate button? On the river? After that evening in the citrine bed? Or had it started long before that? "It wasn't an argument. We were discussing his condition. And I was just saying goodbye."

"Is that why he attacked you? He didn't want you to leave?"

My attention drifted back to the church, then to George. I couldn't leave now. I had made a promise. I had sealed it with a kiss. Vic crossed the parking lot and shooed away the police babysitting George. She surveyed the crime scene with a professional level of detachment. She gave me a quick nod. I watched ashes pepper her hair and fall into her mouth. What did they taste like? Were they bitter with regret? Or sweet with victory? What did James's ashes taste like?

"For the first time in over a century, I watched the sun rise. It was beautiful."

DCI Helderman continued with questions. The only words that escaped my mouth were, no...no...no.

How much of James's blood had George been given

through dialysis? When was his last treatment? How much of his blood had been contaminated? Would his blood behave the same with James dead? Would he spontaneously combust or just disintegrate into dust once the sun touched his skin?

The fog rose above the trees, the white claiming the black soot from the air. My heart stopped as the first rays of sun pierced the fog, glimmering with subtle alarm. When the rays clawed their way across the lawn, I stood from the ambulance.

DCI Helderman shifted his stance, attempting to block me in.

"I need a little air," I said. I turned my eyes toward the cold air to make them water. I would perjure myself to save George from burning. DCI Helderman moved away.

I walked with urgency toward George. Which he noticed, since everyone was staying still and stoic, very British. Twenty meters away, the sun lit up the tombstones and I sprinted.

The umbrella of the white willows lent some protection from his inevitable fate. He heard me shout as the sunrise lit up the front of the chapel ruins.

"The sun. Get out of the sun."

Vic froze with concern and I leaped into the air and tackled George to the ground, covering him with my wool blanket.

"What the hell, Abby?"

"The sun is rising."

I stared into his aggravation and held my ground. My legs straddled his hips and my hand was planted over his heart. His beating heart.

"I've watched the sun rise. Crimes are usually called in at daybreak. And I like to swim early."

"What?" What was happening? This was like day one all over again.

George slowly raised his hand above his head, as if he was being arrested, but he was reaching for the sunlight.

"Don't."

"Abby, if I'm going burn for my sins, might as well get it over with. If this is how all this works."

I held his face between my hands. I wanted him to know I was there for him, good or bad. That I wasn't afraid. That I wouldn't run away. But also wanting to be ready if this was to be our first kiss and knowing I wasn't ready for it to be our last.

His fingers touched sunlight.

Nothing happened.

He turned his palm, drowning it in sun.

"You're okay." There was a whiff of bewilderment in my voice.

"You're bleeding again."

Drops of blood splashed onto the collar of his shirt.

"Shit." I yanked my hands from his face.

"Ouch."

"Sorry." In my haste to blot the blood from his shirt, I had pulled a few strands of his hair, which I slid into my trouser pocket.

"How about we try standing up?" he asked.

Once we were standing, I grew a little light-headed. George held me steady. How had I managed to tackle him to the ground?

"It's amazing what adrenaline can do," George said.

"Can you hear my thoughts?"

He held my gaze, acknowledging nothing. So either it was a harmless comment or poker faces were genetic. "I think it's time for you to go to hospital. I'm alright."

He reached into his pocket and pulled out my passport. It was only slightly bloodstained. "One of the uniforms found it." He handed it to me. Was this his passive aggressive way of telling me to go?

"I don't need it."

"Take it."

I placed it in my coat pocket, snagging my finger on something as thin as my ego. The photo. Three friends smiled back at me. Three friends who had probably believed they would never betray one another. I wiped the photo on my shirt and handed it to him. "I'm not going anywhere."

He stared at the photo of Padma and Nate and him. The past. His past. Not mine.

"The night of your accident, it wasn't James. It was—" But before I could finish, he nodded.

"I know what happened. Mystery solved." His tone was firm, official, and all bluff.

"Sergeant?" I asked Vic. "Can you give me a ride to the hospital?"

"Sure, pet." Vic cast George a quick glance. "I'll give you a ring later?"

George nodded. He looked at me and I gave him the same gaze we had shared under the blanket.

"I'm not going anywhere," I said. I didn't need him to read my thoughts. I wanted him to hear the truth.

He turned away. Vic grabbed me by the shoulders. I hadn't realized I was losing my balance. She guided me across the lot and the menagerie of police cars and emergency vehicles. Once I recognized the coroner's van, I stopped.

"You alright? I can have them bring a wheelchair?" Vic asked.

"Is he in there?"

She chewed her top lip.

"Can I say goodbye?" I was surprised I had gotten the words out. I was still living with the idea the undead lived forever. Could never perish.

She cautiously cased the parking lot.

"He was my patient." My voice cracked on its own accord. "Please."

"Make it quick," she said. She turned her back and I quickly slipped into the back of the van.

Despite the thick body bag, the unmistakable scent of burned flesh and bone cut away the courage I thought I had left. I quickly covered my mouth. What was I doing? I don't like dead bodies. They don't have anything to say. What little was left of James was in that bag. And he didn't even fill it. Death was always painful with irony. But I needed him one last time.

I watched my hands tremble. And instead of reaching out for him, they locked together and I did the unthinkable.

I prayed.

For a miracle.

With a swift bang, the miracle was delivered. The sky clapped with thunder, shaking the van. A bolt of lightning struck a tree not far from the church, splitting it in two. Another strike of lightning hit a squad car in the parking lot, causing officers to run for cover. Everyone's attention had been stolen by the violent weather. And my hands made quick shrift of their task.

By the time Vic remembered to check on me, I was already jumping out of the van. The rain came down in a torrent, and the police quickly moved in multiple directions in order to preserve the crime scene.

"You okay enough to make it to the car?" Vic asked.

I nodded. "I don't think I can feel my arm."

She managed to get me to the emergency room in less than ten minutes.

A BAKER'S dozen worth of stitches and a shot of antibiotic had me home by lunchtime. Not the hotel, but the only home I had come to know—the clinic. I wasn't sure where else to go. I wasn't ready to see the packed suitcases waiting in my hotel room. There were some still relatively clean running clothes in my desk, but once I had taken a seat, I wasn't very motivated to move. It was exhaustion mixed with failure and disappointment. Loss had a lot to do with it too.

I had cleared my collections from various pockets of clothing, hoping that would persuade me to shower and change. But I examined my samples, the loop of steps playing out in my head. I could process them in my sleep. But again, I wasn't quite feeling up for it.

In one clear plastic bag were the strands of hair I had pulled from George's head. Funny, I never believed I could play a weakness into an advantage. I'm clumsy. In a larger plastic bag were the six bones I had managed to steal from the body bag. I will never, ever in my life forget the sensation of how James's singed fingers snapped free. Brittle like driftwood. Salt coated my tongue and I swallowed my sadness.

If Detective Inspector Cooper was going to cooperate, he was going to need proof he was James's last descendant. Irrefutable proof.

I would have the truth waiting for him. It was a starting point.

ACKNOWLEDGMENTS

First, I'd like to acknowledge writing is a strange, challenging endeavor. This book took years to write. First, because I had to learn how to write a novel, and then, I had to learn how to revise it. There were times when I wanted to pull the escape hatch, but Abby and George and James wouldn't let go.

I would like to thank my editors, Stephen Parolini www.noveldoctor.com, and Reina Williams www.rickrackbooks.com. I hope this book proves that I listen. The gorgeous book cover was done by Lance Buckley www.lancebuckley.com.

Writing is a lot like walking through a thick forest at night with no flashlight. You follow your instincts, you track constellations of ideas, listen to little noises in your head, but most of the time you get lost. Sometimes you're fortunate enough to meet kind strangers, fellow writers, who hand you a book of matches—Danita, Ron and Dan thank you for those matches!

As you pick up survival skills and grow thicker soles on your feet, if you're lucky, you meet someone who takes your box of matches and lights a torch, making a path clear and inevitable. I've been truly blessed to have two torch bearers — Gayle Parness and Suzanne Tierney.

Gayle, thanks for sitting with me faithfully on Mondays at Peet's and making me believe in magic. Because writing a book takes skill, practice, patience and whole lotta magic!

Suzanne, thank you for setting the bar high and excepting no half-ass attempts at being clever. But most of all, thank you for understanding my voice and giving it substance, grace and courage.

I only hope I can hold the torch as bright and as high as you both have for me. Me loves you both.

ABOUT THE AUTHOR

Kristina Kairn is an emerging award-winning author of paranormal suspense and fantasy fiction. She hails from the Bay Area, where she lives with her witty husband, two amazing soccer kids, and an aloof Holland lop bunny.

If you would like book release updates, exclusive give-aways and free stories, please subscribe to her newsletter at www.kristinakairn.com.